The Family Way
Tabor Heights, Year 1, Book 5

Michelle L. Levigne

M Zion Ridge Press
Books Off the Beaten Path

www.MtZionRidgePress.com

Mt Zion Ridge Press
295 Gum Springs Rd, NW
Georgetown, TN 37366

https://www.mtzionridgepress.com

Published in the United States of America
Publication Date: August 15, 2024

Editor-In-Chief: Michelle Levigne
Executive Editor: Tamera Lynn Kraft

TABOR HEIGHTS

Welcome to Tabor Heights:
A friendly little town on Ohio's North Coast, where sweet romance is always in the air.

Here you'll be able to explore the lives of the members of the congregation of Tabor Christian Church in the space of two years. The stories overlap, and there's no one right place to start.

Just like any small town, you come in, you meet someone, you hear their story and get to know them, and they introduce you to their friends, tell you something about them, and you learn those stories. As you get to know these new friends, they introduce you to other people, and tell you about other interesting stories in town.

It's the same way with Tabor Heights. Start with the story that interests you the most, and then branch out.

Settle back and enjoy your visit.
Welcome!

<u>Year One</u>

THE SECOND TIME AROUND
DETOURS
COMMON GROUNDS
WHITE ROSES
THE FAMILY WAY
FORGIVEN
FIRESONG
BEHIND THE SCENES
THE MISSION
ACCIDENTAL HEARTS
A QUIET PLACE

<u>Year Two</u>

COOKING UP TROUBLE
THE WRATH OF BUBBLES
INVITATION TO A WEDDING
TRUCK STOP ANGEL
A BOX OF PROMISES
WHEELS
THE TEDDY BEAR DANCER

Chapter One

Saturday, February 15

Lisa knew better than to buy her pregnancy test kit in Tabor Heights.

Mrs. Enright at Beckley's Drugstore spied for her father-in-law, Arthur Montgomery. Lisa knew that for a fact, because the one time she took her reading group at the Mission on a walk and brought the children into Beckley's to buy them Popsicles, Mrs. Enright was the only clerk on duty. Two days later, Mr. Montgomery commented on the outing.

"You should think more about your duties as a good Christian wife and stop making it possible for lazy mothers to shirk their responsibilities. You've been married more than a year now. It's time you had a child of your own to take care of. Not someone else's," he had pronounced at the obligatory Sunday dinner at his house.

Lisa didn't dare use Beckley's or any other store in Tabor Heights where one of her father-in-law's supporters might see her. Mr. Montgomery would be waiting at the apartment door by the time she got home, ready to accuse her of "embarrassing the family" by keeping secret such an important matter. He had practically ordered her on her wedding day to start producing grandchildren. He would demand that she take the test right that moment, while he looked on. He wouldn't care that she wanted to wait until Todd got home from his business trip. As clan patriarch, his right to know first was more important than Todd's, the baby's father.

Despite that, the hope that she might finally be pregnant made Lisa smile. Even without the constant pressure to produce, she did want a baby. And maybe, just maybe, a baby would finally get a nod of approval from him, if nothing else ever did.

Considering the challenge of obtaining that test kit without being seen and outed, Lisa chewed her lip and stared unseeing at the blank sheet of paper on her drawing board. Nearly 10a.m., and she hadn't even drawn the frame for her next cartoon strip, let alone planned what would happen in it. The possibility she could be pregnant had grown stronger, until she nearly blurted the news to Todd on Wednesday before he left on his business trip. Here it was, Saturday, and she needed to do something to be sure, if only to settle her thoughts so she could get some work done.

Going out of Tabor to buy the test kit presented a problem. The car had a flat, which was why she hadn't driven Todd to the airport on Wednesday. He could have hitched a ride with the three men from DeWitt-McGregor going on the trip, but he had asked his father. Lisa knew she would hear from him about that on Sunday, as if it was her fault the car had a flat. The car was Todd's territory. She didn't even know if it had a jack, let alone the first step in changing a tire.

She might ask Bekka Sanderson for help in changing it, but Lisa had no idea if her neighbor in the Parkview Towers building was home. It was too nice a day, despite the icy temperatures, to stay indoors. She would be outside, except she had a deadline for her cartoon strip, *P.K.* Besides, she might spill the news while Bekka helped her. Todd had to hear the news first, and he wouldn't get home until Tuesday.

Lisa lowered her gaze to the blank paper neatly taped to her drawing board. Should she add her pregnancy to the storyline of *P.K.*? Maybe one of Katie's friends could think she was pregnant? Or maybe Katie herself? Many events in Lisa's life were reflected in the adventures of Katie, the quintessential Preacher's Kid. Why not this, too?

One problem solved: she knew the main storyline for the next year, maybe two. Now, back to the problem of secretly obtaining the test kit. She had loved Tabor Heights, ever since her freshman year at Butler-Williams University, but sometimes the small, quiet college town was just a little too small. Like living in a goldfish bowl. Especially married to the only son of an elder statesmen of the town and Tabor Christian Church.

The pencil clenched in her fist snapped. Lisa sighed and tossed the fragments into the wastebasket.

The answer hit her with a jolt that made her laugh at her own silliness. She needed a new box of art pencils. She could take the bus to Padua to Kingsbury Mall, to get her art pencils. Or, she could be totally decadent and take the bus into downtown Cleveland, to Knickerbox and stock up on art supplies. There were three drugstores between the bus stop and Knickerbox, where she could get her test kit. She could put the kit in the green paper Knickerbox bag, which no one could see through. No matter how many people she ran into on Tabor's streets, walking home, no one would ever guess what she had inside it.

Lisa sighed as she put on her coat and grabbed her purse. Was it just her imagination, that life would be so much simpler if she hadn't married Todd?

No, Todd wasn't the problem. It was his Pharisee of a father, and Lisa had known what kind of man he was before she agreed to marry his son. Prominent lawyer in Tabor, hand-in-glove with arrogant Judge Foggerty, long-time deacon and officer at Tabor Christian Church, head of the group that believed good Christian women shouldn't wear pants or hold a job outside the home.

Lisa had walked into her marriage and joined the Montgomery family with her eyes wide open. Pastor Glenn and his pre-marital counseling had made sure of that. She loved Todd, and believed she could put up with a lot because he loved her, and would protect her.

The phone in the kitchen rang just as Lisa turned to pull the apartment door closed. She checked her watch. Ten a.m., as usual. Despite knowing better, she listened. The answering machine clicked on and Todd's cheerful voice ran through the greeting. After the beep, nothing. Not even heavy breathing. Then the hard clatter as the person on the other end slammed the phone down.

Did the caller know Todd was out of town? Lisa shivered. She didn't like the thought that the caller knew anything about her and Todd's schedules or their lives. Every weekday, and on weekends when Todd was out of town, 10a.m. and 2p.m., someone called and never left a message. She had tried using star sixty-nine a few times, but the number was always blocked. And that wasn't a good sign.

If only she could figure out Todd's old-fashioned answering machine he had had since college. She needed proof of the recorded hang-ups and the date stamp, the same time every day. She had told Todd about the calls once, but when she tried to play back the recording, nothing was there. She needed that proof to make him believe her. How did she manage to erase the recordings every time?

This time, she would leave the answering machine alone until Todd came home.

After all, a baby meant they had to make triply sure of the security of their home. Maybe they should move, if someone was harassing them at the apartment? They needed to make changes in their lives.

"Please, God, let things change," Lisa whispered as she locked the door and hurried down the hall to the elevator.

~~~~~

Takeishi, a friend from life drawing class at Butler-Williams, was on duty at the checkout counter next to the door at Knickerbox, when Lisa walked into the store more than an hour later. He looked around in response to the piercing sound of the chimes on the door. Lisa held up the drugstore's semi-opaque white bag to show she was bringing something into the store. He grinned and gestured for her to go on in, meaning she didn't have to check her bag with him. She was known, she was trusted, and her secret was safe. For a second, though, Lisa wished she had saved the drugstore stop for her return trip to meet her bus.

She grinned at her silliness. Takeishi was the last person in the world to tell anyone in Arthur Montgomery's clique that he had seen Lisa walk into the art supply store with a pregnancy test kit. Every time Lisa had broken up with Todd during their years at BWU, Takeishi had tried to fix
~~~~~

her up with one of his friends, who he said were twenty times better for her than Todd Montgomery. He would keep her secret.

Clutching the incriminating test kit close, with the big neon pink letters threatening to bleed through the drugstore bag wrapped around it twice, Lisa headed for the pencils, chalk, and acrylic paints aisle. No leisurely wandering up and down every aisle on this trip, dreaming about the day she could indulge in the most expensive colored pencils and luxurious papers for her cartoons. She had to be even more careful of her expenses, budget, and time from now on. She was going to be a mother. She had to think about her baby's future, after all.

Lisa picked up three boxes, enough to last her three weeks at her current rate of drawing and erasing and re-drawing. She turned, and ran into a faded army surplus backpack, hanging from a shoulder draped in a pea coat spotted with melted snow. She knocked the pencils and the drugstore bag from her hands. Lisa froze and watched everything hit the floor. The pencil boxes stayed closed, but the drugstore bag opened and the test kit slid out, exposing those incriminating yet glorious words.

"Sorry!" Bekka Sanderson went down on one knee, laughing, and scooped up Lisa's pencils.

Lisa could only stare. What was Bekka doing Downtown today, of all days?

"Amy's birthday," Bekka said, getting back to her feet. She gestured at the handful of pink, plumed pens she had slipped onto a shelf before she bent to pick up the pencils.

Lisa realized she had spoken her thoughts aloud. Then she remembered that Amy, Bekka's roommate, would only write her poetry with pink plumed pens on lavender paper. She claimed the color combination sparked her creativity. Kat, Bekka's other roommate, had confided in Lisa a few weeks ago that Amy only said that to torture her on-again, off-again boyfriend, Joe. Knickerbox was the only store in all of Northeast Ohio that sold the specific pink plumed pens and lavender paper Amy insisted on. When Joe was desperate to make up after another of their ridiculous fights, he usually had to trudge Downtown to get the pens or paper or both.

"You okay?" Bekka tucked her pens into the crook of her arm with the pencil boxes and the drugstore bag and reached out her free hand to grip Lisa's shoulder. "You look kind of shell-shocked. Something wrong?"

"No. Everything's... fine." Lisa reached for the drugstore bag, barely stopping herself before she snatched it out of Bekka's grasp and started another avalanche.

"Are you heading back home right away? Could I hitch a ride?"

"I don't have the car. Flat tire." Lisa breathed a prayer of relief and gratitude as Bekka slid her bag and boxes into her grasp without even looking at the all-too-visible label.

"Let me guess. Saint Toddy is too busy helping his father with something to fix the tire, so you had to take the bus on a day like this." She laughed as they headed down the aisle for the register.

"He's out of town. He had to get a ride to get to the airport."

"Tell you what. Buy me a hot chocolate at that donut joint on the corner, and I'll help you change your tire when we get back to the apartments."

"You are my hero," Lisa groaned, earning laughter from Bekka and a grin from Takeishi, when they reached the register just that moment. "No, honestly, you are saving my life," she said, continuing the conversation after they had both made their purchases and stepped out into the sharp, cold gusts of wind that came straight from Lake Erie, down the canyons formed by the buildings. "The car is Todd's domain, and I never learned how to change a tire or the oil or do anything more complicated than add windshield washer fluid."

"It's the least I can do for a neighbor." Bekka took the big, dark green Knickerbox bag from Lisa's hands so she could slide the drugstore bag inside it. "And an expectant mommy," she added, handing the bag back to her.

Lisa stumbled, and an especially hard gust of wind nearly knocked her against the building they walked past. Bekka slipped an arm through hers, holding her upright until Lisa got her feet underneath herself again.

"Please -- don't tell anyone."

"My lips are sealed. I just love keeping secrets from my roommates. And you have no idea how hard it is to keep something hidden from those two snoops. They made my Dove dark chocolate hearts evaporate less than a day after I bought them."

"They're not who I was thinking about, but thanks, now that you mentioned it." Somehow, Lisa was able to breathe again. Maybe it was the understanding light, warm in Bekka's eyes despite her crooked grin.

Bekka said not one word more that even vaguely hinted at Lisa's pregnancy. They talked about the news from the Guardians training camp in Arizona and the recent Superbowl disappointment on the long, bumpy, chilly bus ride to their stop in the center of Tabor. They went to the parking lot next to their apartment building and Bekka changed the tire immediately, making short work of the task. Lisa marveled at how self-sufficient she was, how much she knew how to do, and how generous she was with her time. Especially on an icy, windy day. It occurred to Lisa that she and Bekka had more in common than most of their mutual friends. They were both orphans, raised by elderly relatives: Lisa by cousins who did their minimal required duty, and Bekka by paternal grandparents who wanted to do her thinking for her. Lisa had been on her own since she graduated from high school, while Bekka had lived with her grandparents until last fall, when the Sandersons moved to Florida. How had Bekka become so much more independent and assured? She had to fight for everything she had, to keep it safe from people who would take away her individuality and her dreams. Lisa had grown up fairly solitary, with few threats. Life had been quiet and simple and relatively easy.

Until she met Todd Montgomery.

"What wrong?" Bekka asked, as she finished hooking the jack back into the compartment in the trunk.

"Too many deep thoughts and too many deadlines."

"Want me to hold your hand while you wait for the test results?" She grinned and gestured at the white drugstore bag sticking out of the Knickerbox bag.

"I'm thinking of waiting until Todd gets home. To do it together."

"That has got to be true love, because if it was me, I'd have gone into the bathroom at the drugstore and taken the test. Of course, I would never have married Todd Montgomery, but... Does that big jerk know how much you love him? Because I swear, I'll get some of the big backstage guys from the tech crew, and I'll have them take him up to the balcony and drop him on his head a few dozen times until he straightens out."

"Todd isn't that bad. And he'll change his ways, once..." She patted her flat stomach.

"He'd better. That's all I can say." She slammed the trunk for emphasis.

~~~~~

The answering machine clicked off just as Lisa returned to the apartment in triumph, carrying the pencils, the test kit, and a bag of dark chocolate espresso beans Bekka had insisted on giving her from the stash she had bought at her favorite coffee shop Downtown. She checked her watch, even knowing it was 2p.m. on the dot. Repressing a shudder, Lisa made sure the security chain and deadbolt were firmly in place before hurrying to her office.

The answering machine for her private phone line flashed and the number three showed on the digital readout. Lisa fought a wave of nausea. The caller hadn't found her unlisted office number, had he?

"Hey, Lisa, it's Genevieve. I know, you're wondering what I'm doing in my office on a Saturday. Honey, I have fantastic news. Call me!"

Lisa grinned and sat down, feeling a little weak in the knees from sheer relief at hearing her agent's cheerful voice. She and Genevieve had made each other's success. One hesitant cartoonist paired up with one fledgling agent who knew how to make people smile even when she refused to take 'no' for an answer. When *P.K.* exploded on the Christian publishing scene, Genevieve's reputation expanded with it. Even though
~~~~~

she now employed two other agents in her firm, she insisted on handling all Lisa's business personally.

The second message was Genevieve, announcing she was heading out to lunch, but she would be back in half an hour, and demanding Lisa call her before she exploded with the good news.

The third message was Genevieve. She had to leave by 1:30 for her niece's ballet recital and wouldn't be back in the office until Monday. She grumbled good-naturedly and said it was high time Lisa stuck a crowbar into her wallet and bought a cell phone, then condemned her to endure a restless weekend of wondering what the good news was. She would email all the details to her first thing Monday morning.

"Good news, huh?" Lisa hugged herself and finally took off her coat. She spilled her bag onto her second worktable and read the label of the pregnancy test upside down. "Maybe we'll have two things to celebrate when you get home, Toddy."

She could wait until Todd came home before she took the test. Being part of the Montgomery family had certainly taught her patience.

~~~~~

Todd didn't even know the name of the mall where he wandered. The other men in the team sent out by his company had found things to do: sitting in the bar, watching a football game, or sleeping, or indulging in the hotel's indoor pool. After the fourth "What's your problem, Montgomery?" his foul mood wouldn't let him stay with his peers. Even if he knew what had him feeling like he had an anvil in his gut and an incipient explosion in his temples, he certainly wouldn't tell any of them.

What kind of an idiot sends us out on business in the middle of the week, then makes us sit around in a second-rate hotel for an entire weekend, doing nothing? He stared vacantly at a window display, watching a clerk with multiple earrings and purple swatches in her hair take down the display. Then the shimmer of light on red foil broke him out of his haze. She was taking down the Valentine's Day display.

His mood plummeted, hitting sharp rocks. Yesterday was Valentine's Day. As usual, Lisa had bought him a little token, tucking it into his suitcase when he wasn't looking. Did he remember to leave anything for her? Did he take two minutes from that leisurely schedule of meetings and long breaks yesterday to call and wish her happy Valentine's Day and tell her he missed her?

Of course not.

He could probably take advantage of all the after-holiday sales in the card stores and candy shops and get something really spectacular for Lisa without breaking the bank. The problem with a plan like that was that he had forgotten about Valentine's Day last year too, then forgot to take the sale stickers off the little pink bear and the enormous lace-covered box of
~~~~~

chocolate. Lisa had been hurt at this evidence that he didn't think about her until after the fact. She didn't say anything, as usual, but Todd was positive he had heard her crying in her office.

"Do it, you coward," he told his reflection. Fortunately, there was no one nearby to hear him talking to himself.

What use was a cell phone if he didn't use it? The company wouldn't fire him for making a personal call. His boss had specifically told him the cell phones were provided to help the traveling members of the staff stay in touch with their families, since they were away from home so much. He would just dig into his jeans pocket, pull out his cell phone, call Lisa, and promise her dinner at the Mediterranean when he got home next week. Just the two of them. It was their favorite restaurant when they were dating. They hadn't gone out to eat there in months. In fact, Todd couldn't remember the last time they had gone out to eat, period.

He had a hard time wrapping his fingers around the cell phone and pulling it out of his pocket. He didn't even know why. Todd walked down the main walkway of the mall, dodging the loud, laughing, hurrying streams of teens. Their energy and enjoyment of life made him feel old. He had been down in the dumps since he got on the plane to fly out here.

The phone rang and he jumped, almost dropping it. For a second, he transposed the numbers and thought Lisa was calling him. Guilt made him choke. No, that was his father's home number, not Lisa's office number. They were almost the same numbers, just arranged differently.

"Hi, Dad." He settled on a bench facing a fountain. The sound of the water muffled some excited screaming down one wing of the mall.

For two heartbeats, he flashed back to the ride to the airport, and his father grumbling that Todd should get a new job that wouldn't take him out of town so much. No good would come from leaving a flighty, self-centered girl like Lisa alone for days at a time with no supervision. Todd had tuned it out, like he always did.

Not this time, though, he realized. Not entirely. Some of that heaviness in his chest had landed during that ride to the airport.

Chapter Two

"What was that, Dad? Sorry, I'm at a mall, getting some exercise, and there are a lot of kids making noise. I didn't hear you." Todd grinned at the blatant lie, but it was easier to blame someone else than admit he hadn't been listening. His sisters ignored their father whenever possible, and he refused to do that to him, even unintentionally.

That set his father off on a tirade about the rudeness of modern teens and how, when he was their age, he had something useful to do on a Saturday afternoon. Eventually he shifted gears to grumble about the deacons meeting at church that afternoon, still trying to talk sense into the spendthrifts who wanted to throw more money at the Mission and expand the services of the old school building the church had bought.

Todd thought the Mission was a great idea, and the more outreach they could offer to the surrounding communities, the better. Lisa spent time at the Mission two or three times a week, helping the seniors with crafts, or reading to the children in the daycare center, or helping organize the latest donations to the food and clothes cupboard. He had gone several times to help her, and enjoyed the feeling of giving something back to the community. Todd knew better than to tell his father he thought the Mission needed a larger portion of the church's budget.

He reached the anchor department store at the end of the mall and was halfway back to the fountain before his father finished grumbling about church politics and asked how Todd's business trip was going. As usual, he complained about how DeWitt-McGregor didn't fully appreciate his son's talent and skills. By the time Todd returned to the fountain, walked around it, and started back down the mall walkway, his father had run out of words, and Todd felt a little better. He didn't know how he would get along sometimes, without his father encouraging him.

Todd took the next shuttle back to the hotel and joined Bill Whitlock in the bar to eat wings and watch Ohio State smear Michigan yet again in football. The other two members of their team from DeWitt-McGregor joined them, and when the football game was over, they found a basketball game. It was nearly midnight by the time Todd crawled into bed. He was half-asleep when he realized he hadn't called Lisa yet. Making a mental note to do that in the morning, before she went to church, he let himself fall asleep.

His dreams were a jumble of images. He hurried through their apartment, looking for Lisa to tell her something important, but she wasn't there. He kept running through the empty rooms, calling her name. Again and again.

Sunday, February 16

Sunday, Lisa gladly filled in for Jeannette Marshall in the Middlers class during the second service. Jeannette, Pastor Glenn's secretary, had stayed home with her little boy, BJ, who had a fever. Lisa thought about Jeannette, widowed just after she found out she was pregnant, raising her son without any family.

No, Lisa corrected herself, Jeannette had the entire congregation of Tabor Christian to help her raise BJ. Pastor Glenn and Rita couldn't have been better grandparents to the little boy if they were blood relatives. Thinking about Jeannette's situation and how she coped encouraged Lisa. She had Todd and his four sisters, even if she had no family of her own. Her baby would be spoiled rotten. She would never lack for babysitters. Everything would be fine.

If she was pregnant. She thought about that test, sitting on the top shelf of the cabinet in the bathroom, and wished she hadn't bought it. The temptation was excruciating.

Still, hugging her delicious secret to herself helped her endure Mr. Montgomery's icy fury when he caught up with her in the hallway after the second service. He informed her he would drive her to his house for the ritual Sunday meal, since Lisa obviously couldn't figure out how to change the flat tire. Even better, she had a valid reason to decline. She always served in the kitchen for the Autumn Fellowship's luncheon on the third Sunday of each month. Her regular service to the elders of the church wasn't enough to mollify the man, and she could still feel the sting of his offended gaze on her neck as she hurried off to the kitchen to start working. Why did he want her to spend the afternoon with him if Todd wasn't there? He didn't like her, so why make them both miserable?

~~~~~

Todd got up later than he intended Sunday morning, too late for him to call Lisa before she left for church. She didn't have a cell phone, and even if she did, she wouldn't have it turned on during either class or the service. He didn't feel like searching the phone book to find a church to attend, and his co-workers were still asleep and probably wouldn't stir until it was time for a football game to start. He decided to take a chance that the mall would be open.

The first store he saw was just rolling the cage security door up into the ceiling. An art store. Inspiration struck. What were those fancy
~~~~~

imported French colored pencils Lisa drooled over, but never bought for herself? He would be a hero if he came home with those pencils. And chocolate. His sisters always insisted that chocolate was a necessary part of asking forgiveness. Not that he ever had to ask Lisa to forgive him. She knew he loved her. She always forgave him. Still, it wouldn't hurt to hedge his bets by investing in some chocolate along with those pencils.

Todd couldn't figure out the map of the mall, and had gone down two wings, trying to find the candy store before he realized there was a second floor. He finally located the escalator and got upstairs and had the candy store in his sights when the cell phone rang.

"You are quitting that job if they don't have the sense to give you duties that let you stay at home," Mr. Montgomery growled before Todd could finish saying hello. "That selfish--"

"Dad, please don't. Not on a Sunday." Todd had learned a long time ago that appealing to his father's sense of propriety stopped quite a number of diatribes on the launch pad. "What happened?"

"That wife of yours refused Sunday dinner with me. She made up some flimsy lie about doing church work to avoid her duty to me as your father. She knows I'm watching her, to make sure she doesn't embarrass you while you're out of town. Rebellious, that's what she is. Lying, devious, rebellious little—"

"Dad! Stop. Lisa always helps with the Autumn Fellowship luncheon at church on the third Sunday of every month. That's why we never have lunch with you on that day. Every month. Regular as clockwork." Todd sighed and settled down on the edge of a planter. He had been feeling fine until the phone rang.

"She has no business traipsing all over town while you're away. She doesn't care anything about you."

"Lisa loves me. Dad, she put chocolate and a card in my suitcase, so I'd have something for Valentine's Day while I was out of town."

"That's her duty as your wife." He snorted. "She's only doing it to trick you into trusting her. Or out of guilt."

"So if she didn't give me little gifts and show me all the time how much she loves me, then that means she really does love me?"

"Don't you sass back at me, young man. I'm looking out for your welfare. You have no business spending so much time away from home, so young, so early in your marriage. Until you have her trained, until she gives up her ridiculous scribbling and settles down and devotes herself to her duties as your wife, nothing is certain. Do you have any idea what she does while you're out of town so much?"

"Yes, Dad. I know exactly what Lisa's doing right now." He checked his watch. "She's in the kitchen at church, packing up the leftovers from the luncheon to take over to the Mission. Go on over to the church and check. It's the same routine, the third Sunday of every month. She'll be there until 2:30, then she'll take the leftovers to the Mission kitchen. If it's nice weather, she'll walk. Then, she'll go home and... if I was at home, we'd spend the afternoon on the couch relaxing, watching TV or working a puzzle or reading."

"If you were at home. But you're not, are you?"

Todd couldn't remember what he said to get his father off the topic of Lisa doing something irresponsible while he was out of town. He found himself on the shuttle bus to go back to the hotel with the pencils and a box of chocolate covered cherries, so he had managed to take care of his errand to the candy store, even though he couldn't remember doing it. The heaviness had settled back in his gut.

Monday, February 17

The sound of her fax machine chirping and then the hum of paper feeding through it woke Lisa at seven the next morning. That had to be the promised news from Genevieve. The only reason she had the fax machine was because her agent didn't trust sending documents through email.

She rolled over and stared at the clock on the bedside table, on Todd's side of the bed. How had she managed to sleep in so late?

Could it be her pregnancy affected her body already? Lisa giggled as she swung her legs out of bed and felt around with her big toe on the cold linoleum, trying to find her slippers. Would Todd be one of those expectant fathers who would treat her like glass, at her beck and call, ready to massage her feet and carry her everywhere?

It would be a nice change, wouldn't it?

Her smile faded and Lisa firmly pushed aside the discontent that had been festering for months. Todd used to insist on a night out every weekend and bought her flowers two or three times a month. Nowadays, his idea of a fun night together was take-out Chinese, a rented movie, and eating out of the ice cream carton together while they sprawled on the couch. And that didn't happen very often.

Things would change, now that she was pregnant. Everything was going to be perfect.

The fax machine beeped, signaling it had finished printing and the phone connection ended. Lisa scurried down the short hall to her office and scooped up the scattering of papers on her floor. What was Genevieve's big news?

She turned on her computer and sorted through the faxed papers while she waited for it to boot up. Her heart stuttered as she caught the gist of the news. Somehow, though, it wouldn't gel into a cohesive, understandable whole. She had to read the papers three times.

Then, to be doubly sure, she got online and looked for Genevieve's promised email.

"A contract for books," Lisa whispered. She pressed both hands over her mouth, positive she would let out a whoop that might wake everybody in the apartment building and half of Tabor.

She wanted to get up and do a little dance, but her office was too crowded. She wanted to scream and run down the hall and grab Todd and tell him the good news, but he was in Sacramento. Besides, it was only a little after 4a.m. in Sacramento, and she knew better than to wake Todd before 6:30.

Lisa smiled at her wide-boned face framed in sleep-tousled, straight, dark brown hair in her computer monitor, and shuddered with silent laughter.

Who would have thought it?

P.K. had become a hit. Even with the help and connections of her friend, Anne at the Arc Foundation, and four-digit royalty checks every other month, Lisa hadn't really thought she could make a living with her artwork.

Who would have thought that a humorous look at a minister's family life could generate any audience at all?

Someone obviously did, when a major Christian publishing house wanted to do a series of small gift books, starting with Pastor Appreciation Month in October.

The editor wanted the black-and-white panels colored and ready to be assembled into the first book by June. He wanted some ideas of different themes, and an entirely brand new collection of stories to lead off the advertising campaign.

"Oh, I have a great idea for a new story," she whispered, and pressed a trembling hand over her flat stomach. "It'll be just perfect."

Lisa had imposed many of the happier, amusing details of her life and courtship on Katie, the oldest daughter of the minister's family. Why not this pregnancy? Didn't she have a handful of panels scribbled during her engagement and put away somewhere, preparing for the happy event? Lisa thought so, and wondered just how accurate her daydreams had been. Todd would laugh when she showed him. He would be so proud of her for finally making that big sale, and happy about the baby.

Without even pausing to change her clothes or wash up for the day, Lisa got to work. She flung open the closet of her office and pulled out the binders full of her originals. She had sorted them by theme and storyline, to make it easier to refer back to older stories. That would make it deceptively simple to pick out the panels for different books. She had put

Katie's family through all the ups and downs of life, magnifying the events through a spiritual perspective. All the good and bad in ordinary life. Sending children off to college. Facing illness. Moving to a new city. Explaining the facts of life to small children. Facing the deaths of the elderly and ill. Courtship and marriage.

Outside in the kitchen of the three-bedroom apartment, the phone rang. Lisa glanced at the clock over the tiny sofa. Yep, 10a.m. She held her breath, listening for a voice leaving a message. A shiver ran through her when she heard only silence. Again.

"Get a grip on yourself," Lisa scolded, and turned her attention back to her work.

Nothing, she decided, was going to ruin her day. She had a book contract offer; a chance for *P.K.* to go international. Money coming in from her artwork. Maybe now Todd's father would stop his snide remarks about her wasting her time and money *pretending* to be an artist.

"Your grandfather thinks I'm a silly girl who doesn't take good care of your daddy," she whispered, pressing her hand over her stomach.

Lisa frowned as she realized what she had said. *Grandfather* sounded so formal. Mr. Montgomery was the only grandparent her baby would ever have, and silly as she supposed it sounded, she wanted her baby to have a *Grampa*, not a *Grandfather*.

Not that Mr. Montgomery would ever relax enough to allow such an informal label.

Or would he? Maybe he would finally accept her as Todd's wife, once she gave his only son a child. She just barely had his approval because she worked from home, instead of taking a job outside the home. He still didn't approve of her career as a freelance artist, or the fact she had a career at all other than being a housewife. He seemed to think it should take her all day to keep the apartment clean, cook feasts for Todd every night, and do the laundry. Lisa had learned long before her engagement not to point to all the other wives in their church who worked outside the home and had perfectly happy, balanced homes and obedient, healthy children who did well in school. When Mr. Montgomery made up his mind, it was a waste of time showing him that facts proved him wrong.

"I'm warning you right now, junior, if you know what's good for you, you'd better be a boy. Girls are way down on the totem pole in the Montgomery clan."

Enough of that train of thought. Lisa settled down to make notes of what themes and strips she wanted to offer for the collections, then put away the binders.

She had to leave in another half hour to walk to the Mission and do story time, then stop by Homespun Printing and drop off the new designs Joel Randolph had commissioned, which she had finished last night, then do a little shopping at Heinke's Grocery. Todd was due home tomorrow and she wanted to make a special dinner to surprise him.

They were going to have a lot to celebrate!

~~~~~

"Perfect." Joel Randolph shook his head as he looked through the folder of pages Lisa handed him. The husky-built owner of the Homespun Theater and Homespun Printing grinned and sank down in the creaky wooden swivel chair at his desk. "I don't know what we'd do without you, Lisa." He raked a big hand through his salt-and-pepper mop of hair. "With the new production starting in a few days, and this new partnership with the Royal Community Theater — have you met Tyler Sloane yet? You will," he hurried on, when she just shook her head. "Nice guy. He's bunking with Xander Finley until he finds his own place. They were college buddies. Em knows him a little, since she started the theater program at Southeastern Christian in Iowa and he's been teaching there the last ten years or so. Dan Morgan and I are trying to talk him into attending church with us this week, but... well, what can you say? He taught theater at a Christian college, and he didn't have any trouble with acceptance there, but he's leery of trying to find a new church home here until he knows the area. And the people. The theater has one reputation, and too many Pharisees have given the church another reputation, and never the twain shall meet."

"Without an explosion," Lisa muttered. She grinned at Joel's burst of laughter, but her stomach twisted a little as she remembered Mr. Montgomery's tirade, three Sundays ago at dinner.

He was incensed that Pastor Glenn and Rita still socialized with the Randolphs. It wasn't bad enough that Emily Keeler-Randolph had been a rising starlet in Hollywood, but her daughter Max was illegitimate and no one would say who her father was. Lisa had bitten her tongue to keep from pointing out that, first of all, Max's parentage was nobody's business. And second, her birth-father's identity didn't matter, because Joel had adopted Max when he married Emily.

Obviously, Mr. Montgomery never forgave any sin, even if God did. Even if the sin wasn't directed at him, personally.

"You're going to get a lot of design business from Ty." Joel opened his drawer and pulled out the big checkbook. "Do you mind if I give him your office number, so he can tell you what he's looking for?"

"I'll take all the business I can get." She smiled, thinking of the rocking horse wallpaper she had seen in the Floor-to-Ceiling Store's display window as she walked through town. Her baby was going to get the absolutely best nursery she could assemble.

"Lisa! Sweetheart, I didn't know you were here." Emily stepped through the door that came in from the lobby of the Homespun Theater.
~~~~~

The theater itself was an old barn, transformed through Joel's carpentry skills. A smaller barn attached to it served as the lobby and box office. A shed attached to that, tucked up against the end between the theater and the refurbished firehouse where the Randolph family lived, served as Homespun Printing. Joel and Emily had started the business because there was no printer in Tabor Heights when they opened the theater twenty years ago, and to make ends meet in between productions. The business had thrived, and Lisa was grateful because it had given her a steady thread of income since the day she saw a help wanted notice in the art building at Butler-Williams.

Emily and Lisa hugged. It was all Lisa could do to keep from blurting the news about *P.K.* and the coming baby.

Sometimes, she still found it a little hard to believe that she was on a first-name basis with Emily Keeler, star of a handful of movies that played regularly on cable. Lisa wondered what she would have become if she had stayed in Hollywood. Who really cared, nowadays, that she had a child outside of marriage? The oddballs in Hollywood were the ones who *stayed* married.

"You'll stay for dinner, won't you?" Emily continued. "The boys have a meeting at church. It'll just be us and Max and Tony."

"Scratch Max and Tony." Joel stood up to lean over the desk and hand Lisa the check.

He had paid her fifty dollars more than they agreed on when he gave her the design job. Lisa knew better than to argue by now when he gave her bonuses. She smiled and thanked him. From now on, every extra penny would go into a fund for the baby's college expenses.

"What about Max and Tony?" Emily frowned. "They have that book they're working on. For all I know, Tony is camping here for the duration. They have to get that book finished before he goes away for that writer-in-residence program."

Chapter Three

"That's exactly what I mean," her husband said with a wink for Lisa. "They'll eat, but it'll be like pulling teeth with your fingers to get any conversation out of them while they're in the throes of a book."

"They ought to get married, they spend so much time together," Lisa said with a chuckle.

"That's what I think, but I doubt Max knows Tony is a boy, or he knows she's a girl."

"Don't go any further, Mr. Randolph," Emily said. "Matchmaking your daughter isn't going to help anybody. Especially when they have a deadline looming over their heads."

"Speaking of deadline," Lisa said, seeing her opportunity. "I have one. I'd love to stay for dinner, but..." She shrugged.

After getting another hug from Emily, Lisa slipped out the door and hurried down the street. Maybe it was silly to go walking when the skies looked gray with storm clouds, but she felt so good she wanted to skip. What was the use of living in a nice, quiet college town like Tabor if she couldn't walk everywhere she wanted to go?

Lisa cut down Kiln Street to get to Cook, then to Span to cross over the Metroparks road back to the center of town and her apartment building. As always when she walked the winding street lined with big weeping willows and pretty, whitewashed picket fences, she closed her eyes before she reached the dream house. It had golden and gray stone facing on the front of the cottage and an archway over the gravel driveway, revealing just a small glimpse of a yard lined with tall hedges down the sides and two apple trees across the back. She and Todd had promised each other that someday, they would rent the dream house.

Counting to fifty, walking slowly because of the snow making the slate sidewalk slippery, Lisa kept her eyes closed. The house had no lights or decorations when she and Todd drove by at Christmas, as if the people who lived there didn't care about the holidays. She had avoided Kiln since then, afraid to see a "for sale" sign—or worse, "sold"—in the front yard. Until today. Today, everything seemed possible.

"Forty-nine. Fifty," she whispered, and opened her eyes. Her face red from more than the cold, she glanced in all directions to make sure no one had seen her acting silly. Then she turned to the house.

Lisa rubbed her eyes and blinked hard, willing the vision before her to stay solid. She took a step onto the snowy lawn, putting her feet where the realtor had stepped into the snow when he hammered the sign into the frozen ground.

"Perfect," she whispered, and reached out to stroke the "for rent" sign. She slid her backpack off her shoulder, pulled out her sketch pad and pencil, and scribbled the realtor's phone number and web address.

Moments later, she headed down the sidewalk as quickly as she could, despite the patches of ice everywhere. She had shopping to do. Cornish game hens, apples for a Waldorf salad, and Moose Tracks ice cream. Todd's favorites. They would have a lot to celebrate and plans to make when he got home tomorrow night.

~~~~~

Todd stood in the doorway of an office cubicle at Knight-Baron and swallowed down the snarl that kept trying to emerge at the worst possible times. He should be happy, like the other members of the team. They had accomplished the company's business this afternoon instead of having one final meeting tomorrow morning. He could take an earlier flight and be home in the afternoon instead of the evening. Wasn't that something to be glad about?

He knew he should pull out his cell phone to call Lisa and let her know he would be home early, while the other three men talked with the HR clerk responsible for re-scheduling their flights home. He would have to call her again anyway, when he had the definite flight time, so why waste the time? He kept telling himself that, even as he knew it was a lie. His head hurt from trying not to listen to the happy comments from his co-workers or remember the things his father had said yesterday. Of course he knew where Lisa was, almost every hour of the day. She stuck to a strict schedule to get her cartoon work done on time, and managed to take care of the apartment and do ministry work for the church. And she made sure he knew where she would be so he could contact her in an emergency, because she didn't have a cell phone.

Todd had told his father that several times, when Mr. Montgomery insinuated that Lisa was never at home and she lied about her activities. Each time, his father responded with, "Well, do you ever call to check on her?" He said nothing, just snorted or scowled when Todd admitted that no, he didn't check on Lisa.

Every time Todd said he trusted Lisa and there was no need to check on her, his father gave him that disapproving look or lectured him on being too trusting.

"You ready, Montgomery?" Rupert Evans said, stepping back from the HR clerk's desk and gesturing for Todd to step up.

"Yeah. Thanks." Todd shoved his father's voice to the back of his thoughts, but it didn't quiet down until he decided he would call a taxi to
~~~~~

get him home from the airport. He wouldn't tell Lisa he was coming home early, to have her come pick him up. He would go home, walk in the door, and find her exactly where he knew she would be.

Tuesday, February 18

Tyler Sloane called late that afternoon. He needed posters for the coming season of plays at Royal Community Theater, on the border between South Royal and Stoughton. The board of directors for the theater had chosen the plays and announced them to the patrons before Tyler had signed his contract. Lisa liked the fact that though the former drama teacher didn't like some of the plays, he was willing to make the best of it.

"At least they didn't do the casting for me," he said, chuckling in his velvety, dark brown voice.

"Thank God for small blessings."

"That's for sure." A sharp rapping sound came through the phone. "That's my wake-up call. Time for another meeting. So, do you have enough to start out with? I haven't given you too much?"

"I can probably get you the preliminary sketches for the posters by the end of the month. If that's soon enough? There's another project I'm working on..." She smiled, thinking of the coloring she had done today on a dozen panels of *P.K.*

"No hurry. Take your time. I'm grateful Joel told me about you." Tyler chuckled. "I'll talk to you later, Lisa. I think we're going to like working together."

Everything was perfect, she decided for the twentieth time since getting Genevieve's fax.

Steady income doing posters and programs for Royal Community Theater, her already-existing design job for Homespun, occasional work illustrating editorials at the *Tabor Picayune,* and now the *P.K.* books. Plus she didn't have any morning sickness yet. Jeannette had laughed at that baby shower two months ago, when she talked about morning sickness five years ago when she was pregnant with BJ. Despite her good spirits and fondness for every memory of her pregnancy, Lisa had shuddered over the smallest discomfort her friend suffered without the support of a husband. Todd would be her rock, her source of strength. He would baby her through every discomfort, just like she babied him through every cold. Sure, he had to go out of town ten days of every month, but he would move Heaven and Earth to be there when she needed him. She knew he would, no matter how much his job meant to him.

Lisa smiled as she sniffed and caught the heavenly perfume of creamy cheesy potatoes and Cornish game hen cooking in the oven. After dinner, before bringing out dessert, she and Todd would go in the bathroom and take the pregnancy test.

The entire evening would be perfect.

The apartment door rattled, and there was a sound like someone trying to slide in a key. For a heartbeat, Lisa froze. Sometimes she thought she had heard someone trying to get into the apartment at night, thought she heard a key in the lock, when Todd was away on business trips. His plane wasn't due for another hour. She had to take a shower and change her clothes before heading out to the airport to pick him up. But how could she do anything, with a stranger in the hall, trying to pick her lock?

"Don't be silly," Lisa whispered harshly. She wished she had left her radio on, just to have some noise in the apartment, enough to let someone outside know there was indeed someone home. The average burglar wouldn't try to get into an occupied apartment...would he?

It was all her imagination. Just like all those other times she thought she heard someone trying to get into the apartment. The times when she would quietly lock her bedroom door and huddle in her bed, listening for the slightest sound. She never heard the slightest telltale, no matter how long she held her breath and strained her ears. And when she got up in the morning, not a thing was disturbed or missing throughout the whole apartment.

The door opened, creaking on the stiff hinges that the management had been promising to replace ever since Lisa moved in with Todd more than two years ago. Lisa picked up an art knife in each hand and headed down the hall before she really thought about what she did.

"Todd?" She quickly stashed the art knives in the bathroom. "What are you doing home so early?"

"Finished early." Her husband stepped into the apartment far enough to turn and kick the door closed, still holding his bulky, black leather suitcase and matching computer case and carry-on.

"But I was just getting ready to wash up and head out to pick you up." Lisa fought down an urge to run into her bedroom and change from her faded jeans and sweatshirt, into the maroon jumper and plaid blouse Todd's sister, Karla, had bought her for Christmas. She always dressed up for him when he came home from his business trips.

Too late now. She quashed that impulse as she hurried to take his luggage from him.

"Well, now you don't have to." His pale gray eyes looked faded with weariness, contrasting with the dark smears under them. His golden-white hair had that dull, matted look that meant he had spent his days in rooms that reeked of cigarettes and bad ventilation, despite all the "healthy office" regulations.

Lisa held her breath as she went up on tiptoes to wrap her arms around his shoulders and pull his head down to give him his welcome home kiss. The last thing she needed was to find out that the stink of cigarettes and travel brought on pregnancy nausea.

Todd's kiss was little more than brushing his lips against hers. It was hard to put passion into the kiss when he didn't participate. Usually Todd was the one who demanded kisses and prolonged them until she couldn't breathe. He shed his coat and tossed it over his saggy brown leather easy chair, ignoring Lisa's hand reaching out to take it, then dropped into the dented cushions. With a groan, he let out a deep breath, closed his eyes and leaned his head back.

"Rough trip?" she murmured. Todd answered with a grunt. "I made cheesy potatoes and Cornish hens for dinner." She paused to give him a chance to respond. He opened one eye, a sure sign of curiosity despite his weariness. "I missed you, Todd."

"Must have, to make that." He opened his other eye and managed a lopsided smile. "Maybe I should take you with me on these trips. But you'd be bored, sitting in the hotel room all day while I'm at meetings."

"I'm never bored, you know that. But I have so many commitments here in town, at church..." Something twisted in the pit of her stomach when his smile faded and he got that glassy look that made him the image of his father. "*Could* we afford for me to go with you? A couple times?"

"Probably not. Company wouldn't pay." He closed his eyes and lifted his legs one at a time, to drop heavily on the lumpy horsehair hassock.

"I could get a lot of sketching done, though. It'd be really quiet in a hotel room." She sat down on the hassock edge, just brushing his leg with her hip. Todd grunted, opened one eye, and moved his leg over a few inches. "So, did you meet anybody new on this trip?"

Todd sighed, but a few lines around his mouth vanished. It was necessary, Lisa had learned, to get him to talk about his business trips right away. Usually he could unload and unwind in the car riding home from the airport, so he was ready to relax and snuggle on the couch and hear what she had been doing while he was gone. No matter how good her news, Todd wouldn't be able to appreciate it until he got the frustrations and highlights of the trip off his chest and out of his brain.

He scowled at the beginning, his voice a growl. The growl left but the scowl turned into a deep crevice between his eyebrows even as the lines relaxed around his mouth. Lisa didn't understand one-third of the technical words he grumbled. She could run the software needed to access the Internet and handle her accounting, she could make minor repairs on her computer when it acted up, but the things Todd did as troubleshooter and designer for DeWitt-McGregor Computer Systems were as far above her as a shuttle pilot was above a kid with a remote-controlled model airplane.

"And after all that, it looks like I'll have to fly back out to Knight-Baron in a couple weeks," Todd finished. He let out a sigh and dropped his head back against the soft-worn leather cushion and fell silent.

"You're home now and I plan on spoiling you rotten." Lisa picked up his heavy, long-fingered hand in both hers.

Todd flinched a little, but didn't open his eyes. His hand lay limp in hers and that bothered her. Usually when she did that and tried to tickle his palm, Todd would grab her, pull her onto his lap and tickle her instead.

Tonight, nothing.

He must have had a far more demanding, draining trip than usual. Lisa wondered if he would ever climb high enough in the company's hierarchy that he wouldn't have to travel anymore. She stopped that thought as soon as she recognized it as an echo of Mr. Montgomery's usual complaint about his darling son's career.

She waited, but Todd said nothing. Once he got his work off his chest, he always asked what she had done while he was away. It was better to let him ask, rather than risk interrupting a thought about his work that he was preparing to share with her. Lisa had learned while they were dating to let Todd initiate any change in the conversation.

"Are you hungry?" she finally ventured, when the silence grew a little too thick in the apartment. Todd grunted. She shivered and decided it had grown too dark, nearly 5:30 already. He had been talking a long time. She got up to turn on the torch lamp next to his chair. "Todd, I have so much good news to tell you."

"Some good news would be a nice change," he muttered. He flinched when she settled on the arm of the chair and rested a hand on his shoulder.

What was wrong with him?

"You had plenty of good news on this trip, you grump." She shook his shoulder, trying to tease a smile out of him. Todd barely acknowledged her words. "If you're going to be such a sourpuss, I'll just save my good news for later, when you can appreciate it." She slid off the arm of the chair, sure he would stop her.

Something tightened in her throat when she got two steps away and Todd still hadn't moved. She reached back to touch him, positive he had fallen asleep. He opened his eyes and the pale gray had something dark behind them as he looked up at her.

"I'm really not in the mood for your games, Lisa. Why don't you just tell me? I could use something to smile about."

"Okay." She clasped her hands tightly together. "I think I'm pregnant."

No, that wasn't what she meant to say. She meant to tell him about the book contract. Then she would tell him the money would come in handy, to lead into telling him about the baby.

But Todd just sat there, not a speck of change in his pale, weary face or the darkness behind his eyes.

"Todd? Did you hear —"

"Is it mine?"

Something twisted, sharp and tight deep inside her, just before numbness filled her, brain and body. Todd just sat there, waiting.

He looked like his father, when the man had just made a pronouncement that he would let no one contradict or question or even comment on.

"What did you say?" she whispered.

"I said, 'is it mine?' What's so hard to understand about that?" Todd flung himself out of his chair and stomped across the living room to where Lisa had put his luggage. Then he just stood there, looking at her as if she had no reason to feel like he had ripped her heart out of her chest.

His words rang in her ears and still didn't make sense after he repeated them.

"No, I guess it isn't hard to understand at all." Lisa took a step backward. Between her churning stomach and the dizzy feeling wrapping around her head, she had a vision of pitching forward on her face.

This was something she would have expected from Mr. Montgomery, but not from her husband.

That thought swept away the dizzy sensation. Suddenly, her head felt so clear and light, she thought she could fly. Lisa clenched her fists and turned sharply on her bare heel and stalked down the hall. She paused just long enough to retrieve the art knives from the bathroom. Then she continued to her office. Her ears strained, waiting for Todd to say something. Anything.

Nothing. She slammed the door, and locked it.

Her fingers itched to pick up something heavy to throw through a wall, or break something expensive and fragile. But this was her office, her sanctuary, the place where she made the world make sense, even when everything outside her door refused.

The heavy bookshelves lining two walls begged to be toppled. Lisa considered, just for a moment, the satisfying crash they would make. Then she thought of Todd, somewhere in the apartment, listening. She wouldn't give him any satisfaction in knowing he had hurt her.

He was just like his father inside, making a lie of his handsome, youthful looks and pleasant smile. Playing nasty games with words, riling people into fury, and then triumphing over them when they couldn't think straight. She had thought he was different, that he had escaped growing up to be like his widowed father.

Lisa saw she was wrong, now. She had tried to do the Christian thing by swallowing Mr. Montgomery's two-edged remarks, his grudging compliments. Because she loved Todd, she had endured every miserable encounter with her father-in-law.

How could she endure, now that Todd had turned into his father? She *wouldn't* play his game.

How had his mother ever endured it? According to Mr. Montgomery, his late wife was a saint; the perfect housewife and mother; always graceful and demure and refined. The kind of woman his son deserved but hadn't found.

Lisa had learned strong internal control since Todd sauntered into her life and dragged her out of her quiet, happy, isolated little world. She had never needed control before, because there had been practically no one to threaten or challenge her.

She closed her eyes and sat down in the chair between her two art tables. On one lay that day's coloring work, the preliminary sketch sheets for the next story line, and the daydream sketches she had done for *P.K.* during her engagement.

A sob rose in her throat, catching there like she wanted to vomit and couldn't. Lisa had mailed copies of those roughs to Genevieve just that morning, to show the editor her plans for the new collection. She had been so happy and proud, wanting to tell the whole world her good news.

She had grown up with nothing but memories of her parents. No siblings, no grandparents, just her elderly cousins who did their bare minimum duty and shoved her out into the real world as soon as they could. She had created a huge family in her imagination and gave them life with her pen. The cartoons she had mailed that morning showed Katie and Bob announcing her pregnancy. They had both been so happy.

"Stupid," Lisa whispered. She closed her eyes and turned her back on that art table to keep from ripping the paper off the pad. Why punish an innocent cartoon for her stupidity?

Chapter Four

She had been warned, the first time she met Mr. Montgomery. But she had let Todd's promises and sweet words talk her out of common sense and self-preservation. Todd's father had given her neatly pressed broadcloth trousers a scandalized look, and then sneered when Todd told him she was an art student. She should have dumped Todd right then. Permanently.

"Too late," she whispered and stepped to the second art table.

Spread over it lay wallpaper, carpeting and material swatches to decorate the baby's room. After seeing the dream house was for rent, she had spent a happy afternoon gathering samples and catalogues from Floor-to-Ceiling. She had downloaded a floor plan of the dream house from the realtor's website this morning and cut out scale model slips of paper to arrange their furniture inside it. There was a third bedroom for the baby's room. The timing had been perfect. Until now. The lease on the apartment was up this month, and they could move into the dream house without any delays, if they acted right away.

Those happy dreams felt like a lifetime ago. Right now, Lisa didn't care if she ever saw those samples and sketches and catalogues again. She threw all the paperwork and samples into the wastebasket. She poured her unfinished chocolate protein drink on top of them.

The tears burned, pressing hard at the backs of her eyes. How could Todd say that? What did he mean, asking if the baby was his? Of course it was his! He was the only man she had ever slept with. The only man she had ever kissed.

Lisa swallowed hard and rubbed at her eyes. She refused to cry. She had cried too much since marrying Todd Montgomery. Too many secret tears, believing she was being overly sensitive and silly. She had thought Todd was on her side, and she didn't want to put any more stress on him than necessary. Just knowing Todd loved her and that he *would* side with her when necessary had made it easy to hide her tears.

That was another delusion, wasn't it? Well, Lisa now resolved, she wouldn't give him or his father the satisfaction of knowing she had cried over this wound, either.

And on top of everything else, Todd had forgotten Valentine's Day. She had tucked a card and a bag of chocolate covered peanuts into his luggage when she packed for him. Todd hadn't called to thank her or wish her a happy Valentine's Day. Nothing had come. Not a card. Not even a few wilted carnations. He certainly hadn't picked up some overpriced flowers in the airport, like he had done two other times he was away on a business trip and missed an important day. She had told herself on Friday that she was being silly, and Todd would bring her something nice from his trip.

Should she have been warned then, and worried? Were there other signs of trouble she missed?

How could Todd say such a thing?

A harsh beeping penetrated the spinning, angry thoughts that seemed to go nowhere fast. Lisa almost laughed when she recognized the smoke alarm in the kitchen, and realized she had been sitting here for more than forty-five minutes, her mind and heart caught in a repeating loop of pain.

"Why not?" she muttered, and pushed herself out of her chair to totter to the locked door. Her perfect plans for a happy evening of dreaming had been wrecked. Why not dinner, too?

A thin layer of smoke hung across the kitchen ceiling. Lisa hit the fan button, then strode into the living room and opened the window to let fresh air into the apartment. She took a deep breath of the damp, icy air, then returned to the kitchen.

Opening the oven released a gush of thicker smoke. She snatched up the oven mitts and yanked the rack out, almost losing the casserole of scorched potatoes onto the floor.

The Cornish hens were fine, though. Lisa's stomach tried to come up her throat at the rich aroma and the thought of eating anything.

Her lips flattened in anger. Lisa picked up the little roaster pan and upended it into the sink on the disposal side. The hot meat sizzled against the cool stainless steel. She yanked the refrigerator open and emptied the Waldorf salad on top of the meat. The smell of sizzling, melting mayonnaise made her stomach twist again. She retreated into the living room, and nearly ran into the little bistro table, set with flowers and the good china and crystal.

Lisa fought the temptation to throw the dishes to the floor. They were gifts from college friends. She had fought to have her own pattern, instead of inheriting the china Todd's father didn't want anymore. Hands trembling, Lisa piled the plates together and took them to the kitchen.

"What's for dinner?" Todd's voice, barely above a whisper, startled her so she dropped the salad plates as she lifted them to the cupboard.

Lisa swallowed a little shriek and managed to catch the plates, cradling them against her chest. She took a deep breath and continued putting them away.

"Whatever you can find," she managed to say in an even voice as she passed him to get the flowers and silverware off the table.

"Oh." He said nothing more, but he didn't leave either.

Lisa refused to face him as she came back and put away the silverware. She stepped over to the disposal and turned it on before turning on the water. It growled at her. She scorched her hands on the Cornish hens as she tore them apart to shove down the disposal.

"Smells good," Todd offered, raising his voice above the sound of the motor.

She ignored him, and grudged every second she had to wait until the disposal could handle all the good food she shoved down its maw. Lisa rinsed her hot, greasy hands in the cold water and wished she could rinse the sting from her heart as easily.

"What are you eating?"

"I'm not." She made the mistake of looking at him as she turned to retrieve the scorched casserole of potatoes.

Todd had that lopsided little smile and that unreadable dullness in his eyes she could never interpret. Was he angry? Laughing at her? Sad and trying not to show it? Confused? All through college, he wore that smile in a multitude of situations. She had broken up with him too many times to be counted, because of that smile. Lisa wished she had stayed broken up with him.

"You have to eat. For the baby."

"Why should you care?"

She felt the heat penetrating the threadbare oven mitts and nearly threw the casserole down into the sink. It snapped at contact with the wet metal surface.

"What do you mean by that?" Todd's voice cracked.

"You said it's not your baby, remember?"

"I didn't say—"

"Let me tell you something, Mr. Montgomery." She spun to face him and almost shrieked when she came nose-to-nose with him. She hadn't heard him step into the kitchen. "You're the father of this baby because you're the only man who ever touched me. Right now, I wish you never had." She turned, slammed on the faucet, and stomped out of the kitchen. The casserole crackled loudly as cold water doused it.

Lisa retreated to her office, slammed and locked the door, and fell into the couch. She huddled there, fighting nausea that made her want to empty herself until she was a hollow, cold shell.

Not a sound reached her from the hallway. No footsteps. No apology from Todd, no angry shouts.

He rarely shouted when he was angry, preferring to talk through clenched teeth in icy tones. He never apologized, but he always did something extra-special sweet for her when he had hurt her.

Had she been an idiot, thinking he was sorry all those other times? Was it only a bribe to keep her quiet and compliant?

It was too quiet out there. What was Todd doing? She could imagine him standing on the other side of her door, staring at it, white with fury like his father. Or did he fight tears like her? Was he too hurt, too shocked by what he had said to say anything now?

Had she finally won a fight? Had she rendered a Montgomery man speechless with anger and hurt? Lisa's eyes ached for tears, but the tears didn't come.

From far at the other end of the apartment, she heard the door slam. She winced, feeling the reverberation through the walls. What were the neighbors thinking? A giggle rose up in her throat, catching there at the same place where her tears had stopped.

When Lisa ventured out into the apartment, she found the water still running in the sink, slowly eroding burned potatoes out of the broken casserole. She turned it off, gently, and finished putting the dishes away from the table. The flowers followed the potatoes into the disposal.

She made herself a nest of blankets and pillows on the couch in her office, with the door locked. Todd had awakened her by making love to her once, after he had totally ruined a special evening she had put together for some friends from their Young Marrieds class at church. The very idea that he would try something like that again, without uttering a word of apology, made her want to shriek.

He had forgotten to pick up the cake from Rick's Bakery and the etched champagne flutes with Joyce and Larry's first anniversary date. Then he decided to go bowling on the spur of the moment with some buddies from work. He didn't bother calling on her office phone to let her know what he was doing.

He got home just as their friends were leaving, after a relatively pleasant evening despite the disasters. Todd had stumbled through apologizing to their departing friends, but when he was alone with Lisa, he hadn't said anything. He was silent as he helped her clean up the dishes. She went to bed, worn out from the strain of entertaining without bursting into tears.

Todd had kissed her awake. His hands were cold and pressed too hard. He smelled of the bowling alley, greasy food and cigarette smoke. He still wore his shoes. They jabbed her ankles as he moved over on top of her. His knees bruised her thighs as he maneuvered the blankets down to climb in next to her.

"Don't."

"It's okay, honey." Todd smashed her lips with a long, invading kiss. "You know I love you, don't you?" he whispered, his words muffled as he trailed more kisses down her cheek to her ear.

She had wanted to scream that no, she didn't think he loved her at all, but Lisa had kept silent. She had let him make love to her because she believed he was sorry and trying to apologize.

Todd had been tender and attentive and adorably sweet for nearly a week after that.

Lisa knew he would try that trick now, simply because it had worked before. She couldn't stand the thought of him touching her. She wished he had never touched her. Lisa tried to think back to when she had enjoyed making love with Todd.

Had it been so long that she couldn't remember? Or had she always given him what he wanted, whether she got any enjoyment or not, simply because she loved him?

Did he ever love her, or had he been using her to get what he wanted? Clean clothes and house, home cooking and someone to snuggle with on the nights he didn't go out with his friends. And for sex.

"We never made love," Lisa whispered, and was surprised to hear how steady and cool her voice was. "To make love, you have to be in love, and Todd never loved me."

Somehow, hearing the words eased the pressure deep and hard and sharp in her chest. It was true, Todd didn't love her.

He had laughed when she said that in her fury, one other time he had tried to kiss and snuggle her out of her anger. Lisa had pushed him away and told him she wasn't interested in sex.

"We're gonna make love, honey," Todd had said, and laughed as he reached for her.

"You can't make love if you're not in love. You certainly don't love me, and right now I wonder why I ever fell in love with you."

She had stormed away then. Todd had wisely left her alone for a few hours, then brought her flowers and took her out for dinner and told her silly stories about his buddies from high school.

Todd should have been hurt by her words. He should have been angry. He had just been quiet, with that odd glitter in his eyes that made her think he was going to laugh at her.

If she told him now that she didn't love him anymore, and that she knew, was positive, that he never loved her, what would Todd do or say?

He would probably look down his nose at her, just like his father, and walk away.

~~~~~

"Lisa?" Todd's voice at her door startled a squeak out of her as she came awake. She wrapped her arms tight around herself, expecting the door to give way under one thunderous blow.

"Go away, Todd." She smiled, proud of how calm her voice sounded. All the aching twisting through her was too tangled to touch her voice.
~~~~~

"Come on out and let's talk about this."

"You think I'm a whore. What's there to talk about?"

"I didn't say—"

Silence. She couldn't hear anything, not footsteps stomping away or a hand fiddling with the doorknob. What was he doing? Leaning against the door in the weariness he had brought home?

Exhaustion flooded her. Was that the problem? They were both tired, both prone to depressing thoughts? Had Todd meant to say something else, but his tongue had twisted, the words came out wrong, and then she had blown it out of proportion?

His father constantly accused her of that when she made the slightest protest to his unkind or critical remarks.

"What's wrong with us?" Lisa whispered. She choked, refusing to weaken and give in to tears now.

Todd had hurt her. She wasn't mistaken about what he had said. She wasn't going to let him smooth things over without an apology or an explanation. Not this time.

"You didn't say what?" She struggled out of the couch. She advanced on the door. "What *were* you saying when you asked if my baby was yours?"

Silence. She waited until the quiet thickened and she heard the ticking of the old mantel clock on the bookshelf.

"I just wanted—" he began softly, muffled by the wood in the door.

"It's always what *you* want! What *you* think! What *you're* feeling. I missed a lot of work I could have gotten done, to put together a celebration for when you got home, but do you care? Your father has nagged me since the day we got married to give you a baby, and it *is* yours, but—" She choked, feeling as if she would vomit.

Todd said nothing while she gasped for breath. She refused to let out one sob, one more tear. Never again.

"I have a book contract, you selfish jerk! We should be celebrating, but do you care?" She waited, but he gave her no answer. "Well, I don't care either. Not anymore."

Lisa stepped back, waiting, hearing a ringing through the silence, like an emergency broadcast signal on the radio. But there was nothing. No sound. No reaction. Again.

She curled up on the couch and closed her eyes, but sleep was a long time coming. The ticking of her treasured mantel clock, one of the few things she had kept from her parents' estate sale, gnawed at the calm as she tried to find sleep. It echoed voices she only vaguely heard, brought up the hard, biting sounds of critical words.

Todd's father had criticized them for wasting money on a three-bedroom apartment, so they each could have an office. He insisted Lisa could content herself with a lap desk in the living room when she had to satisfy her "itch to doodle." Before they were married, Lisa's cartoons were already being printed in denominational newspapers and quarterly magazines. Since then she had graduated to monthly magazines, all eager for several panels a month depicting the everyday, normal lives of a pastor's family. Despite that, Mr. Montgomery considered Lisa's work a waste of time, and inappropriate for a Christian wife.

The third bedroom was Todd's office, but he rarely used it except to store things and to open his briefcase or plug his notebook computer in to charge overnight. His father had filled it with furniture from the big, echoing, dark house where Todd and his four sisters had grown up. Heavy, dark wood furniture with leather upholstery. And books. Lots of books that looked impressive with their heavy bindings and technical words, but outdated before they were even loaded onto the shelves.

Lisa looked around her sanctuary and smiled in bitter triumph. Todd's father thought her office, which she used every day, was a waste of space and money. It wasn't wasted now, was it?

Wednesday, February 19

The sounds of the radio alarm clock and Todd banging around in the bathroom woke her. Lisa stayed curled up on the couch, surprised she had been able to sleep after all. She listened to him thudding around the apartment. She smelled the toast he burned and wondered what mess she would find in the kitchen. She waited for him to knock on her door. She expected him to act as if nothing had happened last night, and demand his good-bye kiss.

Lisa waited, listening to all the usual morning sounds except Todd's voice. She waited until she heard the door close on rapid footsteps. Todd always ran late for work, his first morning back from a business trip.

No farewell. No apology. No pretense that everything was all right. Just silence.

Lisa moved slowly, wincing as she convinced her body to unbend and get up for the day. The morning light sliding through the blinds looked as cold as Lisa felt.

She opened the door and forced herself to go through her morning routine. Most of the mess she neatened was Todd's. As usual. Did she really want to spend the rest of her life cleaning up after a man who thought so little of her? It had been easy when she was in love and dreaming; now it felt like a death sentence, punishment for the crime of being stupid.

Toothpaste globs in the sink. Water spilled across the bathroom counter. Shaving cream can lid sitting in the corner by the toilet. Towels on the floor. Water dripping in the shower stall. Lisa considered leaving all Todd's mess for him to clean up, but she was the one who spent the day here. Besides, the towels were hers. The decorations in the bathroom were hers. She had wallpapered and painted and re-grouted. She had made over every room in the apartment, to make this a nice home for Todd to come back to every day. She had done it herself, with her own hands, buying at discount stores to save as much money as possible.

Mr. Montgomery had criticized her for "wasting" Todd's money on a home that didn't belong to them. Todd got irritated enough to tell his father Lisa had spent only her own money. He then lectured them on the need to save that money for their children, for private schools and college. Then he returned to criticizing his two married daughters and Lisa for not giving him any grandchildren yet.

"Now what are you going to complain about?" Lisa whispered, stopping to press her hand over her stomach at a surge of nausea. She hadn't experienced morning sickness yet, but considering how everything was falling apart around her, she probably would soon.

She spent an hour cleaning up the bedroom, bathroom and kitchen. Todd's burned toast had left a trail of blackened crumbs from one counter to the next. He left out the carton of orange juice, with an inch still left in the bottom, and the butter, but he put the apple butter in the refrigerator. Lisa gritted her teeth to keep from complaining aloud, and put the apple butter back in the cupboard where it belonged.

When she checked the laundry hamper, it wasn't stuffed full of dirty clothes from Todd's suitcase. Where were they? She went into the bedroom, wondering if he had shoved his suitcase under the bed. He had done that once, on his third trip after they were married. Lisa hadn't thought about it because she was so busy decorating their apartment. Todd didn't pay any attention to his clothes until he had to go out of town again and pulled out his suitcase to pack. Lisa had stayed up until 4a.m., doing the laundry. Todd had complained because she barely woke up to kiss him good-bye the next morning. She had blamed it on his running late, and told herself not to feel hurt.

Lisa wondered now if that was the first warning sign.

Chapter Five

Todd's suitcase wasn't under his side of the bed. Where was it?

A hollow chill flashed through her as she considered Todd moving into a hotel. His father publicly embarrassed people who crossed him. She imagined Mr. Montgomery advising Todd to move into a hotel, where people could see him every day and wonder what his wife had done to make him move out.

"I won't think about it. I won't worry about it," Lisa muttered. She finished cleaning up the apartment, then settled down in her office with her Bible and devotional guide.

After ten minutes, Lisa closed the books. Nothing would stay in her head. She read the same verse four times and still couldn't seem to remember what it said as soon as she looked away.

She had been able to find comfort and guidance in her Bible and devotions before, even when Todd's father was at his worst. Why couldn't she concentrate now?

Her stomach rumbled. Lisa smiled a little. Of course she couldn't concentrate if she hadn't eaten since lunchtime the day before. Her blood sugar was down, that was all.

Two bites of fruit salad put her on her knees, gagging in front of the toilet.

What if I lose the baby? wasn't half as shocking as the next thought: *I wish I wasn't pregnant.*

Lisa sat back in the corner, sweat beads dripping into her eyes, her mouth raw from vomiting nothing but acid. She shivered, hot and welcoming the chill of the ceramic tiles.

"Oh, please God," she whimpered. "What's wrong with me? I've put up with this garbage for years. Why does it bother me now?"

She knew a moment later. The verbal battery had always come from Todd's father. She had always had the reassurance that Todd loved her, that he defended her when it really mattered.

This time, Todd was the attacker.

"I'm not putting up with it anymore," Lisa whispered. "I've tried to be a good wife and be nice and make peace. Not anymore. I'm tired of being walked on and kicked around. This time, somebody can apologize to *me* for a change."

When she finally pulled herself to her feet, she saw the pregnancy test sitting untouched on the counter. The plastic seal was broken. The instruction booklet sat on the counter with the plastic wand on top of it, all ready to be used.

Lisa almost laughed when she considered that if she had left the box sealed, she could have taken it back to get a refund. She tore the box to shreds, then the manual. She snapped the wand in half, then tossed it on top of the shreds in the wastebasket.

Then she settled down at her art table and worked on the next batch of cartoons.

She was very careful to keep the occasional teardrop from falling on the panels.

~~~~~

When the doorbell rang at ten minutes to noon, Lisa was pleased to note that she had calmed enough not to jerk at the interruption. And then pleased to note the time. Her work would always be her refuge, her anchor and foundation. Even when she couldn't pray, she could find strength, peace and comfort in her artwork. Her husband might think she was a hypocrite, evil enough to get pregnant by someone else, but at least other people in her life knew she tried to please God.

They did, didn't they?

The doorbell rang again. What was wrong with her, that she just sat feeling sorry for herself instead of answering the door? Lisa did a quick check in the bathroom to make sure she looked all right. She opened the door in time to see Bekka turning away, her arms full of paper bags. The aroma of chili and burgers filled the hallway with a cloud of warm, spicy perfume that made Lisa's knees wobble.

"Guess the angels were whispering in my ear again." Bekka laughed as she shifted her bags to one arm and reached out to steady Lisa. "You've been ignoring everything else for some big splash of inspiration again, huh?"

"Yeah, sort of." Lisa smiled at her friend. When they had first met at Butler-Williams, people thought they were at least cousins, they looked so much alike. The same wide-boned faces and a preference for keeping their dark hair long and pulled back in a ponytail most of the time, the same dislike for makeup and skirts, the same tendency to ignore everything around them when inspiration's siren song called.

Bekka and her roommates were involved in the drama program at Butler-Williams University. Bekka wrote novels, Kat wrote scripts, and Amy wrote poetry. Lisa had felt especially close to Bekka because her grandparents disapproved of her writing and involvement with the theater, just as Mr. Montgomery disapproved of her artwork. The Sandersons, not surprisingly, were good friends of his.

She and Bekka had banded together and laughed at the narrow-
~~~~~

mindedness of her grandparents, who believed Christians weren't allowed to have fun or use their imaginations. Lisa envied Bekka when her grandparents moved to Florida and she had decided to stay behind in Tabor Heights. Kat and Amy had moved in with her and the three friends included Lisa in their circle when their schedules coincided.

"We are celebrating." Bekka set her bags down on the table. "I just sold a dozen devotional pieces to that anthology I was telling you about, the one for single girls written by single girls."

"That's great." Lisa summoned up a smile, but her aching stomach kept trying to deafen her, demanding to be filled.

"And I figured I could bribe you to let me cry on your shoulder for a little bit, too."

"Cry on my —" She shook her head, trying to clear it enough to think. "Bekka, what happened?"

"Well, I was still trying to sort things out when we ran into each other Saturday, and I didn't want to rain on your parade." She grinned and pantomimed cradling a baby. "Friday was Valentine's Day. You know how it is. Amy and Joe were fighting, as usual, and he made up in a big way. Flowers and candy and dinner out. And Kat's newest boyfriend — a total space-case — forgot he got her flowers, so he bought her more. And they all went out together and came back to the apartment with a bunch of mushy movies." She sighed as she finished lifting the steaming, paper-wrapped burgers from the bag.

"And you were alone and flowerless, surrounded by other people's flowers on Valentine's Day. You don't know how lucky you are, being free."

"Yeah, I keep telling myself that, but Amy went and bought flowers for me and had the florist sign the card 'from a secret admirer.' I know her tactics. And Kat was in on it. She has the money and Amy has the ideas." Bekka pried the lid off the cardboard tub, releasing a spicy cloud of chili steam. "Spoons?"

Lisa chuckled and stepped into the kitchen to retrieve plates, bowls and spoons.

"The thing is, I was fine until those flowers came. Didn't feel sorry for myself until somebody else did, you know?"

She peeled off her faded navy pea coat, tossed it onto Todd's chair and came back to the bistro table. Lisa spooned out the chili. Bekka tugged the scrunchie off her long ponytail and raked her fingers through her hair, neatening it before binding it again. She watched Lisa the whole time.

"What's wrong?" she said as they both sat down.

"Wrong?"

"You're always so happy when Todd gets back from one of his trips. Usually, you'd be so excited about something you'd have interrupted me five times by now — not that you're rude or self-centered or anything. Not like that jerk you married." Bekka shrugged.

"You think Todd is a jerk?" Tears stung her eyes, and the heaviness in the pit of her stomach evaporated. The tight feeling in her head loosened. If someone else could see the problem was in Todd, then she *wasn't* being overly-sensitive. Lisa had heard Bekka call Todd a jerk before, but for the first time it meant something.

"Lisa, you nearly worship the guy. You're so happy doing the most menial thing in the world, because it's for him. Half the time, when you talk about what you're doing, you seem more excited about *telling* Todd what happened than any other part of it. And he doesn't seem to notice half the time. He forgot Valentine's Day, didn't he? And I bet he didn't apologize or do anything when he got home, did he?"

"Among other things."

"Men. Can't live with them and you can't blow them into orbit, either. At least, not yet." Bekka toyed with her chili, eyes sparkling. "What did he do?"

"The usual." Her throat closed up at the thought of repeating what Todd had said. Even for someone who understood as much as Bekka did, she couldn't confess the disaster of last night.

Maybe if she didn't say anything, didn't admit she thought she was pregnant to anyone else, and didn't take a test… she would find out it was all a mistake. Her period could come any day now. She had a serious cold two weeks ago. Maybe being sick had delayed her period. It could all be a mistake.

Except for Todd's words last night. Those weren't a mistake. They were a major assault and she wasn't going to let him smooth it over with ice cream and a movie.

"I had so much good news to tell him and he wasn't listening. The world revolves around him and he had a lousy trip, and why should anybody else be allowed to be happy if he's a grouch?" She shrugged and picked up her hamburger. It was far easier chewing and swallowing than she thought, as if getting the words out destroyed the heavy, aching, crowded sensation in her heart and mind, that made her feel as if she had swallowed granite blocks.

"That good news? The guy's a bozo — I bet he never gave you a chance to tell him your good news."

"Something like that. I had lots of good news to tell him. Not just the stuff you figured out."

"Oh, come on, Lisa! It just isn't fair. You're buried under good stuff. Okay, I told you my good stuff. Fair's fair. You gotta tell me yours," Bekka added, putting a whine in her voice like a spoiled third-grader.

A chuckle escaped Lisa, and suddenly it seemed like the sun had emerged for the first time that day. Between bites of chili and hamburger, she told Bekka about the contract offer and all the work she had done so far. She told her about the dream house coming available. She told her about Tyler Sloane wanting her to design the posters for Royal Community Theater, and the extra money the Randolphs had given her.

"They are the greatest people," Bekka said, putting down her empty chili bowl. "I bet if you went to Miss Emily, she'd help you figure out how to straighten out Todd. If she could straighten out the mess she made of her life, like she told us at the retreat last year, she can help you with the problems Todd's making for you."

"Yeah, probably."

"I'm still jealous of you," her friend added, voice dropping to a whisper. "Even if it's a mess right now, you're married to the man you love. He loves you even if he doesn't know the first thing about acting like it. You're both Christians, so you can go to God about it. And I'll pray for you. It'll work out."

"Thanks." Lisa busied herself scraping the last of the chili out of her bowl, blinking hard to fight tears. She knew Todd had never really loved her, and right now she wondered if she had ever loved him.

Someone said love hurt, but it wasn't supposed to hurt like this, was it?

~~~~~

Todd's head hurt. He had already taken twice as much ibuprofen as was safe, and that was half an hour ago.

He raked his fingers through his hair and leaned back in his chair. His gaze roamed the narrow, paper-drifted office, looking for something in the shelves crammed with computer hardware and peripherals to catch his attention. Anything to avoid the unfinished report on the screen in front of him. He spotted his suitcase, still locked and tagged from the airport, with his dirty laundry and Lisa's imported colored pencils inside.

Why hadn't he given them to Lisa last night? Between the chocolate covered cherries and the pencils, everything would have been fine. She would have known he was sorry the minute he held them out to her.

The least he could have done was leave them in front of her office door. Then she'd know he bought them for her while he was out of town, instead of today at lunch. But no, he had been in such a hurry to get out of the apartment, half-afraid he would hear her crying, he hadn't even stopped long enough to put out the peace offering. What good would it do later on? She'd just accuse him of trying to bribe her.

And honestly, wasn't that what it was, anyway?

"Stupid move," he whispered, his voice hoarse. He wasn't getting sick, but his throat ached and his eyes burned.

Lisa had every right to be angry with him. Why had he asked her that
~~~~~

stupid question? She wasn't the kind of girl who could pretend feelings she didn't have. In college, she hadn't been able to pretend friendship with a girl who had treated her viciously the semester before. She wouldn't have welcomed him home so gladly, she wouldn't have sounded so quietly happy when she said she thought she was pregnant, if she had been cheating on him. Lisa wasn't made that way, and he knew that, so how could he have doubted her?

He had spent most of the night blaming his stupid, cruel words on his aching head, empty stomach, lack of sleep, and his increasing distaste for business travel. He had even convinced himself that Lisa had already figured out that was his problem, and when he woke up in the morning she would be there in bed next to him.

But when he woke up, only an hour after he finally fell asleep, her side of the bed was still empty and cold, the blankets undisturbed. He had checked her office, afraid she had vanished during the night. The jolt of relief at finding the office door still locked almost made him sick to his stomach.

Why had he said that to her?

He had to work extra hard this time to make it up to her. Todd had brought his suitcase to work with some half-baked notion of taking everything to a Laundromat at lunch. Lisa would get over her sulk if he took care of his own laundry for a change. He knew how much she hated losing time away from her drawing table to do things like laundry and ironing. The fact that she never complained and even managed to smile or even sing under her breath while she did the laundry always amazed him.

Why had he asked if the baby was his? What had he been thinking?

It was past two, and it looked like he would never get out for a sandwich for lunch. Forget the Laundromat. Maybe he could ask his father if his housekeeper —

"Wrong move." His throat hurt even worse now. Todd wondered if it was better to continue suffering, or tell his boss he was sick and go home.

He certainly couldn't let his father know Lisa wasn't doing his laundry. He would demand to know why Todd couldn't have his own wife do his laundry, and the whole fight would come out in the open.

Fight.

Just thinking about the word made Todd's headache worse.

He had actually had a fight with Lisa. They had bickered about things in college. She had given his ring back to him twice. Or was it three times? She hid in her office and gave him the silent treatment when he forgot things and acted selfishly before. But they had never really fought until now. Slamming doors and broken casseroles and burned dinners certainly counted as a fight.

After the things his father had said about Lisa when he drove him to the airport last week, Todd refused to let him know he and Lisa had fought. His father loved to be proven right, especially when someone suffered for ignoring his input.

Had his father been right? Was it stupid to leave Lisa alone so much of the time, without checking on her, without demanding an accounting of every move she made? Was his father right? Did women feel neglected and unloved if their husbands weren't constantly breathing down their necks?

Todd had stared with bleary eyes at the pregnancy test sitting out on the counter, while he brushed his teeth that morning. The bright pink box glowed, daring him to pick it up. The little testing wand waited to be used. Obviously, Lisa had wanted to take the test when he got home. She had waited for him so they could read the results together.

Lisa was like that, always taking extra steps, always waiting for him to get home before she opened a letter or an email with good news, so she could share it with him. The last time her cartoon strip had expanded to three more markets, she had waited all day, the contract still in its envelope, for him to come home so they could open it together and read the details. She was always saving the last scoop of ice cream for him, waiting for him to get home from business trips so they could see a movie together, always cooking things he liked and she loathed.

"I am a grade-A jerk," Todd told the cloudy sky outside his window. For some reason, that vocal admission didn't hurt his throat.

How could he make it up to Lisa? He couldn't just walk in with flowers and candy and say he was sorry. That wasn't enough.

He had ruined her surprise and her fancy dinner, so he would just surprise her and take her out for dinner.

She had wanted to make a big announcement, hadn't she? To make it up to her, he would let her make the announcement where it mattered most.

Todd grinned and reached for the phone. He chuckled as he realized his headache didn't thump quite so sharply now. He dialed and leaned back and closed his eyes.

His first call was to his father's private line at the law office. He got an answering machine. Good. Leaving a message let him say everything without being interrupted and interrogated.

"Dad, I have something really important to tell everybody. I'm taking the whole clan out for dinner at the Mediterranean Terrace tonight. Be there at seven."

His father would be puffed up with pride by the time the evening was over. He would forget every criticism he had ever leveled against Lisa. He would finally see she was the sweet, loving, Christian wife he had always wanted for his son. Her artwork and career didn't get in the way at all. In fact, it would make things even more convenient for her as she slipped into motherhood. Todd grinned, imagining all the ideas Lisa would get for her cartoon strip, just from pregnancy and motherhood and the baby growing up.

They were going to have a baby. He was going to be a father. He hoped they had a girl, despite his father's insistence on a grandson. Todd wanted Lisa to have a little girl to fuss over and make mother-daughter outfits for. He imagined coming home at night and having both of them come running to kiss him and hug him and fuss over him.

"Oops." Todd pulled free of that daydream and opened up his phone to browser to get the restaurant's number. He had to make sure there was a table to accommodate all of them, after all.

His four sisters, two brothers-in-law, his father, Lisa and him. Nine. Was that enough to justify a private room?

"Yeah, go for it," he muttered as the phone rang and he waited for someone at the restaurant to pick up.

He'd show Lisa he really did want this baby. She would forgive him. Lisa always forgave him. She was the sweetest little wife a man could ever want.

Now Lisa and his father would get along. He would shower her with gifts and treat her like she was made out of glass. He had certainly treated Todd's mother that way, during each one of her five pregnancies. His father had enjoyed repeating those stories of how happy he and his wife had been, looking forward to each coming child, and how he had taken extra special care of her. Todd looked forward to asking his father for advice on how to take good care of his wife and coming baby.

Everything would be just fine.

"Hi," Todd said, as the maitre d' at the restaurant answered the phone. "I'd like to reserve a private room for tonight."

Chapter Six

When Todd called his sisters, they all wanted to know what the big announcement was. He laughed and told them to guess, but he wasn't saying anything until dinner. Karla came close to the truth, but Todd thought he did a good job of giving answers without any hints in them.

"Maybe I should just call Lisa and ask her," his sister said, laughing.

"No! Don't do that." Todd winced as his headache suddenly galloped back at double strength. How could he have forgotten to tell Lisa about the dinner? What if she had other plans for tonight?

No. That was silly. Lisa wouldn't have anything else to do. She always made sure her evenings were free for the first two days after Todd got back from his business trips.

"Why? Haven't you told her what it is yet?" Karla teased. "I swear, Toddy, I wonder sometimes why she stays with you. That girl is a saint to put up with you forgetting about her half the time, and keeping her in the dark the other half."

"Well, you're right about that," he muttered.

"What was that?"

"Lisa knows, but she's not about to tell anybody either. She wants me to keep it a secret until tonight."

If she shows up for dinner, that is, Todd silently amended. He knew he would be busy with meetings up to the last minute, so he asked Karla to pick up Lisa and bring her to the restaurant, then hurried his sister off the phone, so he could call home. He didn't need Karla calling to wheedle the news out of Lisa before he could even tell his wife about the dinner party.

The problem was that he had to apologize before he could tell her about the celebration. Twenty minutes later, Todd still didn't know how to say it. How could he explain to her that he had simply been in a bad mood, he was tired, he hated leaving her alone all the time, and the wrong words slipped out?

The phone rang, jangling his nerves so he nearly jumped out of his chair. He reached for it, praying it was Lisa. She had called him at work and made everything right a few times before. He had never needed to apologize before. She knew he loved her and that made everything all right. How could his father say Lisa wasn't the perfect wife for him? She understood him better than anyone.

"Todd, what's this big news?" Mr. Montgomery demanded the

moment he answered the phone.

"Dad—"

"They aren't transferring you out of state in that ridiculous merger deal, are they?"

"No, Dad." Todd sighed and wished he had never mentioned the West Coast merger to his father. Especially since it wouldn't take place for another year at the earliest.

No one was supposed to know about it, but Mr. Montgomery had a way of worming information out of everyone. He had a sense for secrets, for bad news especially, and badgered until people gave in out of self-defense. The only thing that saved Todd from worrying about his job if the news leaked prematurely was that his father never divulged information to anyone, about anything. His father's attitude was that he had a right to know everything going on in Tabor Heights, but no one had the right to know anything about his life or activities. Todd sometimes wondered how his father had any friends.

"What could be so important then? She's not leaving you. I know you'd be more discrete if that was happening."

"Lisa would never leave me. Just the opposite. It's the greatest news in the world—" Todd groaned and slouched back in his seat. Right on schedule, he had let slip too much. When would he ever learn?

"Opposite, huh?" A sharp bark of laughter rattled the phone. "What could be so great that little sl— No. Did she finally do right by you, son? Well, it's about time she grew up and faced her responsibilities. When's the baby due?"

"I didn't say we were having a baby, Dad." Todd sank lower in his chair. Sure, that was a great defense. Knowing his father, he had just confirmed it.

"Okay, have your way." Mr. Montgomery chuckled. "I'll let you make your big announcement to your sisters. Congratulations, son. Now, take a word of advice. Pregnancy does crazy things to a woman's head. Treat her tenderly. Your mother loved me with everything she had, but I still suffered some bad times when she was pregnant with you and your sisters. She always realized she was wrong and apologized, but those were some tense months, let me tell you. I knew you'd be the one to make me a grandfather."

Todd wanted to bang his head on his desk by the time he got off the phone with his father. He could never win. Why did he even try?

Still, it was good to hear his father laugh. Todd imagined him showing up at the restaurant with roses for Lisa, maybe even hugging her for the first time. No, he was too reserved for that. He disapproved of public displays of affection. Maybe he would do or say something to finally convince Lisa he cared about her.

Lisa. He still had to call Lisa. He still had to apologize.

What was that his father had said about apologizing? His mother had acted crazy during her pregnancy and she had apologized for it? Somehow, that didn't sound right.

Then again, maybe his father was right. Lisa shouldn't have overreacted like she did last night. Maybe her pregnancy was already getting to her.

Todd grinned as he reached for the phone. She wouldn't be angry with him for long. He planned on treating her like glass. He'd shower her with anything she wanted. He'd hire a maid, so she wouldn't even have to get up from her drawing table to make a cup of tea.

How could Lisa ever think he didn't want their baby?

"Todd?" Mr. DeWitt tapped on the half-open door before he stepped inside. "Ready to make your report?"

"Ah... sure." Todd put the phone back in the receiver and reached for his notebook, half-buried under all the paperwork he had brought back from the trip. His boss gestured for him to hurry and stepped out into the hall. He'd just have to call Lisa when the meeting was over, Todd decided. He tugged his tie straight as he hurried to catch up with his boss.

~~~~~

The doorbell rang as Lisa stood up from her art table. She flinched and lost her balance, turning her ankle. A gasp escaped her as she went down. She scrambled for a grip on her chair. Her chest hit the edge of the table.

Panic sent an icicle straight through her chest. Was that how it would happen? One silly, avoidable fall, and she would miscarry?

Lisa landed hard on the floor, narrowly missing hitting her chin on the edge of the table. She closed her eyes, listening to her heart thump.

The doorbell rang again. She considered ignoring it, in the hopes that whoever was outside would go away. Then she glanced at the window, the blinds only a foot above the sill. It was dark outside.

"Thank You, Lord, for small favors," Lisa whispered. Her throat hurt, her eyes were dry, and now her ankle throbbed from the fall. That didn't matter, though, in the face of a bigger miracle.

Once again, she had been able to lose her problems in her artwork. She had spent the afternoon working on her cartoons and never noticed the passage of time.

As if on cue, her CD player clicked and processed through the last disk of the ten in the stack. She hadn't left the room other than a bathroom break and to refill her water bottle. And Bekka's visit. That had been a gift from God. Lisa had been able to talk about her contract and regain that sense of giddy triumph and accomplishment. Bekka had been sympathetic over her usual troubles with Todd and reminded Lisa to pray and turn her
~~~~~

hurt over to God. After she left, Lisa sat down to work with renewed energy and a lighter spirit. She had a reasonable stack of roughed panels in the green plastic tray, and a pile of notes for future panels in the red tray. Best of all, she had six sheets of paper with finished panels in the blue tray. Quite a good output for a solid day's work.

"I wonder if they're any good," Lisa murmured.

The doorbell rang a third time.

"Coming!" She would have laughed if her throat wasn't so dry. Lisa ran her fingers through her hair and limped down the hall to the living room and the door. Her ankle hurt less with every step.

Karla, Todd's oldest sister, and her husband, Kevin stood in the hall. They were both dressed up for an evening out; suits and high heels, that cashmere coat that looked so good on Kevin, and Karla had her hair swept up with the blue and pearl clips Lisa had given her for her birthday.

A stab of envy shot through Lisa, followed by a sharp hunger pang. They were going out for dinner. How long had it been since Todd took her out?

"You're not ready," Karla said, after looking Lisa up and down. She chuckled. "Are we early again?"

"Ready for what?" Lisa stood back and beckoned for them to come in. The mantel clock in her office chimed the half hour.

"Yep," Kevin said. "We're early. How's the cartoon business treating you, Lisa?"

"Fine." She looked back and forth between the McNeals, feeling grubbier with each passing second. "What's going on?"

"Todd said you two had something important to tell everybody, so he made reservations at the Mediterranean." Karla took a step closer, her blue eyes narrowing a little as she looked over Lisa's baggy jeans and sweatshirt. "Don't tell me my idiot brother forgot to tell you what time we were picking you up?"

"He didn't bother inviting me." Her throat closed for a minute, then Lisa swallowed hard and tried to smile. "Look, whatever is going on, I'm really not in the mood. I spent the whole day bent over my desk and my head hurts—"

"What do you mean, Todd didn't invite you?" Kevin said. He and Karla exchanged glances. "He asked us to pick you up since he had to work late tonight."

"This is the first I've heard of it." Lisa considered Kevin and Karla's clothes and tried to think what she had that was ready to put on and didn't need much fussing. She couldn't handle fussing right then.

Something came to a jolting stop inside her. Why should she put herself out to convenience Todd?

"But... Todd said the two of you wanted to take us to dinner," Karla said. "He's been a jerk again, hasn't he?"

"Jerk?" She tried not to burst into tears. Or was it hysterical laughter that caught in her throat?

"He's done this since we were little. Instead of just saying he's sorry, he has to buy a present and do something big to make up for what he did."

"Todd certainly has a hard time saying he's sorry, doesn't he?" She forced her lips into a smile.

Why hadn't she ever seen this before? Todd never said he was sorry when he forgot something they had planned, or he let her down. He made a big fuss the next time they went out together, or he brought her flowers or a full Chinese dinner and rented her favorite movies so they could spend an evening just goofing off at home together. Lisa had always thought he was just being romantic.

It was easier for him to spend money than say he was sorry.

Probably because he wasn't sorry, just doing what it took to keep her quiet and content.

"Well, whatever my baby brother did, it was probably a lulu." Karla gently touched Lisa's cheek. "You look like you've had a rough day, all alone here. I bet he didn't have the guts to even leave you a message on the answering machine."

"Not too rough." No way was she going to admit, even to a sympathetic sister-in-law, how deeply Todd had hurt her. "I got lost in my next strip. And you know something?" she hurried on. "I really don't feel like going out."

"If you don't come, Todd'll never forgive you."

Forgive me? I haven't done anything compared to what he did to me.

Lisa bit her lip against blurting the words.

"Whatever you're fighting about, if you sit at home, Todd will be the winner," Kevin said, shaking his head. "Come on, Lisa. It'll be a great time. Why not live it up?"

"Where did you say we're going?" She just felt too tired to argue.

"That's the spirit." He settled down on the couch. "We have plenty of time. We're just going to the Mediterranean, down the street."

"Oh." Lisa nodded and blinked hard against another more hot pressure in her eyes that would turn into tears. Hadn't she sworn she would never cry over Todd Montgomery ever again? Still, the news hurt. Todd hadn't taken her to the Mediterranean in more than a year. "Okay. I just need a few minutes to change."

Halfway through struggling into her last pair of pantyhose and praying they wouldn't run, Lisa nearly burst into tears.

If Todd was trying to make up with her, why had he invited his whole family to witness it? Didn't it matter to him if someone knew they had been fighting?

Obviously not.

"You know, I think Todd is going about this the wrong way," Karla confided, as she and Lisa waited in the lobby downstairs for Kevin to bring the car around. "He just got back from a trip, you two fought about something, and now he's spending the evening with the whole clan instead of being alone with you. I think it's time to have a talk with our father again."

"Talk?" Lisa wondered if she had missed something.

"He's been complaining that Todd isolates himself with you instead of spending 'quality' time with his family. Good grief, the poor guy is on the road weeks at a time, then he's only home for a few weeks before he has to fly off again. When is he going to have a decent marriage unless he works on it? For all we know, this dinner party is because Todd got chewed out again for shirking his duty to the family."

"Probably," Lisa whispered. She wanted to laugh, but the sound caught in her throat.

In the last four weeks Todd spent at home, he devoted two weekends to working on his father's car. They had to eat dinner with his father every Sunday after church. Mr. Montgomery insisted Todd accompany him during visitation and any other duties he took care of as a deacon at church.

How could Todd be isolated with his wife, when he spent more time with his father?

~~~~~

The evening wasn't turning out at all as Todd had planned. He needed what energy the day hadn't drained away to keep from slouching in his chair at the table and sulking. He couldn't do that. His father would scold him, tell him his bad mood was from lack of sleep or proper food, and then criticize Lisa for not looking after her husband as a good wife. Todd thought of that dinner she had fussed over and then sent down the disposal last night, and wondered how his father could ever say that about Lisa. She looked after him far better than he deserved.

Not that she even looked *at* him now.

Todd glanced around the small, private dining room and stifled a sigh. Darkly elegant wallpaper and matching upholstery, snowy napkins, oversized platters edged in hunter green, and a waiter with a napkin hung over one arm, ready to take care of their smallest need. The atmosphere demanded no one sulk.

His father sat at the head of the table, a stern mountain of proper manners and dark elegance. He didn't dominate the conversation so much as he established it and kept it within the boundaries he required. Mr. Montgomery was in a genial mood. Because he already knew the secret, he took Todd's refusal to make his announcement right away with good
~~~~~

grace. Why couldn't everyone else at the table be in a good mood, too?

His four sisters were quiet, as they always were when the family got together. It drove Todd crazy, because he had seen them giggle and chatter when there wasn't an official family gathering. His two brothers-in-law kept the conversation going with his father, and Todd was grateful. His father liked Kevin McNeal, who was a lawyer too, even if he refused to join his law firm. Stuart Owens had Mr. Montgomery's respect because he very successfully ran his family's storage and moving business. The only thing he didn't like about his sons-in-law was that they didn't go to church.

Todd knew his father would have blamed both men for his daughters no longer attending church, but all four had stopped attending as soon as they turned eighteen. As they had reminded their father through many icy arguments, they no longer lived in his home, so he no longer had any right to dictate their actions.

Why was he thinking of those arguments now, at what should be such a happy occasion? Todd silently grumbled and tried not to sulk. This dinner party was too expensive for him to sit and sulk like a baby.

He glanced at his silent wife. He kept checking on her all during dinner to make sure she was still there, because she was so quiet.

Lisa hadn't looked at him since she walked in with Karla and Kevin. She barely responded when he told her she was beautiful in her dark blue linen dress, with her long, dark hair pulled back and up in an elegant sweep. She didn't seem to notice that he didn't kiss her. His father did, though, and gave him a nod of approval. Todd wondered why he felt more embarrassed that he *hadn't* kissed his wife, than when his father scolded him over public displays of affection.

Lisa ignored his suggestion that she order the stuffed flounder, her favorite. She ordered a Cobb salad. Why? She could get a Cobb salad anywhere.

She said she had a big lunch and wasn't hungry, when he offered to split an appetizer sampler plate with her. She loved the sampler plate. They had laughed and competed with each other over it the last time they ate here. How long ago was that? Todd nearly writhed in his chair when he realized he couldn't remember how long it had been since he brought Lisa here. This was their special place for celebrations. They had made up over big breakups in their relationship here. Didn't she realize what he was trying to do?

He and Lisa sat next to each other at the long oval table, but they might as well have been sitting at opposite ends for all the conversation they had. Todd tried to hold her hand under the table. Her fingers were cold and she tugged her hand free to butter a roll and then kept her hands on top of the table, always fiddling with a utensil or picking her roll apart, crumb by crumb.

It was little comfort to Todd that Lisa hardly talked to anyone else, either. It made for a too-quiet meal, because his father never seemed interested in his daughters' lives. He put them through the same questions he asked every time their family got together, as if their lives could be contained in those boundaries. When he finished his questions, and got the usual two- or three-word answers, totally lacking in warmth or enthusiasm, he left the four sisters alone. As if he could get all the important details of their lives in two hundred words or less, and there was nothing else of interest beyond what he wanted to know.

Didn't his father see that if he just let his daughters talk naturally, at their own speed, he would get just as much information with less work and everyone would be more comfortable? Todd had listened to his sisters talk when their father wasn't around. They laughed and teased and spilled information the family patriarch would never hear, because it wasn't included in his short list of questions. Todd's sisters weren't laughing now, just like Lisa.

No wonder Lisa doesn't talk much. Dad grills her and then ignores her just like he does with the girls.

Lisa was always unnaturally silent during these family get-togethers. Maybe she didn't like the noise or the crowded feeling? Was nine a crowd?

No, that couldn't be it. When they were planning for their life together, Lisa had told him she wanted a big family. She said she envied him having four sisters. She was an only child.

Maybe that was the problem. Lisa still wasn't used to being part of a big family.

An even bigger family, soon. Todd felt his heart thump a little harder at the thought and he grinned.

They were going to have a baby!

The waiter had just finished putting down the dessert; delicate cups filled with warm bread pudding, butter rum sauce and clotted cream. Lisa loved bread pudding, but tonight she didn't pick up her spoon. She even looked a little paler and sat back, as if the aroma of the dessert made her nauseous. Was the baby doing that to her already?

Todd felt that ache return to his throat. He had been cruel last night. Well, in another moment he would show Lisa he hadn't meant it.

Chapter Seven

"We have some great news," Todd said, glancing around the table.

"It's about time." Mr. Montgomery smiled that triumphant smile that always made Todd think of a cat with feathers around its mouth. "I swear, since you got married you're as secretive as a miser. What is it?" He winked at Todd, his eyes gleaming the way they did when he won a court case or prevented yet another change in the government of their church.

"We're having a baby." He slid his arm around Lisa and squeezed her shoulders.

Lisa stiffened. Todd could have sworn her skin grew icy underneath the crisp blue linen. She didn't look at him. She didn't look at anyone, despite the chorus of congratulations and delighted questions from his sisters.

"When is he due?" his father demanded, cutting through the happy clamor.

Lisa didn't answer. She stared at the base of the candle ring in the middle of the table and licked her lips once.

"It's about time you two made me a grandfather." Mr. Montgomery glanced around the table and fixed each of his daughters with that triumphant, tight smile that brought sighs and headshakes and other small signs of frustration from all four. "It's nice to see at least Lisa knows her duty to this family. Lisa, when is my grandson due?" He waited, but Lisa ignored him and kept staring at the candle ring. Todd took his arm from around her shoulders. "Todd?" he prompted, when full silence settled around the table.

"I really don't know." He chuckled, but it sounded weak to him. "We didn't really talk that far."

"Lisa, I asked you a question. When is my grandson due?"

"I have no idea. I'm not even sure if I'm pregnant yet," Lisa finally said, with a flick of her eyes in her father-in-law's direction, but no other movement.

"But Todd just said you two were having a baby." Mr. Montgomery sat back in his chair, resting his arms on the table in that pose that reminded Todd of a judge ready to make a pronouncement. He wished his father wouldn't do that. What little stubbornness Lisa ever showed always came when someone kept pushing, or like his father, tried to guilt-trip her into acting against her will.

"Since I'm the one who might or might not be pregnant, I'm the final word, don't you think?" Lisa's eyes had a brightness Todd didn't like. Maybe she was feverish.

"Honey," Todd began slowly, "when I got home, you said—"

"I said I *thought* I was pregnant." She looked at him for the first time. Moisture glimmered on her lashes. "We didn't get any further than that, did we?"

"Uh oh. Still acting like newlyweds," Charli muttered, followed by a chorus of chuckles from her sisters.

"What do you mean, you *think* you're pregnant?" Mr. Montgomery's voice cut through the momentary lightness.

"I haven't taken any tests or gone to a doctor for confirmation." Lisa picked up her spoon and delicately dipped the tip into the butter rum sauce, avoiding the cream.

"When are you taking the test? I have the right to know immediately, since this will be my first grandchild."

"Oh, Father..." Andrea sighed. Their father didn't react to the exasperated sound, and that worried Todd.

"I'm not going to take any tests." Lisa licked the single drop of sauce off her spoon.

"What?" The single word rang off the chandelier and the brass candle sconces on the walls.

"It's no one's business but mine." She dipped up another drop of sauce.

"Todd, what is she talking about?" Mr. Montgomery demanded.

Todd froze. His gut said this family dinner had been a big mistake. He couldn't quite figure out how or why.

Lisa was furious with him. The more she hurt, the quieter she became. Until she could vanish from the room.

Todd tried to hold onto his smile as he looked at his waiting family, and his head ached with a sickening confusion. What had he done to get her so angry? Didn't she realize he was doing all this to make it up to her?

He had to get out of this. He had always gotten out of scrapes before. All he had to do was control the damage until he and Lisa could be alone. She loved him. She would forgive him. She always forgave him. Lisa never hung onto her anger for long.

Todd relaxed a few degrees. No matter how bad it felt right now, it wouldn't last for long. Lisa loved him. She would forgive him. Everything would be just fine.

"What am I talking about?" Lisa said in a quiet voice that seemed to ring through the room. "Todd doesn't want this baby."

"I never—" The words caught in his throat. His sisters stared, their mouths falling open in identical expressions of horror. His brothers-in-law very carefully didn't look at anyone.

"What is going on?" The ice in Mr. Montgomery's quiet voice filled the room.

"When Todd got home last night, I told him I thought I was pregnant. He says the baby isn't his. Therefore, my baby *isn't* your grandchild. It's no one's business but mine." Lisa licked another drop off the spoon with the lazy grace of a Siamese.

The room crackled with silence. Todd's head pounded and he couldn't breathe for the pressure of everyone staring at him. They wanted him to do something. He knew he had to do something. But what?

Lisa turned and looked at him, waiting just like everyone else. Her face had no expression. Just like his. He counted fifteen heartbeats before she stood up.

"If you'll excuse me, I have to go throw up." She slid out through the curtained door, vanishing into the restaurant.

"Oh, Todd, how could you?" Karla demanded. Her eyes filled with tears. She never shrieked, never nagged, never scolded, but her tears could always make him feel like a two-inch-high pile of dirt.

"It's nothing to worry about," Mr. Montgomery said with a chuckle that shocked Todd. "It's just hormones, Toddy. Just like I told you. She'll be all right. When a woman gets pregnant, it takes a while for her mind and body to settle down." Another chuckle sent a new kind of silence through the room. "I remember what an emotional roller coaster your mother was on, every time she got pregnant with one of you." He nodded and slapped the table, grinning as if he had just won a long-lasting argument at a church board meeting. "I knew that girl would do right by you once she got rid of those childish notions of hers. She worships you, Toddy, and that's the important thing."

"Father!" Andrea groaned. "Didn't you hear what she said? She told Todd she was pregnant, and he said the baby wasn't his!"

"I'm sure he never said any such thing. Did you, Todd?"

All gazes turned to him again. Todd wondered if he could find the women's bathroom, grab Lisa and escape out the back door before anyone realized what was going on.

Then again, the way Lisa had been acting, she would probably fight him every step of the way.

"Actually..." He wished he hadn't eaten the whole appetizer sampler by himself, along with his sixteen-ounce steak. "I said—I was so startled when she told me—"

"What did you say, Todd?" Charli asked. She reached across the table as if she would shake him until he confessed.

"I asked... if the baby was mine." He couldn't look at anyone. It was hard enough looking at his clasped hands on the snowy tablecloth.

"Oh, Toddy... " one of his sisters sighed. It could have been all four in chorus.

"No wonder Lisa didn't want to come tonight." Karla stood, pushing her chair out hard enough to bang against the wall behind her. Kevin stood with her. "You didn't bother telling her about this little dinner party tonight. She was totally surprised when we showed up. Did it ever occur to you to *ask* her if she wanted to go out before you invited the rest of us?" She sighed when Todd could only shake his head. "You are such a jerk, Todd. I'm surprised Lisa stayed with you long enough to get pregnant."

"Karla, how dare you say such a thing to your brother? Apologize right now," Mr. Montgomery ordered.

"I never apologize for telling the truth. It was Lisa's right to make the announcement. He didn't even tell her what he was planning."

"It's Todd's child. Who has better right to tell us the good news than he does?"

"Right? Todd doesn't even think the baby is his. I wonder where he got *that* idea, hmm?"

"Karla Grace Montgomery!"

"The same place Mother got the idea none of us were wanted," Charli muttered.

"Good-night everyone. I have to get out of here before something... unpleasant happens." Karla headed for the door, snagging Lisa's purse off the back of her chair on the way.

She vanished out the door, with Kevin right behind her. Todd wished he could vanish too, but he was held in place like a butterfly in a display case, pinned by the angry, astonished stares of his other three sisters.

~~~~~

She didn't throw up, but Lisa knew if she moved, she would lose everything. Sharp pains shot through her stomach, reaching around her back, arching up her spine to settle into the base of her skull. Labor couldn't be any worse than this.

Tears burned the corners of her eyes, slowly breaking free and dripping down to her chin. The bathroom tiles were cold, slick, lime sherbet green. The room smelled faintly of peach potpourri. She huddled in the stall, her elbows resting on the green porcelain seat, and wished she could just vanish down that little drain in the floor.

The door thudded softly open and high heels clicked on the tiles. Lisa closed her eyes, praying whoever it was would stop at the first stall. She had chosen the fifth stall deliberately to avoid being noticed.

"Lisa?" Somehow, Karla's half-whisper wasn't a surprise. "Oh, honey, look at you." She knelt in the stall and put her arms around Lisa's shaking shoulders.

"No thanks. I'm sick enough as it is." A tiny, cracked giggle escaped
~~~~~

her. Lisa wondered how much rum was in that butter rum sauce. Was this what it felt like to be drunk, or had she simply lost all sense of balance?

"No wonder. Between the hanging judge and the village idiot, I'm feeling a little sick myself. Can you move?" Karla didn't wait for a response. She slid her hands under Lisa's arms and lifted.

In a few seconds, they had settled on the couch in the outer room. Lisa shivered and prayed she wouldn't throw up on Karla's green brocade dress.

"We're taking you home." Her sister-in-law showed Lisa her purse.

Lisa hadn't cried the entire time she knelt in front of the toilet, but now she did. Karla held her, mopping at her gushing tears with a handful of tissues yanked from the jade box in the center of the table.

"Why?" Lisa managed to say, when she could finally catch her breath again.

"You mean, why am I sticking up for you instead of my idiot brother?" Karla snorted when Lisa could only nod. "You're the victim here. It's always been Father and Todd against us girls. He could do no wrong, and we could do nothing right if we weren't worshipping the faultless son at the holy father's side."

"That's awful."

"Sometimes the truth is. We know our father has always been rotten to you, and we've certainly fought to get him to ease up. I honestly don't know how you've avoided running for a gun."

"Me neither." A tiny giggle crawled up her throat and escaped with a painful gasp.

"If you want to stay with us tonight, you're more than welcome."

"If I'm lucky, Todd will go away and leave the apartment to me. It's my place more than his, anyway."

"That's the spirit." Karla hugged her tight once more. "Ready to go?"

Neither Kevin nor Karla said much on the way back to the apartment. Lisa was grateful for the silence. What good would words do, anyway? She was also grateful the ride was so short, barely ten minutes. She could have walked if it weren't so cold out, and her stomach and head so unsettled.

Karla hugged her when Lisa got out of the car, but neither woman said anything. Lisa paused in the doorway of the building, watching the McNeals' car pull away. She almost darted back out through the door to wave for them to stop, almost begged to take Karla's offer. Did she really want to stay in that apartment, whether Todd came home or not?

She had to. It was time to hold her ground instead of always making peace. She was the victim here.

It felt odd to realize she had Karla's full support. From her few words, maybe Lisa had all four sisters' support. She was almost warm by the time the elevator deposited her on her floor.

She couldn't sleep, even if she wanted to. Lisa had a vision of Todd coming home and trying to kiss her into forgiving him, like he had succeeded in doing so many other times. After what he had done, she would accept nothing short of an apology and some huge, permanent changes in their lives. She refused to be vulnerable. Wearing her nightgown, lying in bed would make her vulnerable. Her office was her fortress, her domain. She put her sweatshirt and blue jeans back on and settled down at her art table.

As she had feared, the cartoons she had done during the long day of retreating were... silly. Angry, but ridiculous in their anger. Bickering about silly things like decorations for the nursery and names for the baby. Pathetic little one-upmanship games between both sets of grandparents, conducted through phone calls and deliveries from baby stores.

"It'd work better if it was face-to-face," Lisa muttered, looking over her scribbled preliminary panels.

The problem was that Bob's parents lived three states away. They had caused a few problems for Bob and Katie's wedding two years ago. Lisa had been inspired, using all the grief Mr. Montgomery had given her over her own wedding plans. The distance made it hard for the prospective grandparents to compete or do more than make snide remarks. Besides, a minister and his wife couldn't afford to be nasty people, even in the privacy of their own family. Lisa had set out to make the minister and his wife and their many children into humorous, real, lovable, flawed, yet essentially *ideal* Christians.

The problems with this coming baby had to come from the out-of-state in-laws.

Lisa sat and stared at the panels in front of her for nearly half an hour as the ideas worked through her mind. Maybe what she planned was bitter. Maybe it would be seen all too clearly as a strike back for all she had endured. But she would work out all her pain through the comic strip. She had worked out her dating problems with Todd through her comic strip. Maybe she would find some answers.

Praying certainly hadn't helped yet.

Lisa worked until nearly 3a.m., and Todd never came home. She knew where he was. Faithfully staying at his father's side, letting that cruel, cold man pour more complaints into his mind. According to Mr. Montgomery, the only mistake his wonderful son had ever made was to marry the wrong woman.

Thursday, February 20

Todd overslept in the big hotel bed. That amazed him, since he never slept well on any business trip. From the first night of marriage with Lisa, he had been unable to sleep decently unless she was next to him. It was proof how important Lisa was in his life.

That night after the debacle in the Mediterranean, Todd tossed and turned and stared at the clock for minutes at a time. He thought he saw every hour and half hour change in those ridiculous red numerals. Then, somewhere between 5a.m. and being late for work, he fell asleep.

He still couldn't think clearly when he got to work. His thoughts kept going back to the restaurant, rewriting what he could have said, rewriting what Lisa should have said, until he couldn't quite remember what had happened. All he knew was that his father and sisters weren't talking to each other, again, and Lisa had gone home without him.

For all he knew, she didn't go home, but stayed with Karla and Kevin. He hadn't called the apartment. He knew he should have. He had reached for his cell phone sitting on the nightstand five times, but stopped each time he remembered that he had forgotten to call Lisa on his last business trip. She was probably angry about that, too.

Why hadn't he called her? He always called her when his plane landed and he was settled in his hotel, and then on his last night before coming home. They always made plans for what they would do their first night back together.

Why had he forgotten to call her? Through the growing headache, at only 9a.m., Todd admitted he hadn't exactly forgotten. He hadn't called Lisa because he was angry. Over what, he wasn't quite sure, but he had a growing certainty, as strong as his growing headache, that his anger was somehow connected with her.

For what? What had Lisa done?

Nothing. That was the problem. He was angry with her, yet he knew she was innocent. Somehow that made him even angrier. It was stupid. He hated feeling stupid. Somehow, Lisa was responsible for that.

So he hadn't called her.

Now, sitting in his office, his second day home, he still hadn't done his laundry or given Lisa her chocolate covered cherries and colored pencils. Lisa had kissed him when he came in the door, but he hadn't kissed her yet.

It would have been so easy if he could have come back to the apartment after taking that walk, and found her asleep in their bed, not locked into her office. He could have gone to bed and held her close, and when she woke up in the middle of the night, she would have known he was sorry. She would have kissed him and woke him up to talk about the baby. He should have insisted she eat something. He should have stopped her from putting her fancy dinner down the disposal. That would have proven he did care about her.

Why couldn't he have just found her asleep when he came back from walking off his headache, and woke her up making love to her? He remembered the last time he had put that hurt look in her eyes and the apartment had filled with cold silence. Todd had woke her up by making love to her, and then everything had been wonderful after that. Lisa always forgave him.

To make love, you have to be in love, Lisa had said once when she was angry with him and didn't want him to touch her.

Why did those words echo in his head now? Did she honestly think he didn't love her when she said that?

"Does she still love me?" Todd muttered. She sure hadn't acted that way yesterday.

He remembered the few times she had been angry with him in college. Lisa simply didn't *get* angry. He had to do something awful to get her to glare at him, to tell him to go away, and to give back his ring. One time, she had been angry enough to throw it at him. She hadn't accepted his phone calls for nearly a month. He had haunted the campus mail room and the library where she had work-study and her dormitory, trying to catch up with her and get her to talk to him. Lisa had finally agreed to eat lunch with him one day, and everything had been fine after that. He had been very careful since then, terrified he would get her so angry she would call off the wedding.

He *had* remained careful, until now.

Chapter Eight

Lisa wouldn't leave him, would she? With a baby on the way? She had even told him she was an all-or-nothing girl who didn't believe in divorce as an option. She held to her principles. She believed sex before marriage was wrong, even two weeks before the wedding. Not that he had ever consciously pushed her, but there were a few times when he wanted a little more than kissing and holding, and she had always stopped him.

Despite that, he had been surprised she was a virgin on their wedding night. He hadn't been able to believe Lisa hadn't belonged to someone else before he caught her. Sure, he was raised in church, but he knew plenty of so-called Christians who had experimented before marriage. Lisa hadn't, and knowing she had saved herself for him used to give him a proud glow every time he thought about it.

That thought led him back to her angry words in the kitchen. Lisa wished she was still a virgin, and that he had never touched her. How could she say that?

"I'll tell you how, moron," he growled. "How many times has she wanted to say no, but she gave you what you wanted anyway?"

There were plenty of times he knew, even before he kissed her, that Lisa was in no mood for sex. He had taken advantage of her giving nature, getting what he wanted and telling himself that she eventually enjoyed it.

Now that he thought about it, Lisa never made the first move. Maybe she didn't really enjoy sex? Maybe she had put up with it because she loved him, like she put up with his sloppy habits in the bathroom?

He was going to change that, Todd decided. He would get his clothes cleaned at lunchtime and put them away when he got home. He would clean up after himself in the kitchen and bathroom. He would even empty the wastebaskets without Lisa asking him twenty times. Tomorrow was garbage day, wasn't it? She would see he was sorry and she would forgive him and kiss him and everything would be all right again.

~~~~~

"Jacky time!" a good dozen children called as Lisa came into the after-school care room at the Mission.

"Saved!" a man cried from under the pile of giggling, wriggling children that broke apart to flood to the door to greet Lisa.

"What a wimp." Max Randolph perched on the deep window ledge, reading to the Morrison twins. As dark and square-built as her stepfather,
~~~~~

she had a deep sense of calm and reserve that Lisa envied.

"What took you so long?" Tony Martin called as the last child got off his stomach and tottered across the room to join the dozens wrapping their arms around Lisa and demanding Jacky stories.

There were eight years between Tony and Max, but they looked enough alike to be brother and sister. They were best friends, writing partners, a team that could be counted on whenever the youth at church needed a pair of chaperons. In his mid-thirties, Tony already showed a few streaks of silver in his thick, shaggy mop of black hair. He loved roughhousing with the children at the Mission, while Max always made the readers and dreamers and timid ones her "special ones." They would both make great parents someday.

Lisa thought about what Emily and Joel Randolph had said just a few days ago about their daughter and her best friend. Could a man and woman be so close that they didn't realize what they had? She could see Max and Tony married, going on in their partnership without a break in the rhythm. Or would marriage ruin everything? The thought of Tony touching Max like Todd touched her made Lisa feel slightly nauseous.

"You okay?" Max slid off the window seat with a twin tucked under each arm.

"Fine." Lisa forced a smile and responded to the continuing demands of the children.

She loved the children, their openness, their eagerness, and their energy. She loved being mobbed by little bodies when she came through the door twice a week, loved hearing her name called in so many happy little voices. She even loved the dirty handprints and footprints on her clothes, when she got up from a long afternoon of cuddling and wrestling and laughter. When she first suspected she was pregnant, she imagined her child among these children someday, begging her to make drawings to go with the silly stories Max and Tony helped them put together.

The Jacky stories the children demanded started from a silly, disproportionate drawing Lisa did one day on the chalkboard. Tony teased her about the "mighty artist falling low" and she had teased him right back, challenging him to make up a story to go with the picture, if he was as good a writer as he claimed. The children joined in the game, and by the end of the afternoon, they had named the scribbled character Jacky. No one was quite sure if Jacky was a boy or girl, or even if Jacky was human. It really didn't matter with the children. They brought events from school or home to the Mission and transposed their hurts and victories and questions to little Jacky, who acted them out through Tony and Max's words and Lisa's drawings.

Lisa sometimes grew bored with the character, but the children loved Jacky, and some good had come from the outlet. Even in quiet little Tabor, there were problems, child abuse and domestic violence among them. Through the stories the children made up about Jacky, the adults had caught hints of problems otherwise kept hidden and sent help.

Lisa thought about the children who sometimes cried on her shoulder about "Daddy yelled at Mommy" or "Daddy ain't coming home" or "Mommy ran away." She vowed she would never let that happen to her baby. Todd was going to have to change if he ever wanted to be a father to his child.

She settled down on the floor and held out her hands for the special pad of paper reserved for Jacky's adventures. Three giggling little girls, minus their shoes, scampered across the room to retrieve it. They worked together to carry the oversized pad to Lisa, and all three tried to climb into her lap, so they could see as she drew for them. That brought on peals of laughter from the others, when Lisa overbalanced and fell backward, with all three sitting on her stomach. She didn't fear for the baby, despite the bouncing she took.

How could any harm come from so much love and laughter? She only felt fear and worry for the baby at home. Todd's home. Had it ever been *her* home? Her office was hers, but was that all she could call her own?

Lisa let her thoughts drift as Max and Tony settled down amid the chaos of wiggling, laughing, shouting, chattering children and wove a story out of the tangled ideas shouted to them.

Max and Tony were a great couple. Dark of hair and eye, square-built, sensible, with dry and wicked senses of humor. They were dreamers, just different enough that they filled in for what each other lacked. They certainly loved the children. Lisa could very easily see them with half a dozen children of their own, all with dark mops of shaggy hair, reading and laughing and playing together.

How long had it been since she and Todd laughed about anything together?

Why had she let him get her pregnant? There were so few times Lisa could remember when she had actually wanted Todd to make love to her. She was afraid to say no, and even felt guilty for her lack of desire for him.

Was the problem with her? Mr. Montgomery would say so, but Lisa decided she no longer wanted his good opinion or his approval. It was a freeing sensation to discover that.

Watching Max and Tony working together, Lisa hoped they never changed their relationship. They were better off as friends, best buddies, partners. She and Todd had been friends, back in their college days.

What had happened to the love she and Todd shared? They had been happy once. They used to be able to talk about anything. Lisa used to be able to tell Todd everything, and he used to listen.

What had happened?

~~~~~

Lisa wasn't home when Todd got home, early, with flowers clutched in one hand, his suitcase and briefcase in the other. He slowly shoved the door shut with his foot and stood in the living room, staring at the little bistro table set neatly for one. A salad and silverware waited for him on a plain brown placemat, with a little note saying his dinner was in the microwave.

Woodenly, he dropped the flowers on the couch and took his suitcase into the bedroom. He shoved all his clean, wrinkled clothes into one drawer, kicked the suitcase under the bed, brought Lisa's pencils and chocolates out to the living room and dropped them next to the discarded flowers. He shed his long coat on the way back to the kitchen, draping it over the stereo rack system.

A three-compartment freezer container waited in the microwave. Lemon pepper chicken, roast potatoes and broccoli. Todd remembered the night they had eaten that meal. They had snuggled into the couch afterward and watched the movies he brought home from work. What were the movies? He couldn't recall now.

Todd never ate leftovers. Lisa always saved them for when he went out of town, so she wouldn't have to cook. She didn't like cooking just for herself. She said she liked cooking for him.

Lisa hadn't left a note telling him where she was going or when she would be back. Punching in the time for his dinner, Todd had a horrid thought. Heart racing, he punched the *start* button and raced into the bedroom.

Lisa's suitcase was still in the closet. The clothes hanging on her side of the closet looked the same, no empty hangers or gaps. The two drawers she kept her clothes in were still full.

Todd went into her office and sagged in relief when he saw all her supplies were still where they belonged. Lisa would never have left those behind, even if she left the rest of her belongings.

"She's not going to leave you, stupid," he told himself.

But where was she? Lisa never went anywhere without telling him, either verbally or with a note. He shivered when he thought about his father's words, casting doubt on Todd's claim that he always knew where Lisa was.

He ate his solitary dinner facing the door, waiting for Lisa to come back. Funny how he had never noticed before what good, solid, soundproof walls the apartment had. He couldn't hear anything going on in the hallway outside the door, or in the apartments above or below.

He tried to watch the news, but he couldn't concentrate. All of it seemed bad. Todd turned off the TV halfway through a newsbyte about a
~~~~~

wife who had abandoned her husband and eight children and was found murdered with the trucker she had run off with. The prime suspect was the trucker's abandoned wife.

Todd settled down at his seldom-used desk, plugged in his notebook computer, and got back to work on the spreadsheets he should have turned in that afternoon. There was nothing else to take up his evening. He hadn't planned on having so much free time tonight.

Lisa hadn't planned on you accusing her of sleeping around, his conscience shot back in the silence of his head.

That hurt, but it was the truth, wasn't it? What else would it mean when a man asked his wife if her baby was his?

His head hurt. More ibuprofen didn't seem to help. He finally gave up on his office work and decided to go to bed. How could he sleep, though? Lisa didn't keep sleeping pills in the apartment.

Melatonin. Lisa used melatonin when she needed to sleep and was either too stressed or too wound up to relax right away. Todd dug through the little wicker shelf next to the sink until he found the right bottle. Only two pills left. He had both in his mouth before he thought about reading the instructions.

Only one pill every twenty-four hours. Great. He could feel the little pills disintegrating on his tongue. Todd filled the water glass and washed both pills down his throat. He doubted it would kill him.

Friday, February 21

When Todd woke in the morning, his head clear and his dreams dissolving into nothingness, Lisa wasn't next to him in bed.

He sat up straight in the bed and looked around the room. He nearly laughed aloud when he saw her sneakers sitting in front of the closet door. Still, where was she? There was no sign she had slept next to him.

He got up and stumbled down the hall a few more steps to her office. Lisa was asleep on the couch. Her lips looked swollen, like she had been biting them in her sleep again. When they were first married, her lips had sometimes looked swollen in the morning, from long hours of kissing before they fell asleep.

Maybe she had been kissing someone. A lot. Last night.

"Don't be an idiot," he whispered. Hadn't he argued with himself enough over that?

Lisa mumbled and reached up to rub her nose. Todd considered getting down on his knees and kissing her awake. But what if she didn't like that? While he considered that totally revolutionary thought, her eyes opened and the opportunity evaporated.

"Hi." She sat up, tugging the blankets up to her shoulders as she moved. That made no sense. She wore sweatshirt and sweatpants under those blankets.

"Hi." Todd tried to smile. *Come on, Lisa, just smile at me. Let me know everything is okay and I'll do anything you want.* "Where'd you go last night?"

"The Mission, like always." Her mouth flattened when he just gave her a blank stare. "I do story time two afternoons a week, and last night was art night with the seniors, remember?"

"Oh. Yeah. I forgot." He wished he could bang his head against the wall, but Todd had the horrid suspicion Lisa would laugh at him. It wouldn't be nice laughter, either. "How come you didn't come to bed?"

"I didn't want to wake you up."

"I wouldn't have minded."

The glare she gave him clearly said, *You always mind.* He had to admit it was true. Lisa had made the mistake of waking him up on their honeymoon to watch for shooting stars. She had never tried to wake him in the middle of the night again.

Lisa fidgeted for a moment, as if his bleary-eyed stare made her itch. Then she shoved back the blankets, got up, and slid past him to go into the bathroom. Todd winced, hearing the way her back scraped against the frame of the door. There was plenty of room between them when she passed.

The wastebasket sat at the foot of the couch by the door. Todd saw it was full, and remembered his decision to take care of the garbage without Lisa reminding him. He grabbed up the wastebasket and headed into the kitchen. The tall black garbage can liners Lisa used were in a box under the sink. He opened one and up-ended the wastebasket into it.

A clump of wet papers stuck together in the bottom. Todd sighed and gritted his teeth and reached in to pull them out. Wallpaper samples. Cloth samples. A few catalogs. He remembered how happy Lisa was when she redecorated the apartment.

Wait. He didn't recognize any of the samples. Lisa wouldn't throw them out until the project was finished, would she? A heavy feeling filled his stomach as he slowly pried apart the sticky pages of the catalog and saw the baby furniture inside.

Lisa had to be really angry with him, to throw away all that hard work.

He wished she had waited for him to come home before she started on a big, important project like that. Todd usually didn't know blue from green, but decorating their baby's room together would have been fun.

Right now, he had the horrid suspicion she wouldn't let him help with the baby's room. He remembered the plans and promises they had made to each other, just a few weeks before their wedding. They would take Lamaze classes and pre-natal and childcare classes together, and he would help change diapers if she promised not to make him get up for the midnight feedings.

Todd suspected Lisa remembered all those happy dreams and plans, and the memories didn't make her happy.

Was that really his fault? She *chose* to stay angry with him.

He continued digging. That floor plan didn't look right. He pried apart a few papers and found the specifications for the dream house. It was for rent? Todd nearly dropped the wastebasket as the entire picture came together in his head. Lisa wanted the dream house for their baby. She had started plans for decorating it.

And she had thrown everything away.

The bathroom door opened. Todd shoved the soggy papers and scraps and catalogues into the garbage bag and stood up. Lisa didn't come into the kitchen. He emptied the kitchen wastebasket into the bag, then went into the bathroom.

It only took a moment to recognize the pieces of the pregnancy test in the bathroom wastebasket. His hand shook a little as he reached for the snapped fragments of the wand. He couldn't tell if Lisa had used it or not. He couldn't find enough pieces of the little instruction sheet to determine if there was any sign for either positive or negative.

"What is this supposed to mean?" he demanded, shoving the bedroom door open.

Lisa froze in the middle of pulling a pair of jeans out of her drawer. Her mouth flattened a little more and she backed up a step to match the one he took toward her.

"This." He held out the snapped pieces of the test wand. "You threw it out without using it, didn't you?"

"You know," she said, so quietly he almost couldn't hear her through the thudding of his heart, "there is something really wrong with people who go through the garbage."

"You didn't take the test, did you?"

"No."

"Why not?" He shoved the pieces into the garbage bag.

"It doesn't matter anymore."

"Of course it matters! Lisa, why are you doing this? Aren't you excited about our baby?"

"*My* baby." Her whisper hit him like a two-by-four. "It's not yours, remember?"

Todd dropped the garbage bag and drew back — then stopped short, stunned with the realization he meant to hit her. He wanted to hit her. Lisa looked at his raised hand and her mouth flattened so hard her lips lost all color. She glared at him through the wetness that gleamed bright in her eyes.

"Don't you dare," she whispered, her voice rasping.

Todd made it to the elevator without remembering how he got there. He had his clothes from last night slung over his arm. His keys were in his pants pocket. Todd was barefoot, but he knew he couldn't go back to the apartment. Not now. Not with the air still ringing with the disgust in her soft voice. When he closed his eyes, he could still see the glitter of hurt in her eyes. He didn't know if he was sorry or furious that Lisa refused to cry.

Todd remembered her freshman year at the university. He had been a junior. He remembered when a supposed friend had cruelly betrayed her. Lisa had refused to cry then. It was the first time he put his arms around her. She had shivered and when he urged her to cry and let out the pain, she said something he would never forget.

"I'll never give her the satisfaction of knowing she hurt me."

Did she refuse to cry now, because she thought he *wanted* to see her cry?

Todd dressed in the elevator and made his way out the side door to the parking lot without anyone seeing him. His gym bag with his sneakers and workout clothes were in the trunk. He put his sneakers on without socks and was halfway to his father's house before he realized where he was going.

"I almost hit her." The words, even spoken aloud, made no sense. Todd clenched his fist and stared at it. The palm of his hand stung as if he had actually done it.

"I want to hit her." Todd closed his eyes, fighting the angry, burning tears. "Why did she have to say that? Couldn't she see I was sorry? Why won't she let me make up with her?" He pounded his fists against the steering wheel, jerking half out of his seat when he hit the horn. At least there was no one else on the road right now.

Chapter Nine

His father was pleased to see him come in the kitchen door. Mr. Montgomery called to the housekeeper to fix Todd a big breakfast and then grilled his son about his job, the trip to Sacramento, the delays in the merger. Todd found it hard to speak while the housekeeper was there in the kitchen; a skeletal, gray-haired woman who never said much of anything. He was grateful for the hot coffee, though. Grateful for the pancakes, the warmth of the kitchen and his father's constant questions. He was grateful for the interruptions, because the mental gymnastics made it hard to think about what had happened at home.

Todd remembered how Lisa listened so intently to him, never saying much of anything. She didn't know much about computers but she was interested because it interested him. He listened to himself stumbling over his tongue as he pushed for more details to impress his father. With each "Of course, only you could see that," or "It took them long enough to wake up and do it your way," his ragged feelings smoothed out and he relaxed. Little by little, enough slipped out so he confessed he and Lisa had argued. He didn't tell his father that he had nearly hit Lisa. He couldn't. He didn't want to see the disappointment his father usually only dished out to his sisters. Todd knew all the stories of how his father had tended to his mother's every need and guarded her and sheltered her from the storms of life. He would never approve of a man hitting his wife, or even wanting to hit her.

"It'll be all right, Toddy," Mr. Montgomery rumbled with that warm, satisfied chuckle in the back of his throat. "Lisa's just afraid you won't think she's pretty."

"I don't think that's it at all." Todd crammed an entire sausage link into his mouth. He remembered that look in her eyes, the quiet steel in her voice.

Had Lisa always done so much for him because she feared he would stop loving her? Maybe now she didn't care? Why didn't she care? Had she found someone else, someone who was always there?

Someone who didn't accuse her of sleeping around, and who didn't threaten to hit her?

"It's hormones. Just give her some breathing space and everything will be fine again. We have to take very good care of Lisa now, because of the baby."

"I don't think she wants this baby, Dad," he admitted. "She threw away the testing kit, and she threw out all the plans she made for decorating the baby's room."

"It's just a phase." Mr. Montgomery reached out and squeezed Todd's shoulder. "You just be patient and take care of her. Lisa will come around. She worships you, which is the only reason I've put up with her for so long. Once she gets her head straightened out, she'll see that she was wrong and she'll apologize and everything will be fine again."

"Lisa isn't—"

"Better eat up. You'll be late for work. I know DeWitt-McGregor is going casual, but you aren't wearing those sneakers with your suit, are you?" He laughed and stood.

"No. Dad, Lisa really isn't—"

"There are still some clothes you left behind when you moved into that ridiculous little apartment." Mr. Montgomery took a step toward the kitchen door, then paused. He looked Todd up and down, and for a moment his smile chilled his son. "You know, I have all this extra room. No one but me in this huge old house. You and Lisa should move in with me. New mothers need all the help they can get. I'll hire a nurse for her. Nothing is too good for my grandson."

"It's a little early to know what we're going to have," Todd protested, through the sudden sense of panic filling his chest.

"It's a boy. God wouldn't let me down now." Chuckling, Mr. Montgomery strode out of the kitchen and down the hall.

Force Lisa to live in this house, raise her baby in this house, and put up with a nurse his father had chosen? Todd was glad he was sitting down, because he felt nauseous and dizzy. Lisa hated this house. She hated the dark rooms and the old furniture and the feeling that nothing had changed since the day his mother died. She always tried to be pleasant when they came for Sunday dinner, but he felt her tension whenever they walked through the door. She was always exhausted once they escaped back to their apartment. Even if he was furious with Lisa over how she was acting now, he would never force her to live here.

~~~~~

The phone rang as Lisa finished putting yeast into the bread machine. She closed the lid and hit the 'start' button. The phone was in Todd's name, the answering machine was his. No one would call her during the day on Todd's phone. She had her own phone in the office that Genevieve and her friends called her on and knew not to share the number with anyone. Jeanette knew her number and called that phone for church business or Mission business, and the Randolphs always faxed her about anything they needed for Homespun. If Bekka, Amy or Kat needed her for anything, they would come to the door. Who would call on Todd's phone,
~~~~~

except telemarketers and people she didn't want to talk to? Such as that mysterious 10a.m. and 2p.m. caller?

"Lisa." The sound of Mr. Montgomery's falsely hearty voice made her stomach turn. "I know you're there. Pick up the phone." A pause. "I know you're there. You don't have a life outside your scribbling. You and I need to talk right now. You're upsetting Todd. You're not doing any good for that baby, the way you're behaving. You straighten out, young lady, and straighten out now. Pick up the phone!"

Lisa giggled, and immediately clamped a hand over her mouth. It was ridiculous, she knew. He couldn't hear her.

"Todd agrees with me. You are giving up your pretensions at being an artist, and you are moving in with me. I want my grandson taken care of properly."

A little yelp escaped Lisa. She stumbled back against the wall.

In the cartoon panels roughed out just that morning, Bob's parents had demanded he and Katie move back to his hometown so they could help take care of the baby. Bob had decided his parents were right and was looking for a new job. Katie didn't want to give up her job or leave her parents. When she got angry enough to admit she would turn to her mother for help first, Bob's mother played the martyr. Bob and Katie had started arguing, at the point where Lisa put down her pen to start dinner.

How had she predicted this so accurately?

Life reflected art. Todd's father wanted to take over Lisa's life and control her baby.

"I'll run away, first," Lisa whispered. She fled down the hall to her office, pressing her hands over her ears to drown the sound of Todd's father telling her she was unbalanced and self-centered.

Maybe he thought she was so unbalanced she wouldn't be allowed to raise her own child?

~~~~~

When he got home that night, Todd was relieved to see the table set for two. That was more like it. Maybe his father was right, and Lisa just needed to get used to being pregnant.

Then he saw the wilted bouquet of flowers sitting on the sofa where he had dropped them the night before, along with the chocolates and pencils. He picked up the flowers and found the pencil and chocolate boxes discolored where the decaying flowers sat on them.

"Lisa?" He was half-afraid he wouldn't get any answer.

His heart skipped a beat when she stepped out of the kitchen, dressed in her usual comfortable baggy jeans and sweatshirt, her sleeves pushed up past her elbows, with five colored pencils tucked into the braid wrapped around her head.

Lisa's eyes flicked down to the flowers he held. For a moment, her
~~~~~

mouth began to smile. Then it flattened and she seemed to catch her breath. Had she been about to cry? She turned back to the kitchen.

"Those need water," she mumbled, barely turning her head enough to be heard.

"Yeah. I forgot when I got home last night. You didn't see them lying there?" He followed her into the kitchen.

"I was working all day in my office." She opened the oven.

"Five-layer casserole?" Todd's mouth watered as the aroma of sirloin, green peppers, tomatoes, onions and potatoes swirled through the tiny kitchen. "That's great. We haven't had it in a long time."

"I know." She pulled out the serrated knife to cut the thick loaf of fresh bread sitting on the counter.

He hurried to stuff the flowers into the wastebasket and closed the lid.

"Here. I got you these when I was in Sacramento. They're the ones you wanted, right?" He held out the box of pencils, almost as a shield. Lisa wouldn't hurt him with that knife, would she?

"Right." That hint of a smile returned. Lisa met his eyes for the first time in what felt like years. "Thanks, Todd. That was nice of you."

"I like doing nice things for you." He leaned down for a kiss. Lisa didn't kiss him back, but she didn't hit him either. That was an improvement. "I got you these, too. I missed Valentine's Day." He handed her the candy box.

"Again," she whispered, but one corner of her mouth twitched up in a smile and he was positive she was teasing him.

"Yeah, well, you know how it is when I'm getting ready for another road trip." His stomach dropped when her smile faded before it could reach her eyes.

He regaled her with the office doings while they ate. Lisa never took her gaze off his face as he talked. Todd loved it when he had her full attention. He couldn't imagine life without Lisa in it. She never nagged, never compared him to anyone else. She never complained that he hadn't earned a larger bonus, or hinted that his co-workers were out to get him or that he just didn't have the gumption to live up to his full potential. He had heard enough variations of that from his father to last him for the rest of his life.

"What did you do today? The usual?" he asked, as Lisa got up to take the dirty dishes to the sink. A few seconds later, his conscience twinged and he hurried to pick up the casserole and pile the breadbasket on top of it, and carry them over for her.

"The usual."

Maybe her voice was a little too quiet, but Todd blamed that on the baby. His father was right. Lisa had to get used to being pregnant before everything could go back to normal.

Lisa asked him to check his answering machine, saying she thought she heard someone leaving a message. When he found nothing waiting, she went a little white around her mouth and eyes. When he asked, she said she was tired. She only watched half the movie Todd picked out that evening. When she got up, he thought she was going to the bathroom. Then, when ten minutes had gone by and she didn't come back, he hit the pause button and went looking for her. She was curled up on her side of the bed, eyes closed. Todd doubted she could fall asleep that quickly, but if she was tired, he wasn't going to disturb her.

Sunday, February 23

Lisa stayed tired, saying little, only leaving the apartment when she had obligations. She stayed home from church Sunday, claiming she didn't feel well. Todd brought food home for her from his father's house. He didn't want to go without Lisa, but he knew she understood his family obligations. His father smiled when Todd explained her absence. He didn't complain about Lisa's lack of devotion to her husband's family. That was a change, and Todd hoped it was a good sign. Maybe this baby would bring many positive changes into their lives.

"Dad's worried about you," Todd said, coming home late in the afternoon, after doing some yard work for his father. Lisa was busy in her office. As usual.

"That's nice," she murmured, and leaned down close to smudge the lines between two shades of blue.

"How are you feeling?"

"Fine. Just tired." She didn't look up.

"Let's go for a ride. Let's stop by Heinke's and get all sorts of goodies and have a picnic down at the gazebo by the lake, okay?"

"It's freezing outside." A bit of a smile curved her lips.

"Who cares? It'll be fun."

"Why?" Now Lisa looked up.

"Because it'll be fun."

"No special reason?"

"No." He couldn't figure out what she was getting at. "I just want to."

"Oh. You want to." Lisa nodded and went back to her work. "Well, I don't want to. You go on and have a good time."

"Come on, Lisa. You hardly ever leave this office anymore. We haven't gone out in weeks."

"Months."

"Okay." His face warmed. "Months. I'm sorry. I've been busy with work and—" Todd shook his head. This was ridiculous. He stepped into the office, tired of hovering in the doorway and feeling like an intruder. He settled down on the end of the couch. Her full work tray caught his attention. "Big new project? What are you working on?" He rifled through the stack of sheets, picking one at random to read.

It occurred to him that he hadn't seen Lisa's work in weeks. Usually, she showed her newest story line to him, wanting his input. Todd liked feeling as if he had a contribution to make to her work.

Katie and Bob were having a baby. Katie had told Bob and he bought her a dozen roses even though they couldn't afford it, then he carried her out to the car, both of them laughing, so they could go tell her parents.

Why couldn't it be this way for us? Todd's eyes burned. He blinked hard, hating the nearness of tears.

"So, you're telling the whole world about our baby, huh?" He finished reading the second sheet and reached for the third. Lisa didn't answer.

Bob's parents immediately hopped on a plane to come visit them. Everybody was happy, eager to share the news with the whole world.

"So." His voice caught. He coughed to clear his throat. "Who have you told about the baby besides my family?"

"You're the only one I told. You told your family." Lisa shrugged. From her tone of voice, she could have been talking about a mediocre sale at the grocery store.

"Aren't you happy about this baby?"

"I haven't decided yet."

"You'd better decide soon."

"Don't tell me what to do, Todd. You don't have the right." Again, delivered in the same even, careless tone of voice.

"Of course I have the right!" He stood, almost dropping the stack of sheets. "We're having a baby."

"No, *I'm* having a baby. You just happen to be the man I'm married to." She didn't look up from her work.

Todd wanted to rip the paper off the worktable. He felt hot and his throat hurt. His father's words of caution pounded in his head. Lisa was still out of sorts, so fresh in her pregnancy. He didn't want to get her any more upset.

"Look. Sweetheart." He leaned on the edge of the table. "We have to fix this, work it out, for the sake of the baby."

"For the sake of the baby." The pencil clutched in her hand suddenly snapped. One end flew across the room. "Is that all you care about?"

Her eyes gleamed with tears, red-rimmed and starting to swell. How long had she been fighting tears?

"What do you want me to do?" He kept his voice soft, otherwise he knew he might yell and grab her and shake her.

"I think we need to get some counseling. At church."

"What?" He would have laughed, but for the sick twisting in the pit of his stomach. Only failures went in for counseling. People who couldn't figure things out for themselves. He wasn't a failure. Lisa wasn't a failure.

Not yet, anyway, a quiet voice whispered in the dark corners of his mind.

"Sure. Make the appointment. Whatever you want." He turned and walked out the door.

That night, when he tentatively reached out and put an arm around Lisa in bed, she didn't stiffen or move away. She might have been asleep already, but that didn't matter. Todd fell asleep with a smile.

Monday, February 24

Monday morning, just after Todd vanished out the door to go to work, the doorbell rang. Lisa rinsed the toothpaste from her mouth and hurried to answer the door. It was Bekka, still in her uniform from Biscuit Heaven. She worked opening shift every morning before class. Common consensus was that the fast food restaurant only existed to give college students jobs and contribute to the proverbial Freshman twenty pound gain.

"What's up?" She stepped back, beckoning for her friend to come inside.

"Well, I saw Todd in the parking lot and he looked pretty happy. Did he finally apologize?" Bekka brought a bag from behind her back. "Feel like the double-grease special?"

Lisa snorted. Bekka rarely ate at Biscuit Heaven because she was exposed to it every day. Right now, the aroma of sausage-and-cheese breakfast biscuits made Lisa's stomach growl. She smiled, realizing she was hungry for the first time in days.

"No, actually, he hasn't apologized, but he agreed to go for some counseling. I'm calling to make an appointment with Dr. Harris as soon as the church office opens up." She took the bag. "Thanks. I'm eating for two now, so... "

"So it's official?"

"Well, not really official. I didn't take the test yet. Please don't talk about it to anyone else yet, okay?" She led the way to the kitchen, dropped the bag on the table with a sodden, warm thud, and paused in the doorway to eye the teapot. It looked like there was enough spice tea for both of them.

"Because of your problems with Todd?" Bekka sank down in his chair at the table and opened up her jacket. "Are you happy? About the baby, I mean."

"I think so. Things were so bad right after he got home." Lisa sighed, needing to share with someone. She could trust Bekka to understand, as well as keep her secret. "I actually ripped up the test kit, I was so furious with him. But we've agreed to fix things. It's going to take some time. If I could just send his father to another planet..."

"Tell me about it. Did you know that Pharisee chewed out my grandparents for 'letting' me take an apartment with two heathens?" Bekka snorted, then nodded thanks for the tea Lisa brought over. "He told my grandparents I would end up in Hell just because Kat and Amy don't go to church. Did it ever occur to him that I might be a good influence on them? How are they ever going to want to know Jesus unless they see some love from the people who claim to know Him?"

"Mr. Montgomery only knows about love that's directed at him." Her face warmed as soon as the words left her lips. "That wasn't nice—"

"But it's true. I think it's safe to tell you that the whole time you were dating Todd, he was working with my grandparents to force us into being a couple. That's reason enough never to date!" She slouched dramatically in her chair with a groan, earning a giggle from Lisa. "Every once in a while, Max talks about starting an order of Protestant nuns so we have an excuse to refuse to date some of the losers in our church. We've dedicated our bodies to God, so hands off, boys!"

"It would never occur to some of the guys in our church that being dedicated to God means hands off. They'd take it as a challenge." Lisa hid a grin as she sipped her tea.

"Yeah, but some of us would actually get dates once in a while." Bekka shook her head violently enough to make Lisa's neck ache in sympathy. "I'm not going there. Let's just say I wasn't so desperate for a boyfriend that I'd put up with all Todd's baggage. You really have my admiration for surviving. You're braver than I am."

"I wouldn't say brave..." Her composure threatened to crack. Lisa forced another grin. "So? Tell me your good news?"

Chapter Ten

Lisa opened the bag and sighed at the sight of four sloppily wrapped breakfast biscuits with cheese melting all over the paper. Bekka brought her the mistakes some mornings, so they could relax and complain about their chosen artistic careers.

"Well, for some reason that probably breaks a lot of rules in the publishing industry," Bekka said, "I suddenly have an agent."

"But you weren't looking for one."

"Nope. A publisher is interested in my North Pole book. Max hooked me up with her agent back when that scam artist was trying to fleece me, and he said he liked my work so... I called him when somebody in New York showed some interest. My name was all over the place in connection with actually nailing that jerk who tried to steal my book. Who am I to argue, when it sure looks like a miracle?" Bekka took a big gulp of her tea. "They want to have it ready for the Christmas rush, and I'm going to go crazy doing rewrites for the next month... but it's worth it."

"I bet Kat and Amy are going nuts."

"They don't know." She smirked.

"What?"

"They've been giving me a hard time about keeping secrets from them. Half the time, they don't know what's going on in my life because their lives are too busy to notice I'm even there, and the rest of the time they don't listen... sheesh, listen to me whine! I figured I'd give them a little taste of what it really meant to be secret."

"Oh, I don't know, keeping secrets from your best friends doesn't sound good. You have to talk. I mean..." A sob pressed against her chest and Lisa had to take a deep breath and swallow hard to keep talking. "If Todd and I would just talk more, maybe we wouldn't have so much trouble." She forced herself to smile. "We're going in for counseling. We'll work through it."

She nodded for emphasis. It would work out. They would fix their problems. They had to, for the sake of the baby if no one and nothing else.

She almost cried, though, when Bekka promised to pray hard for her, and in the next breath asked if she was sure about pony décor, so she could start shopping for the baby shower. How could she admit to her friend that she had thrown out all her decorating ideas, just because she was so angry with Todd and hoped the baby was just her imagination?

~~~~~

After Lisa went to bed that night, the phone rang. Todd hurried to snatch it up so it wouldn't wake her.

An emergency had developed at the Colorado office of DeWitt-McGregor's biggest client, and he had to catch the 6a.m. flight the next morning to handle it. His tickets would be waiting at the airport.

Todd knew better than to argue. While he tiptoed around the bedroom and packed, he had the niggling feeling something was wrong. He had forgotten something, he just knew it.

Tuesday, February 25

Before Todd left at 4a.m., he wrote Lisa a note, explaining what had happened, and put it on the bistro table.

Halfway to Denver, Todd remembered what had been bothering him last night: today was their first appointment for counseling at church. He groaned and closed his eyes and reached for his cell phone. It was in his bag in the overhead compartment instead of his pocket. He sternly reminded himself to call Lisa as soon as he landed. He didn't want her to think he had deliberately skipped their first counseling appointment.

~~~~~

Lisa slept in late that morning. When she sat up in bed and looked at the clock and realized it was nearly nine, she wondered if she was getting sick. Usually Todd woke her up no matter how quietly he tried to move around in the morning.

No crumbs trailed across the kitchen. No orange juice carton or butter dish sat out. A little mess in the bathroom, but not the usual. Maybe Todd was finally learning. She smiled as she made her breakfast and picked out what to wear for their counseling appointment, then settled down to work. She could put in two hours before Todd picked her up.

~~~~~

Debbie, the IT tech liaison for the client was waiting at the gate when Todd landed. She launched into the problem that had brought him to town the moment he left the gate area, and talked practically non-stop down the concourse, out of the airport and across the parking lot to her car. Todd had worked with Debbie before. She was too controlled and composed to let much of anything bother her, but she looked upset, bordering on panicky now. He thought once of interrupting, so he could call Lisa, then decided to wait until he had the whole situation explained.

~~~~~

At noon, Lisa went downstairs to the lobby to wait for Todd to come with their car. By 12:15, no sign of him. Their appointment was set for

12:30. She debated going upstairs to call Todd's cell phone and find out when he would arrive, but she had done that twice before when they were running late for something, and each time Todd had been pulling into the parking lot when she reached him. By the time she got downstairs again and climbed into the car, they would be officially late. She decided to simply wait.

At 12:20, Lisa decided to get moving. Maybe Todd forgot he was supposed to pick her up, and she would find him waiting in Pastor Glenn's office. She stepped outside in the gusting, icy wind. Todd had made it clear he wasn't happy about going for counseling, and she didn't want to give him any excuse by her absence to turn around and leave at the last minute. She moved as fast as her new boots would allow, expending her nervous energy so the usual twenty-minute walk across the center of town to Tabor Christian Church only took ten minutes.

When she reached the church, Todd's car wasn't among the few cars in the parking lot. Lisa settled down in the little waiting room outside Pastor Glenn's office and folded her hands and waited.

At quarter of one, Pastor Glenn and Dr. Harris both came out of their offices, looked at each other, then glanced into the waiting room where Lisa sat all alone.

"Lisa?" Pastor Glenn gave her that uncertain smile that always made her feel good. It told her he was human and didn't have all the answers, and wasn't about to judge her.

"I guess Todd's running late," Lisa said with a shrug. "Maybe we should get started without him?"

"Sorry, that's not... ethical," Dr. Harris said. She tugged a strand of silvery hair back into the tight crown of braids wrapped around the back of her head. "The worst thing we can do toward solving your marital problems is to talk to one spouse without the other one there to hear what's said. Marriages that might have been mended have dissolved because careless counselors appeared to side with one spouse against the other."

"Oh." She nodded. "I guess that makes sense."

Lisa walked home, though Pastor Glenn offered to drive her. She wasn't up to making small talk. She couldn't take the idea of his sympathy. Silence with someone she liked and trusted would be unbearable.

She dropped her napkin at dinner, and when she bent down to retrieve it, she found Todd's note where it had slid under the table. Lisa read it twice through. Nothing about missing the appointment. Nothing about being sorry. Nothing to indicate when he would get home. And there had been no message from him on her office answering machine. He hadn't thought about her once all day.

What had happened to his habit of checking in with her, just to talk, every time he went out of town? She supposed that sweet habit had vanished about the time he decided she was carrying someone else's baby.

"Fine," she whispered, crumpling the note. "Don't bother coming home at all."

Lisa couldn't finish her dinner. She took her plate to the sink, scraped it clean, and ran the disposal a long time.

~~~~~

Todd didn't reach his hotel room until 10p.m. and didn't think of Lisa until he was in the shower, trying to relax enough to sleep. It was past midnight, Ohio time. Far too late to call and explain. Besides, he had left a note. What was there to explain?

Wednesday, February 26

Todd's phone rang at five the next afternoon. Lisa sat back in her chair in her office and arched her back a little as she listened for a message. She had spent so much time in her office, she wondered if her chair would become a permanent part of her anatomy. Todd's message played, then the machine beeped to signal the caller to leave a message.

No one spoke. Todd's friends left messages. His sisters left messages. His father left blistering lectures. Who would call and not leave a message after listening to the outgoing message all the way through?

Maybe the mystery caller was changing his schedule? Surprisingly, she didn't feel that chill that usually came when she let herself wonder about the stranger. Maybe she was too tired, too headachy about other problems, to let that bother her anymore.

Twenty minutes later, the doorbell rang. Lisa jerked, nearly leaving a bright pink streak across the bottom of the panel where Katie priced cribs and Bob wandered off through the store to look at baseball equipment. Sighing at the near miss, she got up and went down the short hall to the front door.

"Hi. You're being kidnapped," Karla announced the moment Lisa opened the door. Charli stood behind her, grinning ear to ear. Both sisters wore blue jeans, plaid flannel shirts and vest jackets.

"Huh?" Lisa found it a little difficult pulling her mind away from Katie and Bob's arguments to focus on the present.

"You need a night out with the girls, and we are the girls to do it," Charli said. "Where's that brat, Todd?"

"Todd, we're kidnapping Lisa and you can't do anything about it," Karla called, stepping further into the apartment.

"Denver." Lisa sighed as she said it.

"What?" Charli's mouth dropped open. "Todd went out of town
~~~~~

without telling our father?"

"How do you know that?" Lisa would have laughed if she didn't feel so strangely out of step.

"Father always complains to at least one of us about how badly the company mistreats Todd, sending him everywhere around the country. Then in the same breath he gloats about how important he is."

"So," Karla continued, taking up the narration, "if Father didn't gripe, then he didn't know Todd was away. When did he go?"

"Yesterday." Her voice caught. "The coward left a note that I didn't even find until last night," she added, and didn't care what it sounded like.

Lisa was tired of supporting Todd and making him look good, swallowing her pride and hurt feelings a dozen times a week for his sake.

"Uh oh," Charli whispered. "Girlfriend, you definitely need a night out. Come on, change your clothes. We're going to the cabin. Bring a sleeping bag and warm pjs."

"But—" She shook her head. Lisa realized she had been about to say no, that she had to wait for Todd to call or come home. Why should she? "Okay," she said before she lost her momentum. "Give me two minutes. Should I bring anything along?"

"We could use some more marshmallows and hot chocolate mix," Charli said.

"Ransack the cupboards and take anything you want," Lisa said as she stepped down the hall to the bedroom.

Her phone rang as she was reaching for the sleeping bag Todd had tucked into the top shelf of his office closet. Lisa flinched and jumped out of the way as the dusty roll came tumbling down at her. She hurried into her office on the third ring. Her machine kicked in.

"Lisa, this is Todd. I know you're there. Talk to me. Please?" Silence, while he waited for the phone to get picked up.

She frowned, hearing a whining note in his voice. Had it always been there and she had never noticed? Todd sounded uncomfortably like his father at his most self-righteous.

"Lisa, you're acting like a spoiled brat, and that just isn't like you. I'm worried. Dad said you're off-balance because of the baby. Talk to me, would you? Are you mad because I didn't wake you up to say good-bye? Lisa, come on."

"Drop dead, Todd," she whispered. "Just stay away. Stay in Denver until we're both old and gray."

"He hasn't said he's sorry yet, has he?" Karla asked, startling a tiny shriek from Lisa.

She turned around and saw her sister-in-law in the doorway. Lisa shook her head. She tried to say something, but all that came out was a sob. She didn't resist when Karla wrapped both arms around her.

"Todd needs a good kick in the head," Charli muttered half an hour later.

All three were curled up on the couch together with the kitchen cupboards still hanging open from being ransacked, the sleeping bag still on the floor of Todd's office, and Lisa finally drying her eyes. Her throat hurt from crying and her eyes felt swollen, but amazingly she felt lighter, better than she had since Todd asked if the baby was his.

"Several," Karla agreed. "Oh, Lisa, we really thought Todd was treating you better than this."

"Usually he does, but..." Lisa shook her head.

After all the talking she had done, spilling everything that had happened in the last week to her sympathetic sisters-in-law, she had run out of words. It helped enormously to be able to tell someone and be believed, be supported. She hadn't really expected Todd's sisters to believe half what she said, or to be as angry as they were.

"It's all Father's fault, of course," Karla added.

"Don't start," Charli said. "We'll be here all night, griping. We came here to get Lisa to have some fun, remember?"

"How are you handling all of this? Don't you ever get the urge to hide a knife under your pillow and —"

"Karla!" Lisa laughed despite her shock. She'd never imagined her lovely, elegant sister-in-law had a vengeful streak.

"Oh, not to hurt him. Just scare him a little. Fortunately, Kevin is a decent human being who understands there are other people who matter besides him. I only have to yell at him once or twice to get him to wise up."

"You must be going crazy in here," Charli said. "How have you put up with Todd and Father all this time?"

"Well..." Lisa stopped, her mouth open. How could she explain the way she worked out all her problems and hurt through her artwork? Words wouldn't work. Unless she showed them. "Come on." She led them down the hall to her office and spread out her panels. "I've had an awful lot of inspiration lately."

"These are great," Charli said with a giggle, after looking through the first dozen.

"The great thing about Katie is that she can say all the things I can't seem to get out of my mouth," Lisa admitted. "She can tell Bob he's a jerk and he actually listens. Most of the time, anyway."

"Fortunately, Katie's in-laws live in another state," Karla pointed out.

"And Katie has a mother to support her."

"That, too." She put an arm around Lisa's shoulders. "We're here. We've suffered through Father's tirades all our lives. Todd is the center of the universe and we simply exist to please the prince. I don't think Father will ever forgive us for getting married before Todd."

"For goodness' sake, Kar, you were ten when he was born!" Charli said with a giggle. "Only a lunatic would expect you to wait until Todd got married before you got a boyfriend. Oh, yeah, wait a minute. We're talking about Father, aren't we?" She winked at Lisa, earning a choked giggle.

"Whatever." Karla shrugged. "You're really working things out here. Expectant fathers had better learn something from this." She turned a few more panels over, reading through Bob's refusal to go to the church-sponsored baby shower. "Does Todd read any of these?"

"The last one made him angry. He couldn't understand why Katie and Bob's families could be happy about the baby and we're not." Lisa shrugged and swallowed hard against a thickness rising up in her throat.

"You're not happy about this baby at all?" she whispered. She put an arm around Lisa and hugged her again.

"I was... I haven't taken a test yet or gone to the doctor. I keep hoping my period will start and prove I was wrong."

"How far along do you think you are?"

"Not even two months." She shrugged. "Can we just forget about this and go have our fun?"

"You bet. Todd's a skunk and he deserves the silent treatment." Charli saluted. "Permission to continue searching for supplies, Commander?"

"Permission granted." A tiny snorting laugh escaped Lisa. Her face warmed as she remembered thinking that she couldn't expect any support from Todd's sisters.

Thursday, February 27

"I should probably tell you something, Lisa," Karla said.

It was past midnight and the winter wind howled down the chimney. The Montgomery cabin was warm and snug, full of deep shadows made darker by the flickering light of the fire. The other three sisters were asleep, curled up in their sleeping bags on mattresses on the hardwood floor.

"We liked you so much when we first met you, we nearly warned you not to marry Todd."

"Huh?" Lisa smiled sleepily and snuggled down a little further in her sleeping bag. Funny, but this was the first time she felt really comfortable and warm in weeks.

"We just thought you were too good for Prince Toddy. Father complained the minute you left the house, saying you weren't good enough for him. You were too thin, you wouldn't be a good cook, you were an artist and that meant you were unreliable. On and on."

"Well, when he told me Uncle Benjamin was going to walk me down the aisle and give me away, instead of Dr. Holwood, who has been like a father to me the whole time I was at BWU, I kind of got the idea he thought I was brainless." She laughed softly, and that amazed her.

"We figured Todd needed you. Maybe with enough time, Father's influence over him would fade." Karla sighed. "With all the dirty tricks he's been pulling, I guess we were wrong."

"If he'd just say he was wrong and he's sorry, I could forgive him."

"He probably doesn't even remember that he did anything to hurt you." She rolled over and sat up. "Father's been pestering you from the beginning to have a baby, hasn't he?"

"Every Sunday at dinner, he asks about my health and says I'm not eating enough and I can't get pregnant if I'm not healthy."

"I decided not to have children because I didn't want him getting his hands on them."

"What?"

"Sshh. Don't wake up the others." She glanced at her sisters, lying in shadowy lumps on either side of them. "Charli was anorexic all the way through high school and college, thanks to him nagging about her figure. He said she was built like a hooker. Too many curves. So she tried to skinny down, you know? Andrea miscarried twice. Nerves, the doctors said. The four of us have pretty much decided not to expose innocent children to him."

"That's horrid." The odd thing was, Lisa wasn't shocked by the revelation.

"If you can, get Todd to move before the baby is born."

"Hah."

"I know. If you weren't such a... well, such a good girl, Lisa, I'd tell you to leave Todd."

"I wish I could. He hasn't done anything I can really leave him for."

"Other than being a total, self-absorbed jerk?"

"Talking about Todd again?" Andrea murmured, waking up.

"Boring," Lisa said. Muffled giggles answered her. She laughed with them.

How long had it been since she really laughed? Other than a few short chuckles, some snorts, she hadn't been able to relax and really laugh, long and loud, hard enough to slouch in her chair and get tears in her eyes, in a long, long time.

Chapter Eleven

"I just wish I knew why," Lisa whispered as quiet settled in a thick blanket through the cabin.

"Why what?" Karla said, her voice so soft it blended with the howl of the wind.

"Why did he ask if the baby was his?"

"That's definitely King Arthur's fault."

"You think he's been telling Todd I'm fooling around behind his back?"

"Oh, no, he'd never say anything like that outright. He just hints and asks innocent little questions that only come up with one answer. He killed our mother that way."

"What?" Lisa flinched as she jerked upright. "I thought your mother died in a car wreck."

"She did. She was running away before her loving husband could have her committed to the psycho ward."

"Committed?" She had no trouble believing that. There were times she thought Todd would drive her crazy. Or at least drive her into eating whole cartons of ice cream in one sitting.

"When Mom was pregnant with Charli, he treated her so good. I remember. And I remember how he ignored me, and kept talking about his son. And then Charli was born and he... he didn't want Charli. He was so cold to Mom. He said she cheated on him. And he made a big production about forgiving her, as if she had done something wrong in giving birth to a girl instead of a boy."

"What happens if I have a girl instead of a boy?" Lisa whispered.

"He'll accuse you of cheating on Todd, same as he accused Mom of cheating on him every time she had a girl. Until she got Todd. I saw how differently he treated her after Todd, and I knew he was nasty to her when I was born, too." Karla raked her fingers through her hair. In the shadows from the fireplace, she looked pale, with deep circles under her eyes. "He was so nice to her... until the doctors said Mom would die if she had another baby. He wanted more sons. He tried to sue the hospital for not taking care of Mom. Then he got nasty. He decided it was all her fault, that she had committed some huge sin so God only let her give him one son. And... she had a nervous breakdown just before Todd's second birthday."

"She ran away from the hospital?"

"No, not really. I remember the doctors gave her medicine and she came home and she was very quiet, but she smiled more and he left her alone. For a while. And then he started in again, making her cry. Never yelling. Never arguing. But all the little things he would say... When he said he was sending her back to the hospital, she couldn't take it. She hugged us and said she was going somewhere she could get her thinking straight, and then she would send for us. She got in a taxi. And we never saw her again."

"The car wreck."

"It was snowing. Almost a blizzard. And you know what the worst part was, after the funeral and the police and when things quieted down?" Karla turned to stare into the fire with tears in her eyes. The kind of tears that would burn and never fall. Lisa knew them too well. "All of a sudden she was a saint, the most loving, devoted, wonderful wife a man could ever have. And he pretty much told us if we didn't turn out to be just like Mom, we were going to Hell."

"So when he talks about how perfect she was, how she never worked outside the home, how all her energy was devoted to the house and the babies..." Lisa had to stop and swallow a huge lump of hundreds of angry words that rose in her throat.

"Mom handled the books at church, and she prepared returns on the side during tax season. She was good. Todd gets his head for figures from her, not from our father."

"How does he get away with all this? Doesn't Todd realize what a big hypocrite he is?"

"Todd was too young to remember Mom, sad or happy. And we were just kids. But we learned early to be perfectly behaved, perfectly dressed, good little girls. It was easier to just play along and earn perfect grades and go to church until we were old enough to make our own lives. If you live by our father's rules, he loves you. If you don't — "

"You could lose your mind." Lisa shuddered. "I'm not going to let Todd do that to me. And not his father, either."

"That's the spirit. And remember, the four of us are here. We have lots of practice in handling Mr. Wrath of God. We'll protect you and the baby, no matter what."

~~~~~

Todd got back into town on the red-eye flight, 5a.m., and waited by the baggage claim until six. Lisa didn't come get him, as he had told her to do in the second message on her answering machine. Fuming, he called the apartment. Still no response, though he tried both phones, twice each, assuming she might have slept through the ringing once or even twice. He wasn't about to yell into a public phone, where everybody in the two-thirds empty, echoing Cleveland Hopkins terminal could hear every word
~~~~~

he said.

He took a taxi, finally arriving home at 7:30. The car wasn't in its parking space. Maybe Lisa was running late and on her way to the airport now. He started to grin, glad she would be just as frustrated as him when she got there and couldn't find him. Then he thought about how depressed and tired she had been before he left. Worrying about him wouldn't be good for the baby.

The apartment was dark. Two cupboard doors hung open. Dirty dishes sat in the sink. Todd stormed into the bedroom and Lisa wasn't there. He went into her office. The answering machine light blinked and the number three glowed red. Three messages.

Maybe she never got his message? But where would she go, that she would stay out all night and into the morning?

Fear rose up in his throat, making him feel sick and faint. He ran for the phone and jerked the receiver off the hook. He didn't know the number of the hospital. Todd stumbled into the kitchen and ransacked two drawers before he thought to look on the shelf of the little table where the phone sat. Right on top of two thick phone books.

He heard the muffled giggles outside the door. He sat down on the floor, watching in disbelief as the apartment door swung open and in walked Lisa, with all four of his sisters. Lisa carried a backpack. Karla had his old blue sleeping bag tucked under one arm. Charli carried a plastic grocery bag. Andrea and Terri carried nothing.

"Well, look who's home," Charli murmured, when Todd and the women just stared at each other for a few long seconds.

"Where have you been?" Todd demanded. He got up and took a step toward Lisa. His anger turned cold when she backed up a step in return, retreating toward his sisters.

"She was with us. Is there a law against that?" Andrea shot back.

"I needed a ride home from the airport." He realized how petty and stupid that sounded the moment the words left his lips. There was no way to take it back.

"You should have called —" Lisa began.

"I did! Three times."

"As soon as you knew your travel plans? I was home all day until just after five."

Todd nodded. He had called at 3:30, Denver time, to let her know he was on his way home.

"You know, Toddy," Charli said, "the sooner you realize your wife wasn't created to wait on you hand and foot, the happier everyone else in the world will be."

"What's that supposed to mean?"

"If you don't have the brains to understand a hint to be nicer to Lisa, you wouldn't understand an explanation, now would you?" She patted him on the cheek — he had always hated that — and headed for the door. "It was fun, Lisa. We have to do this again."

"I was going to make breakfast for everybody," Lisa said. "Stay?"

"I don't think we should," Karla said. She gave Todd a meaningful look, dropped the sleeping bag at his feet, and hugged Lisa before heading for the door. "Call me if you need any help, okay?"

"What kind of help?" Todd muttered. None of his sisters answered as they filed out the door, but they all gave him that look he hated. The one that meant he had done something very wrong, but they weren't going to help him figure out what it was. "Just get out of my life, would you?"

"What was that?" Lisa asked. She bent over to pick up the sleeping bag. Todd snatched it up first.

"I'll put it away."

"Thanks." She managed a thin smile. "Hungry? I was planning on making this big breakfast for the five of us."

"Where'd you go?" He wrapped his arms around the sleeping bag roll.

"The cabin. We stayed the night. Girls' night out."

"Did you have fun?"

"It was great." She smiled as she picked up the grocery bag and took it into the kitchen. "I haven't just hung out with the girls since we got married."

"Why not?"

"Because when I'm not taking care of this place and working at the Mission, I'm trying to earn a living. Keeps me kind of busy." Her voice went a little flat, but Todd couldn't be sure what she was thinking, with her back turned to him and her face hidden.

"Oh." He went down the hall and put the sleeping bag away. On the way back to the kitchen, he realized what he felt.

Relief.

He was relieved to learn she had been with his sisters, not with another man. A boyfriend, maybe. Todd mentally kicked himself for those suspicions. They had made him miserable enough on his last business trip.

Lisa didn't say anything while she cooked. She didn't ask how his trip was or why he had to go away on such short notice. None of the usual questions that made him feel so good, knowing that she was interested in his life. They ate in silence, until he got tired of it and started talking about his trip. Lisa didn't seem to pay any attention, as if she didn't care about his job anymore.

What happened to the hug and kiss, the smile, and "I missed you so much"?

"Where's the car?" he asked, when he had run out of complaints.

"I have no idea. Where did you leave it?" Lisa concentrated on her cup of hot chocolate.

"At the airport parking... Oh, heck. I didn't tell you where I parked it, did I?"

"No, you didn't. I didn't find your pitiful little note until Tuesday night, by the way."

"Oh." He cringed, hearing the icy snap in her voice. When he looked up again, she was watching him. As if waiting for something. What? Todd didn't know, and he didn't like not knowing. He bowed his head and gobbled his hash browns.

When she picked up the dishes to clean up after breakfast, Todd noticed Lisa had left half her food on her plate.

"Are you all right?"

"Fine." She headed into the kitchen without looking back.

"You didn't eat much."

"That's because I wasn't hungry."

"Is that good for the baby? Shouldn't you eat more?"

"I can take care of myself, Todd." She turned on the water, hard, slamming the faucet. "I'm used to it."

"Okay." He knew better than to try to talk to her when she was in that mood. Todd went into his room to get fresh clothes and get ready for work.

When he got out of the shower, she was hard at work in her office. She barely raised her head to acknowledge him when he said good-bye and left for work.

When he got home, she was still in her office. The doorbell rang at the same moment he said, "Hi."

"That's the pizza guy. Can you take care of it?" Lisa gestured at the stack of cardboard, protective velum, Tyvek mailers, and tape. "I'm trying to get this ready to mail in the morning."

"Sure." He gritted his teeth, not quite sure why he felt so angry, and went back down the hall to pay the pizza delivery boy.

Since when did Lisa send out for pizza for dinner? She maintained pizza was a treat, not something for a regular meal. Unless they were celebrating something?

"Are we celebrating something?" he asked, carrying the pizza boxes back to her office.

Hadn't she said something about a sale, a few days ago? Why couldn't he remember?

"I just don't feel like cooking." She rubbed the last strip of tape over the flap of the oversized, reinforced envelope. "Unless maybe I'm celebrating being ahead of schedule."

"You're ahead? Can I see what you've done?"

"Sorry. Everything's already sealed."

That tiny smile she wore didn't bother him until much later, when she was already asleep and he had been lying on his back, staring at the ceiling for nearly an hour in the darkness. It occurred to Todd that Lisa wouldn't send her originals. She always made copies of everything.

She didn't want him to see her cartoon strip? Why? Because he got mad about the last one? Todd rolled over and looked at Lisa, asleep on her side with her back turned to him. When had she started sleeping that way? They had enjoyed sleeping cuddled up together since their wedding night. He could remember dozens of times when he had got up in the middle of the night to take a phone call for work or use the bathroom or get something to eat, and when he crawled back into bed Lisa would snuggle up against him without waking. And she would always smile when he wrapped his arms around her.

Right now, Todd suspected that if he put his arm around Lisa she would wake up, unhappy. She would probably get out of bed and go sleep in her office. Again.

Todd muffled a groan. He was never going to be able to forget that stupid remark, was he? Lisa certainly wasn't going to forget.

Why couldn't she just let it go and forgive him? Just when he thought everything was going to settle down and get back to normal, he seemed to say something wrong or do something wrong. Why couldn't Lisa just let it go? She had let dozens of other really stupid remarks go without punishing him like this. Why not now?

True, nothing he had ever said or done or forgotten to do had ever made her this angry. She always seemed to be in her office, as if it were her fortress or sanctuary. Sometimes Todd thought Lisa loved her office more than she loved him.

That brought his thoughts back to her cartoon strip. Lisa had packaged it to mail without showing it to him. Usually when she was ready to send off her latest batch of strips, they would settle down on her office couch and he would read through them and then they would do something to celebrate. Even if it was just ordering a deluxe pizza, they always celebrated a deadline reached and another creative hurdle conquered.

They always chuckled over the similarities between Katie and Bob's life, and theirs. It was a game to see what he caught and what he missed when he read the strips.

Todd had a sick feeling in the pit of his stomach. What was she telling the world about their marriage?

He sat up, swung his legs over the side of the bed and stalked out of the bedroom. A few short steps took him to Lisa's office.

Ring binders with neat, hand-lettered and dated labels sat on a series of wire racks inside the closet. The folder on the far right looked half-empty and had no closing date on it. Inside were sheet protector sleeves, each neatly filled with the originals of Lisa's cartoons. Todd sat down on the couch and flipped the binder open. The very last cartoon showed Katie and Bob sitting in their car, fuming. Katie looked out the side window and Bob slouched over the steering wheel.

Todd's sick feeling grew stronger. He almost closed the ring binder, but he knew if he didn't go back to the beginning and see the progression of this problem between Bob and Katie, he was never going to figure out what Lisa wanted from him.

"You have no right!" Lisa flew through the office door and snatched the ring binder out of Todd's hand. "What do you think you're doing in here? In the middle of the night?" She clutched the ring binder to her chest.

"I'm getting really tired of being shut out of your life, Lisa," Todd said, trying to be calm.

"How would you know the difference? Everything has always been centered around you. What you want, what you think, what you believe. Now that you're curious about part of my life, you think you have a right to snoop? Or is that part of what you think about me now? Since you think I sleep around, you have to spy on me?"

"I don't think you sleep around!" He lunged at her.

Lisa yelped and stepped backward, coming up against the folding closet door. The ring binder slid in her grasp. Todd yanked it from her hands.

"That's mine!"

"And you're my wife. I have every right to know what you're doing, and if you won't tell me, then I guess I do have to spy on you, don't I?" He headed for the door as he spoke. Lisa flung herself on him, grappling for the notebook.

He turned, flinging his arm out to shake her off. Lisa went down, sprawling backward across a wire rack full of books. She and the rack went down with a crash, books and folders spilling out on the floor. Lisa let out a tiny shriek that abruptly cut off as her head connected with the corner of her filing cabinet.

"Lisa?" Todd froze in the doorway.

She didn't move for several seconds. When she did, she slowly rolled onto her side and then to her knees. She curled up on the floor, her head hidden in her hands.

"Lisa?" He dropped the ring binder and stepped hesitantly into the room.

"Get out." The growl in her voice could have come from pain or anger.

"Honey, if you're hurt—"

"You're the last one to care!" Her voice rose to a shriek. "Get out! Get out! Get out!"

She wasn't going to stop. Todd scrambled backward across the threshold. For good measure, he tugged the door closed behind himself. When the lock clicked into place, her voice stopped.

He slid down to the floor in the hallway, shivering in his flannel pajamas. His hands clenched into trembling fists. Todd closed his eyes and rested his head on his bent knees.

This was the worst yet. He had hurt Lisa, he just knew it. Enough to lose the baby? Maybe. What did he know about pregnancy?

His stomach twisted and tried to come up his throat. If Lisa lost this baby, she might just leave him. What was there to keep them together? She had shut him out of her life.

Somehow, this was worse than his suspicions that she was fooling around whenever he went out of town on business.

The knock on the front door startled him. Todd struggled to his feet before he could start thinking straight. His knees ached and his bottom was sore. How long had he been sitting on the floor in the hall? However long it had been, he hadn't heard any movement from Lisa.

He hobbled across the living room and opened the door.

"Karla?" Todd gaped at his oldest sister and her husband. "What are you—"

"Lisa called me." Karla shoved past him. She wore a long coat over a sweatsuit, and sneakers. Her hair was a tangle and she still had a few pillow creases on her face.

"What did she say?" He reached to grab his sister by the arm and stop her as she headed into the apartment.

"Don't." Kevin appeared in the doorway. He stopped Todd with a hand on his shoulder. "Karla is ready to deck you. So am I, come to think of it."

Chapter Twelve

"But –" Todd took a step to follow Karla as she vanished down the hallway.

"Lisa asked Karla to take her to the hospital."

"Hospital? How bad is she?" He stopped, listening to Karla knock on the office door and tell Lisa to open up.

"I think the less Lisa sees of you right now, the better."

"She's my wife. I should be taking her to the hospital. I have a right to know—".

"You've been exercising your rights an awful lot lately, haven't you?" Kevin grabbed Todd by the shoulder, steered him over to the couch and shoved him down into it. "You're a real jerk. Sometimes I'm surprised you and your sisters come from the same mother." A snort escaped Kevin. "The rest of the time, I'm surprised Lisa married you at all."

"Would everybody just get off my back?" He started to stand, but Kevin shoved him back into the couch.

"You listen to me. I'm just a lowly business lawyer, but I know how to handle things like restraining orders and I can slap you with a dozen lawsuits faster than you can figure out how to spell habeas corpus."

"Restraining—" The words died in Todd's throat as Lisa and Karla came down the hall.

His sister supported his wife, who held a wet cloth to the side of her face. Lisa wore sweatpants and sweatshirt and her vest jacket. Neither one looked at Todd as they went out the door.

"Please, God, I never meant to hurt her," Todd whispered, as he slumped forward and hid his face in his hands.

"Right now, I doubt even God believes you." Kevin sighed. "Have you two thought about counseling?"

"Yeah, we had an—" He groaned. "We had an appointment Tuesday, but I got called out of town."

"When's the next one?"

"I don't know. We were probably supposed to make another appointment at the end of the first one. Kevin, what am I going to do? I don't want to lose her. I love Lisa."

"Why don't you act like it for a change?" Kevin turned and stalked out the door. He slammed it shut as he went.

Friday, February 28

When Todd came back from a lunch he couldn't eat, he found Pastor Glenn waiting in his office in the chair facing his desk. For two seconds, Todd wanted to turn around and run. Maybe leave word at the main desk that he was taking the rest of the day off. That impulse made no sense. Why would he be afraid to talk to the senior minister of his church? Maybe it was the somber expression Pastor Glenn wore, the frown wrinkles around his mouth and creasing his forehead. Something made Todd think the reason for this visit, especially without an appointment, couldn't be good. Then Pastor Glenn raised his head from contemplation of his hands and saw Todd standing in the doorway.

"Hi." Todd swallowed hard and stepped around to sit down at his desk. "What can I do for you, Pastor? Finally decided to get that software system I offered to design for the church? It'll do everything but fix the plumbing and mow the lawn."

"No thanks, Todd. We prefer to employ fallible people at the church. The human touch." Pastor Glenn smiled, but his usual rumbling chuckle was missing. "I just came from seeing Lisa at the hospital."

"How bad is she?" His voice caught.

"Just three stitches to close it up. Because it was her head, they made her stay for observation. She'll probably be home waiting for you tonight."

"Probably." He knew that was the key word. "What do I need to do?"

"Talk to me, Todd. Karla says you pushed Lisa, so she hit her head. Lisa wouldn't tell me anything. Your sister wants to report it to the police."

"It was an accident," Todd whispered.

"I believe you. Why did you miss your counseling session? That just makes last night's injury all the more serious. You wouldn't have scheduled counseling in the first place if there wasn't some problem. For you to miss without any explanation... What am I to think?"

"It was an accident." The repetition sounded lame. "I got called out of town for an emergency."

"You didn't tell Lisa. The fact that she was caught unawares says something about the value you placed on the appointment... and, I'm sorry to say, on her. She waited at church. She didn't say anything, but the hurt in her eyes spoke volumes."

"I didn't mean to—I left a note, but she didn't find it."

"Todd, things like missing counseling sessions and going out of town for a few days aren't things you leave to notes. Believe me, as someone who has had to leave the house for emergencies at all hours of the day and night, your wife would much rather lose a few hours of sleep and be told face-to-face, rather than read about it in a note. Or worse, hear about it from someone else."

"I know." He felt like he had when the coach scolded him about cheating in basketball.

"You know, but you don't act on it. Todd, your wife is the sweetest, most giving person I've met in a long time. You have to put her through an inquisition to find out anything about her life — she never puts herself into the limelight. A lot of people in our church love her because she's so giving and supportive. They'd be horrified if your marriage fell apart. Lisa wants this marriage to work. The question is, do you?"

"Yes!"

"Lisa can't do it by herself."

"What did you talk about at the counseling session?"

"We didn't have one. It's not ethical to have one spouse talk about the problems in the marriage without the other one there."

"Oh." The intensity of the cool feeling of relief washing over him startled Todd.

"Can I schedule the two of you for another session on Saturday? How about 10a.m.?"

"Sure. Great. Whatever you want."

"It's not what I want, Todd. It's what you and Lisa want, together. That's the first step in repairing your marriage. Working together." Pastor Glenn stood up. "You know, Lisa still loves you."

"How can you tell?" Todd winced at the bitterness in his voice.

"If she didn't love you, this wouldn't hurt her so much."

~~~~~

"You really shouldn't stay here. Not alone with Todd, anyway," Karla said. She had followed Lisa around the apartment like a guardian angel ever since they got back from the hospital an hour ago.

Lisa had taken a shower to get the hospital smell off her skin and out of her hair. When she came out, Karla had a late lunch waiting for her. They ate in silence, then Lisa decided to face whatever Todd had done since she left. She went down the hall to her office and nudged the door open.

Nothing had changed since Karla helped her leave to go to the hospital. The ring binder still sat in the bent heap in the corner where it had fallen when Todd pushed her. A smear of blood still showed on the pale contact paper covering the side of the filing cabinet. Another smear of blood darkened the light green plaid of the carpeting.

"I think Kevin scared him enough he won't try anything. Besides, I'll just ignore him and stay in my office." Lisa brushed past her sister-in-law to head back down the hall. She picked up the mail she had dropped on the couch when they came in, for want of anything better to do.

"Todd still hasn't apologized for what he said about the baby, has
~~~~~

he?"

"Nope. So I doubt he'll apologize about this, either." She gestured at the bandage neatly taped to the side of her head, just above her temple. The doctor had let her know just how close she had come to disaster. Another half inch lower and she could have suffered more damage than a headache and a few stitches.

"Have you said anything to him about it?" Karla sank down onto the corner of the couch.

"What's the use? I told him the baby was definitely his. Erase all the sex I've had with Todd —" A strangled giggle escaped her. "I wish I *could* erase all the sex I've had with Todd. He's the only man who ever touched me, and I told him I wish he never had."

"Oh, I'll bet my studly brother loved hearing that. I used to hate him when he was in high school, sneering about the bimbos he asked out. What always rankled was that Todd was encouraged to do things that all us girls would have been thrown in reform school for, if we let a boy do them to us. Our father was so proud his son was popular and could get whatever he wanted, but it was a different standard with us, and he certainly didn't want those girls Todd dated coming into our house. You're the first girl Todd ever brought home."

"Maybe that's why your father was so cold to me? He figured I was just like all the others?"

"They never went to church, like you did. That should have made a big impression with him. But it didn't, of course." Karla closed her eyes and clenched her fists. Her mouth worked for a moment and Lisa thought she was about to say something and then changed her mind. She opened her eyes and attempted a smile. "So, does Todd know he's the first one?"

"He was certainly surprised by it on our wedding night." Lisa rubbed her eyes. They suddenly felt very hot and swollen, and she could feel the tears waiting to get past her guard. "I think it hurt more that he hadn't waited for me, than the actual physical shock..." She sat down. "You know, I don't think I've ever enjoyed... that."

"Let me guess. Todd only thinks about how much fun he's having and doesn't take the time to see how you feel?" Karla sighed. "Why am I not surprised? Our father brought him up to think about himself first."

"Yeah, well, I wasn't smart enough to see that."

"He's not smart enough to realize that if you waited until your wedding night, you're not the kind of girl to fool around while he's away."

"What hurts most is that it just came out of the blue. No warning. No idea he was thinking that about me."

"He's a jerk, what else can I say?" Karla smiled. "Come on. Pack up a suitcase or two and stay with Kevin and me for a few weeks until Todd's starving and doesn't have any clean clothes, then make him get down on his knees and apologize."

"Your father will just have his housekeeper cook and clean for him and then he'll have real complaints about me for a change."

"Ouch. Yeah. Forgot about that. You can't stay here, Lisa. It isn't healthy."

"I think our whole marriage isn't healthy and never has been." She looked down at the piece of paper she had just pulled from a Parkview Tower letterhead envelope. "Oh, great."

"What?" She scooted over on the couch to read over Lisa's shoulder.

"Todd didn't renew the lease by the deadline. Management is letting us stay for now, but if we don't make an official renewal application within the month, we're out."

"Can you do it?"

"I guess. The point is, Todd said he'd do it. I just can't depend on him for anything." Lisa started to crumple up the official notice, then thought better of it and smoothed it out before folding it and putting it back in the envelope.

The phone rang, startling them. Lisa clenched her fists under the table and waited for the phone to stop ringing, the silence as the answering machine kicked in, and the waiting, listening silence, as if the person on the other end could hear movement in the apartment.

"Two o'clock on the dot," Lisa whispered.

"What?"

"Somebody calls every day at ten and two and whenever Todd's out of... but Todd's *in* town."

"Somebody calls you every time Todd's out of town?" Karla shuddered.

"Lisa!" Mr. Montgomery growled through the speaker of the answering machine. "You pick up the phone right now." Silence, while Lisa and Karla looked at each other. "Out gallivanting around town, you little slut? You're going to act responsibly for a change. That's my grandson you're carrying and I won't allow you to shame my family. Todd is moving the two of you into my house, where I can make sure my grandson is raised properly. No more running around town at all hours, when you should be taking care of my son's house. You're a tramp, but your days of freedom are over, do you hear me?"

The answering machine beeped, cutting him off in mid-growl. Lisa's stomach twisted into a knot. She managed to get to her feet and totter down the hall to the bathroom. She shuddered and gripped the toilet seat and the cool plastic sent shivers up her arms as her body shuddered and emptied. Karla knelt behind her, holding her upright, wiping the sudden sweat from her forehead.

"Well, that answers that question," Karla murmured, when Lisa's shivers finally calmed.

"What question?" Her throat felt burned raw.

"Your mystery caller."

"You think?"

"He's checking up on you, making sure you're home and not running around town meeting with your boyfriend behind Todd's back. He did it to my mother, calling the church office a few times a day. I remember hearing them argue about it. If she didn't pick up the phone, he'd accuse her of meeting someone in a dark closet. As if my mother would have sex in *church*, of all places!" A sputtered laugh escaped Karla, as bitter as the acid Lisa had heaved.

"I never answer that phone," she whispered. "It's Todd's phone. I have my own phone." She thought a moment. "He probably doesn't know I have my own phone."

"Don't give him the number. You'll never get any work done."

"Karla..." Lisa swallowed hard, forcing down the new churning in her stomach.

"He's going to move you in with him. You can't let my father get his hands on your baby."

"I know. What do I do?" Lisa swallowed hard to fight the panic that wanted to strangle her.

"Get your own place," Karla said slowly.

"What?" Lisa stared, positive she had heard wrong. Yet something leaped in her chest, light, almost giddy with relief.

"Get your own place. Be ready to move out the day your lease expires. If Todd doesn't say anything about staying or a new apartment, then you know he's got a really nasty surprise he doesn't have the guts to tell you. He did that constantly when we were growing up, always telling us at the last minute, in a very public place, so we had to go along with his plan or help him out to keep from looking like selfish little witches, according to our father. This way, you have a fair chance of fighting him."

"But that's abandoning Todd. What if—"

"He's already abandoned you. Look, Kevin and I already discussed this. You have to protect yourself and that baby. Take the tape out and save it for evidence. Then the next step is to get free of Todd's bank account and the credit cards you hold jointly. Just in case he tries to snatch your share of the money or saddle you with debts, so you can't do anything. Understand?"

Lisa nodded slowly. She felt numb, but it was almost a welcome sensation. If Karla could counsel her to do this to her own brother, then she wasn't imagining her danger, was she?

"Can you ask Kevin to help me figure things out? What if your father tries to take me to court or something?"

"Of course he'll help you. He told me so while we were waiting for you in the hospital. He'd love to slap a restraining order on Todd right now, if you'd let him. He's been asking for advice and help from the members of his firm who handle these things. The paperwork is set up, just fill in the blanks and sign your name." Karla helped Lisa struggle to her feet in the narrow confines of the bathroom. "You must still love the jerk, not to press charges."

"It really was an accident," she whispered.

"This time. What about the future? If he gets away with this garbage now, what's to stop him from hurting you worse and claiming it was an accident then, too?"

Lisa knew her sister-in-law was right. That still didn't do anything to settle the frightened churning in her stomach and the burning threat of tears.

She had to hunt for the extra mini-cassettes for the answering machine in Todd's office, thankful that he was too lazy to get a new, tapeless, digital answering machine. Karla had to help her figure out how to open the machine and replace the tape. Then they got to work in her office. Lisa took the easier steps first. She called the credit card companies and cancelled all the cards she and Todd shared.

She still had her own checking account at the bank, still in her maiden name. She had never cancelled it, for business purposes and tax reasons, and because it was easier to let Genevieve's checks be automatically deposited, and then transfer money into her account with Todd. She simply wouldn't transfer any more money.

Lisa had just finished canceling the last card when she heard the apartment door open. She stiffened and put the phone down, wondering if it was Todd, praying he had come to apologize. Maybe last night had finally frightened him into thinking clearly. After his visit to her at the hospital that morning, she knew Pastor Glenn would have gone to talk to Todd, even though she hadn't asked him.

"Todd?" Karla whispered. Lisa nodded. "Want me to stay back in here?"

Lisa got up on shaky legs. She ran her fingers through her hair and wished she wore something different. She had changed out of the bloodstained clothes she wore to the hospital, but suddenly she wished she had on a dress.

No, she silently scolded herself. *Why dress up for him?* Why try to look better than she felt?

Wait. Todd hadn't called her name or come down the hall looking for her. That didn't make sense.

Lisa heard a plastic click and the same beep the answering machine made when she replaced the tape. She held her breath and knew instinctively that wasn't Todd in the kitchen. Her heart hammering in her throat, she peered around the corner.

Mr. Montgomery stood in the kitchen, taking the tape from the answering machine. Lisa held her breath. He put the tape in his coat pocket and put another one in its place. She stepped back, out of sight. She thought each footstep was a thud as she tiptoed back to her office. She listened for the sound of the apartment door shutting, and swallowed a hysterical giggle of relief when it did. What if Mr. Montgomery had come looking, to make sure she wasn't in the apartment? Her entire body shook as she collapsed into the couch.

"Lisa?" Concern wrinkled Karla's face. She wrapped her arms around Lisa as she sank down next to her.

"Your father just took the tape from the answering machine."

"He thinks you're not here. How did he get a key? Duh." She shook her head. "Stupid question. Toddy boy gave it to him."

"Oh, Karla, that explains so much." Haltingly, Lisa recounted the regular phone calls with no messages. The times she tried to play back hang-ups for Todd, and there was no time stamp, not even a message light blinking. The times she was sure someone had come into the apartment at night, while Todd was gone. "He's spying on me."

"And making sure Todd won't believe you, with no evidence."

"I thought I didn't know how to use the machine, but he was destroying all my proof!"

"Now you have proof. Plus, you've got me as a witness. I heard the call. And my sisters know the kind of man our father really is. You have to move out, Lisa. You're not safe. Not if he has a key."

"But Todd—"

"If he doesn't straighten out, you're moving out. End of argument." For a moment, as she frowned, Karla looked enough like her father for Lisa to be frightened.

Lisa decided to take comfort from that, instead. If anyone knew how to stand up to Mr. Montgomery and not crumble, they were his daughters. She was going to need their help.

Chapter Thirteen

Lisa had dinner waiting when Todd came home that night. He actually felt his heart skip a beat when he looked at the table and saw that it was set for two. He carried flowers again. This time, he went into the kitchen, found the cut glass vase Lisa always used, filled it with water, and put the flowers into it right away. Then he carried the flowers down the hall, looking for her.

She was in her office. Todd hated her office even more than before.

"Hi." He stayed in the hall with the toes of his shoes scrupulously behind the dividing line between hall carpeting and office carpeting.

"Hi." She lifted her head from the book she was reading. Her hair hung loose around her face. The movement made it shift, revealing the white bandage and gauze tape on her temple. There was no bruise showing from under the bandage. Todd took that as a good sign.

For several long moments she just looked at him. Not angry. Not sad. Maybe a little tired. She didn't smile when her gaze flicked down to land on the flowers.

Shrugging a little, Todd stepped over the line and gingerly crossed the room to put the flowers down on the filing cabinet between the two art tables.

"Can I help with anything for dinner?" He hurried back to his place in the doorway. A bit of hope lightened his heart when he caught a twitch in one corner of Lisa's mouth. Maybe she was just laughing at him, but at least she had come near smiling.

"No. Everything is set."

"Smells great. What are we having?"

"Eggroll Express delivery." Lisa got up and closed her book and walked over to the bookshelf.

"Oh." Todd was glad he wasn't the blushing kind. His gaze followed her, shifting automatically down to the floor where Lisa had landed that morning. The carpeting looked dark, but not with blood. Maybe it was just wet. From cleaning. "Look, Lisa, I didn't mean to—what happened this morning was an accident. You know I'd never hurt you, don't you?"

"No, I'm not sure about anything when it comes to you, Todd." She took another book off the shelf and stood there a moment, her back to him, flipping through the pages. The silence rang, until she sighed and turned around. "Was that supposed to be an apology?"

"I guess." He tried to smile. She didn't smile. If anything, the smears under her eyes looked darker.

"I don't read minds, Todd. Sometimes I doubt you even have—" Lisa pressed her lips tight together, so they almost turned white. She shook her head. "If you're going to apologize and you want me to know you're sorry, you have to say it. Something like 'I was wrong,' or 'I'm sorry.' And some details, so I know what you're talking about. Is that so hard?"

"I'm sorry I pushed you, Lisa. I didn't mean to hurt you. You just got me so mad, and then you fought me and—"

"That's not an apology. That's an excuse. You're justifying what you did. You're making it my fault!" She threw the book down on the couch and stalked out of the room. Her elbow nearly dug into his gut as she walked past.

"What do you want from me?" He followed her.

"What do I want?" Lisa turned, stopping short so he almost ran into her. They both rocked back on their heels. "I want the man I married," she whispered. "You haven't been him in a long time." Then Lisa turned her back on him and continued into the living room.

The doorbell rang, cutting off the half-formed words burning on his lips. Todd glowered in the hallway, hands jammed into his pockets while Lisa paid the delivery girl. She carried the bags into the kitchen without a backward glance at him. When he turned to go to their bedroom to change his clothes, her voice stopped him.

"Do you want to eat while it's hot?"

He stomped over to the bistro table and yanked the chair out and sat down. The waiting mail caught his attention as he waited for Lisa to bring the food to the table. Todd snatched up the letters, scanning them. Mostly computer club queries, offers for credit cards, vacation plans. He tossed each one into the nearby wastebasket as he read them.

Maybe they needed a long vacation. Maybe he and Lisa just needed to get away from everything and everyone and the lousy Ohio February weather. Todd retrieved the travel agency envelope and put it into his pocket.

On the bottom was an opened envelope. Todd opened his mouth to grumble about his mail being opened, but saw the letter was addressed to both of them. His face flushed hot. Maybe it was petty to be angry about something like that. Maybe he just wanted a real excuse to fight.

The lease expiration notice made him wince. He knew he had neglected things in the last few weeks. This was one he couldn't excuse. The last thing he and Lisa needed was to be tossed out into the snow with a baby on the way.

A grin touched Todd's face as an idea blossomed into full growth.

Lisa wanted the dream house. She had given up on it without even telling him. She probably thought he didn't know it was for rent. A yard for the baby to play in when he got older. A lawn to mow. Flowerbeds for Lisa. Maybe a garage for two cars. Lisa would like to have her own car to get around without depending on him or a bus or her own feet.

He smothered a smile as Lisa brought the food to the table. The last thing he needed was to be caught grinning when Lisa was still angry with him. She wouldn't be angry for long, though, once he sprung his idea on her.

Maybe he should surprise her, arrange the lease and pay the movers to pack everything for them. Lisa loved surprises. Good surprises. Todd admitted he hadn't even tried to surprise her lately. How long had it been?

There was that weekend getaway in Canada, but that was part of her Christmas present. Their first Christmas together. Todd ate slowly as he thought, trying not to look at Lisa, praying she wasn't looking at him. He hoped his face didn't give away his feelings, because right now he felt awful. He and Lisa would be married three years in September, and he hadn't once done anything nice for her. Imported colored pencils and an occasional box of chocolate covered cherries didn't quite match up to the dozens of nice little surprises Lisa used to find for him on a regular basis.

Please, God, You have to listen to me. Please, I want to get the house Lisa wants. I'll move us in and surprise her and Lisa will be happy, and I'll never hurt her again. I promise. Just make that house ready for us. Please?

Saturday, March 1

"I don't see why you don't need this furniture anymore." Mr. Montgomery shook his head and watched Todd and three co-workers and basketball buddies manhandle his heavy, never-used office furniture up the stairs to an empty bedroom in the family home.

"I don't use it, Dad. Never did. Besides, we need more room with the baby coming." As Todd had hoped, mention of the baby put a smile on his father's face.

It only lasted a moment before his frown returned. "Lisa doesn't need her office. Never did. She certainly won't have time for her scribbling once the baby gets here."

"They aren't scribbles, Mr. Montgomery." George from Customer Service paused at the bottom of the steps and wiped his sweaty forehead with the back of his hand. "Those are great cartoons. Lisa's one fantastic little artist. You ought to be really proud of her." He headed out the door before Mr. Montgomery could offer a rebuttal.

"I find it hard to believe that man is successful at your company," he growled.

"He's the best, Dad." Todd nudged the boxes of books he had brought in. Books he had never used. He couldn't understand why his father bought them without asking if he wanted them.

"Well, at least he makes up for his mouth by being helpful. I still say the two of you should move back home."

"We can do it ourselves." He cringed, anticipating the arguments that would fall on him in a wave. "We don't want to inconvenience you or change your lifestyle. Besides, the baby crying would keep you awake at night."

"Don't you worry about me. A little crying would never bother me. I loved walking the floor with you, when you were just a handful." He chuckled, a rich, warm sound that loosened some of the tight, aching feeling that lived in Todd's head and chest nowadays.

"Really, it's for the best all around, Dad. You'll enjoy the baby a whole lot more if you see him on visits, instead of all the time."

"If I ever get to visit. I wouldn't put it past that conniving little... Lisa's never liked me, Todd. I wouldn't put it past her to cut me off from my grandson entirely."

"Lisa doesn't even know I'm looking for a new place. It's a surprise."

"A surprise? Why?"

"Dad, this is *my* wife and *my* child. It's my decision where we're going to live. You and Lisa will just have to live with my choices, okay?"

For a long moment, Mr. Montgomery stared at his son, his mouth hardening into a flat line, lips losing all color from the pressure. A shiver crawled up his back. Was he finally going to see the icy temper his sisters had always complained about? That made him feel sick to his stomach. What else had his sisters been right about, that he had written off as jealousy because he was his father's favorite?

"It's about time you finally grew up." Mr. Montgomery's face brightened in a wide grin. He clapped his son on the shoulder. "That's the spirit. Take charge. Be the man of the household. It's your God-given right to rule, and don't you ever forget it. Don't even let your old man tell you how to run your house. I'm proud of you, son."

"Dad—" Todd choked, his thoughts from a moment ago swirling through his mind in a dizzying rush.

"But don't be too forceful. Lisa's in a delicate emotional state. Just like your mother was every time she got pregnant. We can't endanger the baby's health by putting any heavy decisions on her. She needs you to be the ruler of the household. That's the only way she'll be the good Christian wife you need. Remember that, son."

"Sure, Dad. Anything you say." Todd tried to smile, but his father's words echoed oddly through his mind. They sounded right, but something just felt... wrong.

~~~~~

"What do you mean, it's cancelled?" Todd stared at the Kohls clerk and slowly took back his credit card.

"The order was entered in the computer yesterday." The man looked up from the terminal that refused to process Todd's purchase.

Todd had remembered the baby furniture Lisa circled in the catalog that went into the trash. He went to Kohls after his father's house, found and ordered the complete set to surprise her. But now he couldn't pay for it.

"Was it reported stolen?" Maybe Lisa had lost her credit card and had been afraid to tell him. That would explain why she was so quiet and avoided him. She was ashamed and afraid he would be angry. After that fight Thursday night, he really couldn't blame her for being afraid of him. He hadn't know that fury was there. But her fall had been an accident. Just an accident.

"No... the joint account was cancelled," the clerk said. "Do you have a credit card in your own name?"

"Sure." Todd started to dig through his wallet for his separate account card. He and Lisa had a joint account for things they both used. The separate accounts were for things like clothes and gifts. An angry little voice whispered that the baby furniture was something for the joint account, not his.

"Can you hold this?" he finally said, when he had stood there and thought long enough to get the attention of the roving floor clerk and two customers, who now stared at him.

"Of course." The clerk punched the orders into the terminal. Todd waited until all the details were entered correctly, holding a pleasant expression, thanked the clerk for his help, then strolled away.

Walking to his car, he caught sight of a local bookstore, and detoured to stop in. Baby books and prenatal care books were on his list, too. He would show Lisa he really did care about this baby. He would study up on all the things she needed to do or avoid to stay healthy during her pregnancy.

The computer refused his credit card. Another joint account. Todd gritted his teeth, pulled out his MasterCard and paid for the books. He was halfway to the car before he wondered if he should have left the books there.

No, that would be a spoiled child's trick. Lisa could get away with things like that because she was pregnant. He couldn't lower himself to such tactics.

"Where's your office furniture?" Lisa greeted him when he got back home that afternoon. She spent every other Saturday morning at the Mission, helping prepare meals for shut-ins for the next week or people
~~~~~

who came in off the street looking for assistance. Todd had taken advantage of her absence to start the move.

"At Dad's."

Lisa lost a little color. Her mouth flattened and she nodded and headed into the kitchen.

"Are you all right?" He followed her.

"Tired." She poured herself a glass of orange juice with slightly shaking hands.

"When did you cancel the MasterCard and Kohls?" Todd set the bag of books down on the counter.

"When I cancelled the Target and VISA." She took a sip.

"All our joint accounts? Why?"

"We spend too much money. This way, no more grumbling over paying for what the other person bought."

"I don't grumble that much," he mumbled. "I mean, we haven't even bought big stuff on those cards in... months."

"Exactly. Why have them? They're just something else to get stolen. You might as well cut up those joint account cards while you're thinking about it, so you don't try to use them again."

"Okay." He watched her pull the scissors out of the utility drawer and took them from her. He felt strangely numb when he finished the task and tossed the fragments into the garbage can.

Todd felt like Lisa had shut him out of more of her life. That was ridiculous, he knew, but he felt it just the same.

He took the books and put them in his office closet. He would give them to Lisa later, when they were both in a good mood.

Sunday, March 2

Bekka came over Sunday after church, because she had noticed Lisa had again missed the service they both attended. Lisa appreciated her friend's concern, but for just a moment when she saw her in the doorway, something bitter rose up and threatened to choke her, demanding to know why everyone was bothering her and checking up on her and looking over her shoulder. Why didn't anyone give her the credit for being able to think for herself and take care of herself?

Lisa pushed that anger aside, ashamed and surprised at herself. This was Bekka. She knew more than anyone else what it was like to live under the shadow of Arthur Montgomery and his judgmental clique. Bekka cared about her, Lisa, the person, not the outsider who would damage the Montgomery family image if she wasn't kept on a short leash.

"What happened?" Bekka's eyes widened and she gestured like she would touch the bandage strip that now covered the stitches on Lisa's temple, rather than the thick pad the hospital had originally put there.

"Todd is showing his true colors." Lisa clapped her hand over her mouth, surprised that the words had slipped out.

"What did he do?" She stepped into the apartment and Lisa moved out of the doorway.

They ended up on the couch, and by the time Lisa finished reciting the events of the last few days, Bekka shifted from holding her hand to putting an arm around her shoulders. One of the wonderful things about Bekka was that she listened and let someone finish a story before breaking in with her own interpretation or questions.

"And Karla says the best thing to do is move out, before their father moves us in with him and he takes over my baby's life." Lisa hiccupped, fighting sobs and the urge to reveal to Bekka the Montgomery family secret: her father-in-law had driven his wife into a nervous breakdown. He had hounded her until she had to flee to protect her own sanity. And had died in the attempt.

"Yeah, I can believe he'd do that, but Todd hasn't actually told you he's doing it, has he? For all you know, it's just a bunch of threats on the phone. And you said he came in and took the tape, meaning he's covering things up. Maybe he doesn't want Todd to know the threats he's making against you."

"I got home Saturday and Todd's office was completely emptied out. When I asked what happened to it, he said he had moved it to his father's house."

"Maybe he's just doing it to get ready for you to start remodeling it into the baby's room," Bekka offered.

"If that was his plan, he would have told me. Todd never lets anyone assume anything, when he has an idea or a plan. He needs to get credit for it." Lisa fought another hiccup attempting to turn into a sob. She forced a smile and her cheerful tone wavered only a little bit. "So, can I count on you to help with the move?"

"You know I'll always be here for you." She shifted away, leaving Lisa feeling bereft until she caught hold of both of her hands. "But I really think you need to get some help. Go to Pastor Glenn. Or Pastor Dave. Or Dr. Harris. Heck, if I didn't know how much the Ice Man hates theater people, I'd tell you to go to Morgan. He's constantly having students drip all over his shoulders with boyfriend and girlfriend problems. You'd swear he was a father to the entire theater department, sometimes."

Lisa wondered for a moment about the smirk that caught Bekka's lips when she talked about her beloved Dr. Morgan. But the expression was there and gone so quickly, she couldn't be sure.

"We tried counseling. Todd skipped town when we had an

appointment."

"Then how about counseling just for you? Talk to Pastor Glenn. I know you're miserable, but Todd's not entirely a jerk. Maybe if you slap him between the eyes with all the rotten things he's been doing lately, he'll wake up and mend his ways before it's too late. I could ask a couple of the tech guys to take him down a dark alley and pound some sense back into his brain. The tech guys are just as big and muscle-bound as some of the football players." She waggled her eyebrows suggestively, earning a sputtered laugh from Lisa.

"Thanks, but ..." She sighed. "I've tried telling him. It doesn't work. He doesn't know how to apologize—ask his sisters. When he did this to me," she brushed two fingers over her bandage, "he started out apologizing, then he turned it around to make it my fault. Last week, he raised his hand to strike me, but didn't. Then this. I'm not hanging around and letting him do worse things. I have a baby to think about. Maybe it'll be harder to prove emotional and mental abuse, but I'd rather fight over that in court than have the police take pictures of bruises and cuts and broken bones." She swallowed hard against a surge of nausea. "And you can bet his father will turn everything around to put the blame on me, that I'm clumsy, that I'm crazy, that I did it to myself to hurt his precious son."

Lisa stopped, shocked at the ringing, sharp tone of her voice that seemed to echo off the walls of the apartment. For several moments, she sat and stared at Bekka, who stared back at her. Then Bekka wrapped both arms around her again and drew her head down to rest on her shoulder.

"That's been a long time coming, hasn't it?" she whispered. "I promise, no matter what happens, I'm here for you. Even if I disagree with you, you have my support. But go talk to Pastor Glenn, okay?"

Chapter Fourteen

Lisa promised. She felt grateful, then embarrassed, then uneasy as Bekka prayed for her, right there, holding her and rocking her like a baby. She wanted to cry, but the tears wouldn't come. She felt like something big and hard and cold had lodged in her head and in her chest, blocking all feelings except the turmoil and pressure. In a way, it was a relief when Bekka finally left and went to her own apartment. Yet in another way, she felt abandoned.

"Please, God." Lisa choked on the prayer, as she always seemed to do lately. She had to trust that the scriptures were right, and God knew what she was praying, even if she couldn't figure it out for herself.

She went to her office and sat down and got back to work. As usual, she couldn't make herself eat any lunch. She put a plate and fork in the sink, to look like she had rinsed them off after eating, so Todd wouldn't pester her about lunch when he came home from his father's house late that afternoon.

Monday, March 3

Monday morning, listening to a niggling voice of suspicion, Todd got online and checked on the balance of his and Lisa's joint bank account. It wasn't what he expected. Over a lunch he barely tasted, he did a few calculations and guessed what money was missing. Lisa's most recent scheduled deposit wasn't in the bank. There was only enough money in there to cover the electric, water and rent payments through the end of the apartment lease. He needed that money for the security deposit on the dream house.

"What's going on?" he demanded when he got home that night. Lisa was in their bedroom, folding laundry. "There's money missing from our account. What did you do with it?"

"It's still in my account."

"Why?"

"It's my money. I earned it. I put in enough to pay for my share of things." She swallowed hard and looked away a moment. When she met his gaze again, her eyes were unusually bright. "I'm not taking anything that belongs to you."

"I wasn't accusing you!" He flinched when his voice echoed off the ceiling. "I just want to know why you're doing this," he said, trying to use a reasonable tone.

"I have to plan for the future." She concentrated on the laundry she folded as she spoke. "I have a baby to protect."

"For God's sake, Lisa, I'm not some drunk that's going to drink up our savings on a binge!"

"I know that. I still have to protect my baby."

"It's my baby, too!"

"Since when?" Lisa whispered. She kept folding the laundry. Her hands didn't shake at all.

Todd wished her hands would shake. He wanted to look into her eyes and see tears and know she hurt just as much as he did. He had the horrid fear that if he looked into her eyes he wouldn't see any pain at all.

He left, knowing he was running away. He walked nearly an hour, finding himself past the railroad tracks, nearly to the Industrial Triangle as a storm started. Todd dashed into the nearest fast-food place and huddled in the corner in a plastic booth. He glared into his coffee as it grew cold, and thought hard. This was just another phase Lisa was going through. None of this was his fault. It was her pregnancy. That was all.

A smile pushed away some of the ice filling his belly, as he thought about Lisa's delight when he announced they were going to move into the dream house. She would know for certain then that he loved her and he wanted the baby, and everything would be right again. He got up, poured his cold coffee into the drinking fountain at the back of the restaurant, then went up to the counter to get the cup refilled. He dialed three wrong numbers before he remembered the correct number for the realtor handling the rental of the dream house. Chances were good he would have to leave a message at this time of the evening, but to his surprise, the realtor picked up halfway through his message. He got the name of a reputable moving company from the realtor, once they had come to an agreement on the dream house. This time, Todd had to leave a message for the company to call him back. He didn't mind. He felt warm and cheerful again as he walked home, despite the icy sleet hissing through the darkness.

Lisa was still at work in her office, with the door closed, when Todd got home. A sandwich waited for him, wrapped in plastic, with a note that soup waited to be heated in the microwave. He decided to take that as a good sign. Lisa felt guilty about what she had said and done, and she had taken care of his supper to show she was sorry. He could understand that. He decided not to press the issue, but ate his late supper and sat up watching a basketball game, long after Lisa stopped working and went to bed.

Wednesday, March 5

"Hey, Mr. Montgomery, this is Geordi from Dusty's Packers, calling to verify the time you want us to show up on the fifteenth, and how many boxes you'll think we'll need," a cheerful, young tenor voice called from the answering machine that afternoon.

Lisa staggered backwards a few steps, staring at the phone. Since she had caught her father-in-law sneaking into the apartment to steal the answering machine tape, she had taken to getting up and going into the kitchen to listen whenever the phone rang, just in case she could catch another diatribe for evidence. The last thing she expected was a stranger to talk about moving her home. She barely snapped out of her shock in time to grab a pencil and paper and write down the details. The efficient young Geordi gave all the information twice, detailing how many people he would bring to pack up everything in the apartment, and take care of basic unpacking and arranging furniture at the new house.

She felt unusually calm when she went back to her office, and sat at her drawing board, staring unseeing at the latest panels that only needed coloring before she sent them to Genevieve. Lisa realized she had subconsciously hoped Bekka was right, and her father-in-law had been making pronouncements and decisions without clearing anything with his son. That was why the confirmation of her fears now made her feel so unbalanced, like she stood on two different levels that kept shifting in different directions under her feet. She had hoped, deep inside, that Todd didn't know what his father was saying. Or if he knew, he was resisting his father's decisions. That was why he hadn't said anything to her about moving when the lease expired at the end of the month. The notice from the apartment management had disappeared, without Todd saying a word, so she had assumed he had taken care of renewing the lease like he had originally promised and had kept silent so he wouldn't have to admit that he had messed up yet again. Here was proof that she was wrong again to have any hope.

This was even worse than she had feared. Todd not only agreed with his father, but the coward hadn't had the guts and integrity to tell her his plans. He probably thought she would be too surprised to argue with him, and certainly she would be afraid to make a scene in front of strangers, when the movers and packers came to their apartment next Saturday morning. Todd counted on her to be too polite, to give in and go along with his arrangements. And then she would be trapped in his father's home for the rest of her life.

Half-formed plans and ideas congealed into a list of tasks. Lisa was grateful Karla had made her cancel the joint credit cards last week. That was one step toward emancipation and protecting her baby. The next step, after a few phone calls, was to walk up the street to the post office and arrange for a box, and to get a mail forwarding order immediately.

"Could I speak to Kevin McNeal, please?" Lisa said when the receptionist at her brother-in-law's firm answered the phone. Even though Kevin specialized in business, he could still guide her through what she had to do. The most important thing was to document every step she was taking, her reasons, the timeline of everything Todd and his father had done. As evidence against future need.

She couldn't make herself look ahead to see what that need might be. She only knew she had to get out, get away, find a safe nest, and then catch her breath.

"I've been looking at a couple of likely places," Kevin told her, after she gave him the latest details. Karla had kept him updated. Lisa wondered what it was like to have a husband who listened and who put the needs of others first in his life. "Do you want me to look into that cottage on Kiln that Karla mentioned you were looking at?"

"Could you?" Lisa's voice cracked. She wasn't sure she could afford the dream house. She wasn't sure she wanted it, because so many shattered dreams had been tied up in it. But taking the dream house and making her own home there would be a blow for her freedom and independence, wouldn't it? She would be proving to herself, and to Todd, that she could survive and be happy without him.

When she finished with Kevin, she called Bekka's apartment. She had to leave a message. For a moment, Lisa contemplated just hanging up.

"Bekka, this is Lisa. I'm calling in that promise. Some movers just called to verify arrangements with Todd." Her voice caught on a sob she refused to let out. "He's moving us in with his father on the fifteenth. Can you help me pack up and move? My lawyer is looking into places for me right now. Please? Maybe you're right about a lot of things, but I just can't give Todd any more chances." She choked on dozens of more words, but they were all bitter and tear-soaked, and she reminded herself once again that she refused to let the Montgomery men make her cry, ever again.

Amy, Bekka's blonde poet roommate, pounded on the door ten minutes later. She rushed into the apartment and wrapped her arms around Lisa before the door was more than halfway open.

"I was just getting home from class when you called, and I couldn't get to the phone in time and then I couldn't move when I heard your message and—" She released Lisa and shook herself, letting out a sound that was half-growl and half-shriek. "I hope you're taking everything, not leaving a single thing for that scumbag lying brat!"

"Legally, I can't. But you know what's funny? Most of the stuff that belongs to him, I wouldn't want to take with me anyway."

"Honey, you should take the jerk to court and take him and his dictator father for everything they've got. For emotional abuse, if nothing else."

Half an hour later, Amy scurried back to her apartment, leaving Lisa amused at her outpouring of fury on her behalf, and her avalanche of outrageous, vicious, totally impossible plots for revenge on Todd. Lisa laughed, her throat aching from fighting tears for so long, and hurried to her office to make notes before she forgot everything Amy said. She could probably use some of the scenarios in future panels. Amy was so outrageous, always on an emotional roller coaster, so sure that what she believed and felt was right, and yet so giving and supportive. How could anyone hate her, even for her extremes of opinion and her razor-sharp tongue? It warmed Lisa to know that she had the support of all three roommates.

Amy's parting remark, though, had her puzzled, and a little ashamed.

"After what happened with Kat and that creep her mother married, you'd better believe we'll help you get out while the getting is good."

Lisa wondered what had happened with Kat that related to her situation and made Amy so adamant that leaving Todd was the right thing to do. She felt ashamed that she had been so wrapped up in her own life and concerns that she hadn't noticed when one of her friends was having trouble.

"Please, God, when this is all cleared up..." Lisa sighed, knowing this mess of their marriage might not clear up for months. If ever. "Please, make me a nicer person, and help me see when other people are hurting and need help. Help me see more than my tiny little life."

Friday, March 7

Mr. Montgomery stormed into Todd's office at ten in the morning.

"Look at this travesty!" He threw a sheaf of papers in plastic sleeves down on Todd's desk.

He looked into his father's pale face, saw the explosion ready to release, and knew a moment of gratitude that his boss had walked out the door only four minutes before.

It took Todd a moment to recognize the master copies of Lisa's cartoon strip. An ache throbbed through his head as he remembered the last time he had tried to look at them. Was he ever going to be allowed to forget what he had done to her?

"Dad, where did you—"

"I went to your apartment to check on her. I was worried, since she hasn't come to church in two weeks. And just like I suspected, that irresponsible child you married wasn't home."

"Lisa's at the *Picayune* today. Editorial meetings," he murmured.

"That girl has no right traipsing around town when she has a husband and a home to tend to."

"Dad!" Todd met his father's gaze, glare for glare. "I have no problem with Lisa working for the *Picayune*."

"You should," his father growled. "Judge Foggerty has been saying for years they're a bad influence on this town." He gestured at the papers. "Just look at this trash." He threw himself down into the chair facing Todd's desk.

Slowly, Todd flipped through the pages. He had a mental image of Lisa racing into his office now to stop him, accusing him of spying on her. He imagined the entire scene from last week repeating, with more tragic consequences, many more hard, sharp edges for Lisa to fall against, with witnesses.

A cold, hollow feeling moved through Todd. In between the third and fourth pages was a note from an editor at a major Christian publishing house. He felt pride for Lisa, to get praise from someone in the industry, and dismay that she hadn't told him about this. The man congratulated her on daring to explore the reality behind Christian family life with all its beauty and grit. Real life. Real marriage. Real problems. Real loss.

"If you don't file for divorce and custody of that baby, I will do it myself." Mr. Montgomery gripped the chair's arms hard enough the plastic creaked in protest.

Todd shuddered, wondering what his father had seen to prompt those words. He continued reading through the cartoons.

Katie and Bob were arguing in their car. She was furious because he quit his job and took a new one in his hometown without talking to her, first. Bob slouched over the steering wheel, glaring at the road, and Katie told him what a domineering, arrogant jerk he was.

In the second from the last panel, a huge semi-truck loomed down on them from the opposite direction. It hit a patch of ice and skidded. Katie screamed.

The last panel showed Katie, unconscious in a hospital bed. Her parents, brothers and sisters sat by her bed, waiting for her to wake up. One brother asked how they would tell Katie that Bob was dead and she had lost the baby.

"She is mentally unbalanced. I've been telling you that since before you married her. But you wouldn't listen." Mr. Montgomery used that weary tone that had always made Todd sick with guilt. "Now look what you've done. That poor baby, burdened with such a mother. I hope it's not genetic."

"Shut up, Dad."

"What did you say?" He reared back in his chair, poised to launch himself to his feet and tower over Todd. He had moved just that way hundreds of times over the years with his daughters.

Todd was too tangled up over what he had read in Lisa's cartoons to feel any shock or fear that his father would treat him that way, for the first time in his life. "I have a meeting in five minutes and if I'm late, I could lose my job. Go home and let me handle it."

"Obviously, you haven't *been* handling it." He stood slowly and leaned over Todd's desk, making it creak with the weight of his arms pressing down on the surface. "I'll draw up the custody papers this afternoon."

"This is between Lisa and me." Todd slid the pages into his desk drawer. Out of sight, out of mind still worked for his father. It had for years. A new thought sent cool relief through his gut. "Lisa is still working on this series. She hasn't even shown them to me. She never does, until she's completely finished. I know she hasn't sent these out to anyone," he lied. Lisa never filed her masters in their plastic sleeves until copies had been mailed. "Besides, Lisa did these cartoons last week when she was still furious with me—"

"Furious with you? You've done nothing wrong."

"Remember how you told me Lisa needed to get her balance back, after getting pregnant? She's pretty touchy, emotionally. Crying for no reason. Unable to sleep."

Todd saw the struggle in his father's eyes. He wanted to argue, but he couldn't put a lie to his previous words.

"Everything is great between us, Dad. Lisa plans on making this all a bad dream for Katie. You know how pregnant women get. She had a bad dream about losing me and the baby and decided to use it in her strip."

Todd stood, hoping his father would take the hint and leave. Mr. Montgomery looked him in the eyes for several long moments. Todd held firm, willing himself to believe what he had just said. He couldn't let himself doubt for a moment, or his father would know it and the whole argument would resume.

When his father was safely gone, Todd grabbed his coat and briefcase and left, just in case his father came back. He didn't need a lecture on lying, not on top of everything else.

His relationship with his father had always been so good, not like his sisters claimed it was for them. What had happened? Why all this division between them?

Why did he have to choose between his father and his wife?

Todd pulled over at a gas station halfway home and pulled out his cell phone.

Pastor Glenn was busy counseling someone and would have to call him back, according to Jeanette. Todd thanked her and hung up before the groan escaped his throat. He had forgotten the counseling session he had scheduled for last Saturday. The only saving grace in all this was that he had forgotten to tell Lisa about the appointment, too.

~~~~~

"I miss seeing your cartoons." Pastor Glenn handed Lisa a mug of tea and settled down at his desk in his big, book-lined office.

Herbal tea, of course. Since finding out she might be pregnant, she had stopped drinking anything with caffeine. Was Pastor Glenn the only man who cared enough to think about such things? No, she thought after a moment. Dr. Holwood, her former advisor at BWU, had been just as caring and observant. She had felt close enough to him to ask him to walk her down the aisle at her wedding. Lisa thought about going to him for advice, or even better, to his wife, Doria. Shame made her shrivel a little more inside. How could she go to them now, when the situation had become so bad, so impossible to fix? She should have turned to them weeks ago. Maybe months ago.

"Is something wrong? Something I said?" Pastor Glenn added with a grin and a chuckle.

"Something you said?" Lisa nearly tipped the mug into her lap.

She had come to Pastor Glenn for personal counseling. Not marital counseling. If Todd wouldn't come, she at least wasn't too proud to admit she needed help.

Pastor Glenn raked his knobby hands through his graying hair and sank back in his squeaky desk chair. "Lisa, I know something is wrong when you don't show me your latest batch. Usually you ask my opinion before you do the final draft."

"Oh. I never even thought about that." She tried to sip her tea, but the surface rippled, making her slightly queasy when she looked at it.

"You've holed yourself up in your apartment like you expect a war to start and leave you stranded. Don't you do anything besides draw and clean and make yourself sick over Todd?"
~~~~~

Chapter Fifteen

"I do a lot of things." Lisa managed to lift her gaze to meet his, and smiled. "I've been apartment hunting, actually."

"Any success?"

"I found the perfect place. It's right over Rick's Bakery. Just a hop and a skip away from church and the post office and the Easel, for my art supplies. What more do I need?"

"What does Todd think about this new place?"

"You know Todd." She sipped again, this time with success.

"No, I don't." Pastor Glenn sighed. "The few times I've tried to get a word with him on Sundays, I can never catch up with him. Sometimes I think he's trying to avoid me."

You're lucky. Lisa had given up trying to sleep on the couch or going to bed ahead of Todd. He watched everything she did, playing the concerned husband, asking if she should see the doctor every time she went to bed early or got up in the middle of the night to sleep in her office. Telling him she couldn't sleep in the same room with him would just start another argument. Silence was more comfortable. It was easier to just lie still and pretend to sleep, then nap during the day.

She had no idea what her lack of sleep was doing to the baby. Lisa hadn't gone to a doctor. She hadn't bought another testing kit. Part of her kept hoping that if she waited long enough, she would find out she was wrong, and she wasn't pregnant.

"What does Todd say about your cartoons?"

"He doesn't ask to see them and I don't offer."

Todd would never see any of her cartoons ever again. She had a post office box now, and permission to store things in the locker of the bakery basement before she actually moved into the apartment. She had started moving her books, summer clothes and unneeded art supplies there, just a box or bag at a time whenever she left the apartment to run errands or work at the Mission. Today, on her way to the church, she had brought two big canvas bags full of the binders with her past cartoons. Just in case Todd decided to come home during the day while she was away and do more snooping where he had no business.

"That's not good." He sighed and took off his glasses.

Suddenly, Pastor Glenn looked tired, closer to eighty than his sixty-odd years. Lisa wondered how many other people were crying on his shoulder, trying to figure things out and not making any progress. It had to be very frustrating for him. She wondered if she should switch the focus of *P.K.* to Katie's father for a change. It would be enlightening, just like the editor said about her preliminary strips about Katie and Bob's problems.

"That's not good at all," Pastor Glenn continued. "So much silence and holding back between two people sharing a home, a coming child —"

"It's not a home anymore," she said quietly. Pastor Glenn didn't look surprised at her statement. Just more tired.

"The two of you have to talk, Lisa."

"I've tried. He was... Karla calls it 'buying forgiveness.' I told him if he wanted forgiveness he had to say he was sorry and admit he was wrong. What could be clearer?"

"Maybe he doesn't know what he did wrong."

"He knows. Todd has an excuse for everything. Even when he apologizes, he tries to justify what he did." She shook her head and took a deep swallow of her cooling tea. It caught in her throat.

Next Saturday was moving day. She couldn't wait to see Todd's face when his sisters showed up to help her pack. Lisa had decided to use the gift list from their wedding to help her divide up their possessions. Whatever came from her friends, she would keep. Whatever came from his family and friends, she would leave for Todd. Everything from mutual friends, she would divide evenly. If they had any mutual friends. Shouldn't that have been a warning sign long ago?

"He's moving us in with his father," she offered.

"What? When did this happen?"

"He thinks I don't know, but the moving company called while he was at work and confirmed details. His father has already let me know that I'm an unfit mother and that Todd and I have to move in with him. Todd hardly ever says no to his father."

"Lisa... I don't know what to say." There really were tears in his eyes now.

"I'm not going with him."

"Do you think that's wise?"

"I have my baby to think about. I have my own sanity to protect. And my own health, if not my life." She touched the tiny pink scar above her temple. Charli had offered to drive her to the doctor to get the stitches removed yesterday afternoon, and Lisa had taken advantage of the car and her help to haul a whole load to the bakery's basement ahead of moving day. Pastor Glenn winced, then nodded that he understood. "There was a time when, if he had just said he was sorry, I would have forgiven him and everything would have been fine. Now, I don't think I would believe him if he got down on his knees and apologized."

"Sometimes we have to let go, Lisa. Sometimes we have to take a leap of faith and ask God to help us do the impossible."

"What if I don't want to? What if I just want Todd out of my life?" A teary laugh escaped her. "He started talking about our summer vacation yesterday. We never go on vacations. We get hip deep in travel brochures and guide books, trying to decide what we want to do. We end up not going anywhere because we want to be careful with our money... but just planning is fun. *Was* fun. Dreaming." Lisa squeezed her eyes shut, fighting tears. They trickled down her cheeks anyway, two solitary, scalding drops, in defiance of her vows. "I think I've forgotten how to dream. Todd took that away from me."

"A trip might be a good idea. Getting away from everyone and everything might be what you two need."

"He's not sorry," she whispered. "He's just trying to buy my forgiveness. Why can't he just say he's sorry? Why can't he explain why he's so selfish and... and suspicious?" she choked out. "I don't want flowers and candy and dinners out if he doesn't love me anymore!"

"I think Todd does love you, Lisa. The two of you just don't speak the same love language. You use several love languages. You tell people how you feel, and you serve. Constantly. You're always giving. I think you've drained yourself dry."

Lisa nodded. Drained dry was a good description for how she felt. Emptied even of anger. And fear.

Discovering that Mr. Montgomery was her mysterious caller and the nighttime intruder had killed her fears. She wasn't going to let him affect her life any longer. She wasn't going to let either Montgomery man push her into a nervous breakdown, like Todd's mother.

"Todd only knows how to express his love with material things," Pastor Glenn continued. "Buying love, as you said. You have to teach him to express his love with apologies and changing his behavior. Even the way he thinks about things."

"Does Todd think at all?" Lisa shook her head. "I'm sorry. That wasn't nice."

"That's how you feel. Part of the healing process includes bringing all the poison and hurt to the surface so you can wash it away."

Pastor Glenn continued talking. They were new words, personal to her, full of caring. No pre-packaged homilies. Lisa tried to listen, but the words meant nothing. She didn't want to ask God for help in saving a marriage that didn't exist anymore. She felt no guilt for moving out on Todd. He had abandoned her long ago.

Saturday, March 15

Todd got up early Saturday morning and got dressed while Lisa still lay with her back to him, debating how to tell him before his sisters got there. Or should she just let Todd make a fool out of himself in front of his family? She flinched when she heard the apartment door slam. What was Todd doing? Where was he going? Was he going to leave her here to face the movers alone when they arrived? As far as he knew, he didn't have to do anything. The movers had said they would pack everything, and Todd didn't have to do any work except to tell them where everything was to go in the house at the other end of the process.

Was he leaving her to direct the movers, without giving her any warning of what would happen today? What was wrong with him? What made him think that when strangers showed up to empty out their apartment, that she would just stand back and let them?

She imagined Mr. Montgomery waiting at his home, rubbing his hands in glee at the thought of putting everything she valued into storage, or tossing it to the curb.

That wasn't going to happen.

A feeling of lightness washed over her. By the end of the day, she would be free. She had done a lot of thinking while waiting for one word of apology from him, one sign that he wanted to make things right. Lisa had thought that being a good Christian wife meant ignoring all the little hurts and sorrows. It was easy when they were just little things, like forgetting to empty the trash, not helping with the dishes, forgetting to tell her he used the last stamp, or not putting away the butter. The problem was that the little things grew into big things.

Like Todd thinking she became pregnant by someone else.

No more. She couldn't take it anymore. She had tried praying, tried leaning on God for comfort and wisdom and strength. It wasn't working. Todd's sisters offered the only help, the only advice that made sense. Move out, break away from Todd before he ruined her life and their baby's life completely.

Bekka had disagreed with her. She had offered to get some friends from church to drag Todd to Pastor Glenn for counseling. She insisted Lisa should stay with Todd and trust God to work things out.

Lisa had feared she would lose her friend over this, but Bekka had promised to help and support her, no matter what she decided. Kat and Amy promised to help today, too. Thinking about Bekka's two roommates gave Lisa a twinge of guilt. What kind of witness was she, running out on her husband like this? What kind of witness to his sisters, who couldn't stand church because of their father?

Lisa admitted that when it came to a choice between her own mental and emotional stability or her witness, she was just too tired to care anymore. She hoped God would forgive her.

Todd's absence so early in the morning, without a word, made things easier for her. She decided to be grateful. She hurried into the bathroom to get ready for the day.

Karla was the first to arrive, loaded down with packing boxes and newspapers, helped by Kevin and his teen niece, Bridget. Lisa set them to work in the kitchen. She re-arranged the cupboards days ago, everything she was taking in the bottom cupboards, everything she was leaving for Todd in the top cupboards. It would make everything easier, faster, less complicated now.

Charli, Andrea and Terri all showed up at the same time with Andrea's husband, Stuart and the other two sisters' boyfriends. Stuart had donated his moving truck for the day.

Bekka, Amy and Kat showed up only moments after the truck arrived, with more boxes and newspapers they had scavenged from Heinke's and around campus. They hugged Lisa, demanded to know what they could do, and set right to work.

Amy was fully supportive of Lisa's decision. Mostly because she was currently in her "men are the scum of the Earth" phase. She and Joe were separated. Again. For the twentieth time since the three girls had moved into the building. She had also brought decadent, gooey, chocolate, caramel and peanut cookie bars to fortify the workers. Lisa thought about what Pastor Glenn had said about love languages. Amy expressed her feelings through baking and pitching in to help even more clearly than she did through her poetry.

Kat didn't say much, but she had that dreamy look in her eyes that Lisa had learned meant she had a new boyfriend. Lisa almost felt sorry for Kat, who wouldn't date a guy more than twice. Bekka had been worried about Kat for months, and asked Lisa to pray for her. After Amy's odd comment the week before, Lisa had asked Bekka and learned the truth. Kat's stepfather had sexually harassed her for years. Her mother had finally learned the truth during the holidays and immediately divorced the man. There had been some strain between Kat and her mother because daughter hadn't trusted mother enough to tell her the truth years ago. Things were better now and Lisa was grateful. She had prayed for Kat.

Lisa wished someone had tried to warn her about Todd before she gave her heart and life to him. She wondered if anyone was praying for her.

Bekka was, she knew. Lisa raised her head from the slow task of wrapping her good china and looked at her friend. Bekka was against her moving out, but she was still here, giving her support, staying her friend.

"I'm not running away," Lisa had retorted, when Bekka accused her of it in the only argument the two friends had. "I'm protecting myself. And my baby. If he was throwing me around the apartment, wouldn't you tell me to leave?"

"I'd take you to a shelter myself."

"Mental and emotional abuse is just as bad as physical."

After that, Bekka had stopped arguing, but Lisa knew she still didn't approve. Her silent help and her continued friendship meant more to Lisa than the more vocal support of her sisters-in-law.

All her books, her bookshelves and art tables, plus the dishes were packed and waiting in the truck for the short hop across the center of town, when Todd came back. He stumbled through the open apartment door and stared. Lisa was down on her knees, wrapping her mantel clock in bubble wrap. Todd laughed. Everyone stopped what they were doing.

"How did you figure it out?" Todd strode through the mess, carefully stepping around a box of glasses. He knelt next to her and kissed her on the cheek. "You guys are great. The movers are supposed to take care of everything, but this will make things so much faster. Lisa and I really appreciate you helping us out like this," he added, looking around the room. "Hey, what's wrong? You all look like you've stepped on something gross."

"Todd, we're helping Lisa move into her own apartment," Karla said.

"You're kidding." Todd slid his arm around Lisa's shoulders. "Sweetheart—"

"The moving company called last week to confirm details for the move." Lisa braced the mantle clock against her chest and stood. "I'm not going to live with your father, Todd."

"My father? What gave you that idea?" He struggled to get up from his knees to follow her.

"That's a pretty lousy joke," Charli said, emerging from the kitchen. With Andrea on one side, and her boyfriend, Kirk on the other, she advanced on him. Todd backed up until he fell into the couch. "Making arrangements to move without telling your own wife. Who do you think you are?"

"It was going to be a surprise. I got our dream house. I even got rid of all my office furniture so we'd have a room for the baby." Todd held up his hands like a shield when all three towered over him. "What makes you think I'd move us in with Dad?"

"He told me so," Lisa said from the far side of the room. "He calls here quite often and screams at me, telling me what a lousy wife I am, what a horrid mother I'll make, and how you agree with him that we should move into his house."

"That's crazy."

"I never answer your phone, Todd. He calls every day to make sure I'm here. Whenever he leaves a nasty message, he comes over and takes the tape out of the machine so there's no proof. Karla is a witness." She managed a smile, though she felt frozen inside. "Once I realized what he was doing, I made sure I got the tapes first. I have lots of evidence. Why did you give him a key to our apartment?"

"I didn't—" He stopped, a sick look on his face. "I had him check on the place when we went on our honeymoon, and I never got the key back."

"He lets himself in all the time. There is no way that man will ever get his hands on my baby."

"Our baby!" he shot back, his face instantly going red.

"Hi." A total stranger thumped on the frame of the apartment door and stepped in. "Looks like you folks got started without me." He wore a bright green jacket with "Dusty's Packers" blazoned across it in purple letters.

"We're almost done," Lisa said. "When we're cleared out, you can pack up the rest for him." She turned her back on Todd and the mover and took her clock out the door.

~~~~~

"Why didn't she tell me?" Todd wailed, when the mover had gone outside to fetch his people. He turned to Karla, the only one who didn't look like she wanted to stomp on him.

"You didn't tell her about moving, either."

"I wanted it to be a surprise."

"Moving in with Father is not what I'd call a surprise. Surprises are supposed to be nice. Not something that'll turn your hair white!" Karla turned away to finish packing a box with towels and kitchen gadgets.

"I wasn't moving us in with Dad. I got our own house. With a fenced-in yard and lots of room for the baby. Our dream house. Lisa has always wanted it."

"You should have told her, then."

"Why didn't she tell me—I mean, sure, Dad's worried about Lisa. He doesn't want her upset and sick like Mom was. He probably just called and told Lisa he *wanted* us to move in with him."

"He stopped just short of telling Lisa she should be locked up in a rubber room," Charli offered. "I listened to all the tapes. He called her a slut, among other things. Just like he used to call Mom."

"He did not!"

"You were too little to know anything," Andrea said, stepping forward. "You only know what he's told you. We were there, Toddy. We know the truth. And we're not going to let you kill Lisa like he killed our mother!"

"He did not—"

"Lisa was afraid she was reacting too strongly," Karla broke in. "I don't think she reacted fast enough or hard enough."

"Why didn't Lisa tell me about Dad? I would have told her she was
~~~~~

wrong." Todd knew he sounded like a whiny child, but he really didn't care. He sank down on the couch.

"Why didn't *you* tell her? Why should she bother telling you anything, Toddy?" Her voice gentled, sorrow on her face. "You can't be bothered to listen when she does try to tell you what's wrong. Lisa isn't pushy. You have to get her really mad to get her to fight and stand up for herself. I wouldn't be surprised if she never stops being angry with you."

"I didn't mean to hurt her!"

"Just like you didn't mean to send her to the hospital? That's half your problem, Todd. You just don't think beyond your own nose. You don't know how to admit you're wrong and apologize. When you do apologize, you always have to prove that you weren't really wrong, that it's always someone else's fault. I'm surprised Lisa has stayed with you so long. She should have moved out a long time ago."

"You should have listened to your heart," Lisa said, coming into the apartment. "You should have warned me not to marry him at all, like you told me you wanted to do."

"Lisa, why are you doing this?" Todd said.

"Because I don't trust you. Because I can't stand living with you. Because I don't ever want to see your father again, much less live with him."

"We're not moving in with him!" His voice rang off the unwrapped dishes and the windowpanes. Todd's face burned. He knew everyone in the apartment stared, and probably half the people in the building had heard him. "I rented the dream house for us. Don't you want to live there?"

"Liar," Kevin said. "I looked into it, because Karla knew how much Lisa wanted to live there. It's not for rent."

"That's because I rented it! Lisa—"

"Just go away, Todd," she whispered and turned away. "Soon I'll be out of your life."

Chapter Sixteen

"You can't leave."

"Why?" She bent to pick up a box full of newspaper.

"You're my wife."

"In name only. You haven't treated me like your wife in months."

"That's my baby inside you!"

"Prove it."

When Todd could only stare, she turned her back on him.

"Lisa," Bekka said, reaching out a hand to her friend.

"Tell her, Bekka. You know I love her," Todd pleaded.

Bekka turned to him, her big, dark eyes seeming to swallow him up with a sadness that choked him. "You say you love her, but not often enough. You certainly don't show it," she said quietly. "I was against her moving out, Todd —"

"See?" he blurted. "Bekka's on my side."

"But after this, I'm on Lisa's side," she continued. "Why did Lisa say you had to prove the baby was yours? I've heard your father call her a slut, when he's grumbling to his clique at church. Did he convince you Lisa is sleeping around while you're out of town?"

"I would never —" Todd stopped short, choked by a wave of nausea so strong his head swam.

"Love is patient, Todd. Love is kind. It doesn't demand its own way. It endures all things. It believes all things. It's not suspicious or rude or selfish. But Lisa is only human, and sooner or later, love breaks down. She can only give so much love without getting any back. God's the only person I know of who keeps giving love despite everything." She stepped over to Lisa, never taking her gaze away from Todd, and bent to help her friend with her packing.

After a few moments, with everyone else staring at him, Todd snatched up his coat and ran out the door.

Sunday, March 16

"Lisa?" Doria Holwood stepped into the kitchen at Tabor Christian Church, where Lisa was busy scooping ice cream, assembly line-fashion, onto dozens of paper plates holding slices of apple and cherry pie. The

Autumn Fellowship luncheon for the senior citizens of the church was nearly over. "I haven't seen Todd anywhere. Isn't he helping today?"

"He had to put in a command performance at his father's house, as far as I know," Lisa said, summoning up a smile.

Obviously, that smile was even less steady than it felt, because concern creased the older woman's dusky features and she came further into the room.

"That man," she said on a sigh, then pressed her lips together as if to hold back angry words, and shook her head. "Then can I give you a ride home? Rance just stepped outside to help Mrs. Sommersby out to her car, and he said that threatened storm is about to hit."

"Thanks, but I'm practically home already." Lisa felt her smile grow a little steadier. She adored her new little apartment, despite the mess of boxes and bags everywhere. She had awakened to the delicious aroma of baking bread and donuts from downstairs, and had actually laughed at the whimsical thought that she would gain fifty pounds during her pregnancy, just from breathing the air.

"And that means?" Doria slid three plates at a time onto the wheeled cart to take the desserts out to the seniors who had stayed for the musical program.

"I'm renting the apartment over Rick's. One hundred yards down the hill from the post office, and I'm home. I won't even feel the cold by the time I'm inside again."

"That's a very small apartment." She chuckled and paused in sliding more plates off the counter. "Rance and I stayed there when we were first looking for houses in Tabor, and he had to start teaching before we found anything. Why did you and Todd move?"

Lisa sighed. She had dreaded telling her former advisor's wife that she had left Todd, in fear of disappointing the woman whose good opinion meant so much to her.

"I moved out... before Todd could move us in with his father." She held her breath, waiting for that disappointed look, maybe some slightly critical but caring questions.

"Oh, sweetheart," Doria whispered, and stepped around the cart to put both arms around her, almost making Lisa's legs fold in shocked relief. "What you must have been suffering from that self-righteous old man."

"I'm sorry," slipped out before she could think. In retrospect, Lisa thought that was the best reaction. Her only other choice was a gusher of tears.

"For what?"

"For not coming to you."

"Lisa." Doria moved her back, holding her at arm's length by her shoulders. "You don't owe us anything. Rance and I have often thought that we should have stepped back and refused when you asked him to give you away at your wedding. We knew how that man thought of us, and we knew it would make a sore point in your relationship. If anything, we owe you." She released one shoulder to cup Lisa's cheek. "I've been thinking, the last few times I saw you, that you didn't look entirely yourself. Something is very clearly weighing down your spirit, and it shows in your face, your voice, the way you move. I wish I could help."

"You are. Just by caring." She swallowed down one of those ubiquitous hiccups that wanted to burst out and turn into sobs. Lisa rubbed at her eyes with her knuckles and forced a smile. "And I'm free and feeling much better already. Honestly."

She suspected Doria didn't quite believe her. She was proven right when Dr. Holwood came into the kitchen twenty minutes later and informed her that he and his wife were driving her home once the cleanup for the seniors' luncheon was done.

"And if you need anything hung, some help putting things away, let us know. It's been thirty years since we had to move, but I can still remember the disorder that plagued our house for weeks afterward. You never quite settle until the last box is emptied and thrown away," he added with a crooked little smile on his square, dark face. Dr. Holwood turned to leave, just nodding when she stammered her thanks.

She supposed that was what her own father would do and say, if he had been around to help her in this situation.

Wednesday, March 19

"Todd, could you come by my office?" Pastor Glenn sounded more somber and downright sad over the phone than Todd had ever heard him.

"Sure." Todd felt his mouth relax into something near a smile. He could make an appointment for counseling with Pastor Glenn while he was there.

It was hard to remember to call when he was at work. When he went home, he could barely stand to be in the echoing house full of boxes and furniture that didn't even have its cushions back in place. All the happy dreams he had about fixing up the house with Lisa haunted him. Todd usually went for long walks or drives through the neighborhood instead of unpacking and fixing up the house after the move.

"When do you want me to come over?" he continued.

"Right now would be good. There's someone here—I think you should be here when we talk. It'll save time."

He knew instantly: Lisa was there. She had gone to Pastor Glenn, since Todd kept forgetting to go. She wanted to work out their problems.

Three days of silence between them since the move had been more than enough for her, and she was ready to admit she had been wrong.

Todd grinned and almost leaped from his chair to run out to the parking lot right that moment.

"I'm on my way. Be there in fifteen minutes, tops."

Todd whistled as he hurried across the icy parking lot to his car.

Since Lisa moved out on Saturday, he had tried everything to figure out where she had gone. He hadn't seen her in church on Sunday, so he couldn't confront her in public, where she would have to answer his questions just to avoid a scene. His sisters wouldn't tell him where they had taken Lisa, and he had been so busy with the movers, he hadn't been able to follow her moving truck when it left the apartment. He had hesitated going to his father for help, but who else could he turn to for advice? Besides, he had to get that key back from his father, to return to the apartment management.

He had run out of options by Tuesday evening. When he explained to the Tabor Heights police that Lisa had moved out, they refused to help him track her down. She hadn't been kidnapped and she was too old to be classed a runaway. Unless he wanted to file an abandonment report and press charges, there was nothing they could do, since foul play was definitely not involved. Officer Nichols had been on duty when Todd stopped in, and the older man had an odd expression when he asked the required questions. As if he blamed Todd for everything.

That had made Todd angry, but not enough to overcome the sense of shame dogging him, or get him to say something stupid. He had shaken his head, thanked the officer for his time, and got out of there as quickly as he could.

He had checked with the post office Monday morning, to see if they had a forwarding order for Lisa, but they wouldn't release that information to him. Their only answer was to send her a letter at her former address, and they would forward it to her new address. That wasn't any help.

Todd checked the phone company next. Lisa's number had always been unlisted, so they wouldn't release her new address. His only consolation was that she hadn't moved to a new city, because she still had the same number she used at their apartment. She was still living in Tabor, but where?

Why was she doing this to him? Didn't she realize he was sorry, that he wanted to work things out? Why did she have to fight him every step of the way? What did she want from him?

Well, Lisa was waiting in Pastor Glenn's office right that moment, and she wanted to fix things. She would tell him what she wanted. He would do everything and anything, no matter what kind of advice his father had been throwing at him about being the ruler of the household. Todd planned to take her to her new apartment after the meeting and help her pack as much of her belongings into his car as they could fit, and then take her home to the dream house. He thought about carrying her over the threshold, just like he had when they got home from their honeymoon. Lisa would laugh and call him a silly romantic. Everything would be forgiven and forgotten and back to normal.

Jeannette Marshall was on duty at the front desk when Todd reached the church. She gestured for him to go into Pastor Glenn's office as soon as he walked through the door. He grinned at her and hurried down the hall, his steps light. He hadn't felt this good in weeks. In just a little while, he knew, everything would be all right.

"Dad?" Todd stopped short when he saw the man sitting in one of the three chairs facing Pastor Glenn's desk. "What are you doing here?"

"Your father wants me to, as he puts it, talk some sense into Lisa," Pastor Glenn said. "I explained that I have been talking to Lisa for weeks now, and you're the one who won't talk. It's a little hard to help with marital problems unless both spouses are willing to talk."

"I'm willing," Todd began.

"See? I told you. Todd has never been the problem," Mr. Montgomery rumbled in that rich, satisfied tone of voice his son suddenly hated. "It's that Lisa. How anyone can be an artist and claim to be a Christian is beyond me."

"Todd might be *willing*," Pastor Glenn said with that forced smile that always made Todd feel guilty. "However, he never follows through when we make appointments for counseling. In fact, I asked Lisa why you two missed the last appointment we made, and she said you never told her about it."

"That's true, unfortunately," Todd said quickly, to halt the angry denial he saw in his father's eyes. "I keep forgetting."

"It makes me wonder if you really do want to save your marriage."

"Of course Todd wants to save it," his father snapped. "But as I keep telling you, it's Lisa. She abandoned her own husband, the father of her child. If it really is his child."

"Dad!" Todd's face burned. He heard echoes of the night he got home from that awful business trip. "Of course it's mine. Lisa would never cheat on me."

"That's not what Lisa says you believe about her," Pastor Glenn said.

"A genetic test will solve the whole problem." Mr. Montgomery stretched his legs out as he settled back in his chair. "We should arrange a psychiatric evaluation while we're at it. It'll save time later."

"What do you mean?" Todd didn't like that smug look his father wore.

"Your father wants to file court action to take custody of Lisa's baby as soon as it's born," Pastor Glenn explained.

"No! No way." Todd threw himself down into the chair next to his father. "That would—that would kill Lisa. It's bad enough I said what I did, but to do that to her—I can't. I won't."

"It would certainly calm our doubts, Toddy," his father rumbled.

"I don't have any doubts. I'm the one who really matters, right?"

"Why haven't you told Lisa this?" Pastor Glenn asked.

"We haven't talked about much of anything lately," he admitted grudgingly.

"Why is that?"

"The girl is unbalanced," Mr. Montgomery offered.

"Dad, will you shut up?" He stared him down while his father went white and sat up straight and gripped the arms of the chair until Todd thought he would break the dark, glossy wood. Any moment now, the storm would break; the tirade that had always been directed at his sisters, but never before at him.

Todd felt a strange, cool sense of relief, as if he had been waiting for this confrontation all his life and was glad it would finally come, so he could put it behind him.

"Pastor?" Lisa knocked on the half-open door before coming in. "You wanted to see—" Her face went white when she saw Todd and his father sitting in front of the desk.

Todd leaped to his feet and crossed the room in only a few steps. He slid an arm around her waist to steady her and led her to the third chair. He nearly put Lisa next to his father, then thought better of it and sat between the two. She moved stiffly, but at least she didn't dig her heels in and resist.

"I'm sorry I tricked you, Lisa. When Arthur showed up, asking me to talk to you, I knew this was my only chance to get you and Todd together and clear the air." Pastor Glenn studied them a moment. He seemed pleased when he saw Todd's arm resting along the back of Lisa's chair.

Lisa glanced sideways and immediately leaned forward, resting her elbows on her knees. Todd withdrew his arm.

Pastor Glenn cleared his throat. "Lisa, when did this problem between you and Todd start?"

"The day I forgave him and took him back after our first fight in college," Lisa said with a bitter little chuckle.

"Forgave him?" Mr. Montgomery sneered. "Todd had to forgive you! You're just an overly sensitive little—"

"Dad!" Todd stared him down again. To his surprise, his father sat back in his chair and closed his mouth.

"This most recent trouble, then," the minister continued.

If Todd had heard right, Lisa had been coming to him for counseling already. Why had she never told their pastor the root of the problem?

She still loves me. She doesn't want to embarrass me, even here. Lisa still loves me.

"Todd came home from a business trip a month ago..." Lisa shook her head. The thickness in her voice seemed to choke her.

"You have to tell me, Lisa," Pastor Glenn coaxed. "You've refused before. Todd needs to hear what he did, so he can really understand how he hurt you."

"He hurt her?" Mr. Montgomery snorted. "I find that hard to believe."

"Dad, please," Todd said.

"Why not?" Lisa sighed and stared at a point on Pastor Glenn's desk. "I told Todd I thought I was pregnant. I had a special dinner prepared, to celebrate. We were going to do the pregnancy test. When I told him, he asked if the baby was his."

"Oh." Pastor Glenn steepled his fingers. "That's very serious, isn't it?"

"He was joking, of course," Mr. Montgomery said with a light little laugh. Todd wanted to strangle him. "You were just tired. Worn out and irritated with the trip. Weren't you, Toddy?"

"No," Todd whispered.

"Todd, how could you say that to Lisa? Do you know how many girls I get here for pre-marital counseling who point to Lisa as the kind of wife they'd like to be?"

Lisa flinched. Todd stole a sidelong glance at her. She stared at Pastor Glenn, blushing. Didn't she know what others thought of her?

"She loves you," the minister continued. "Anybody seeing the two of you together can tell that. I've visited your home, I've seen what care she puts into everything she does for you. She's a shining example to the single women in our church. Several of our teens have gone to her for advice, wanting to know if it's worth waiting until marriage for sex. Then you ask her if you're the father of her child? Why?"

"I was... I was in a bad mood when I came home." Todd waited for a sarcastic remark from his father. Why was he being silent? Why didn't Lisa say anything? He sighed, realizing he wouldn't be allowed to get off that easily. "I was upset the whole time I was away. I couldn't get it out of my head that I was gone so often, Lisa could get a boyfriend... a lover... and no one would ever know. I guess I was feeling bad because I'm gone from home so much. Lisa never complains. Maybe I figured she didn't complain because there was somebody keeping her company."

"Did you ever ask her?"

"How could I ask her something like that? It'd hurt her too much."

"You cared about hurting her with your suspicions, but you didn't care about hurting her with your accusations?"

"The truth never hurts anyone," Mr. Montgomery muttered.

"Arthur, I'm going to have to ask you to leave the room if you can't be quiet. In fact, maybe you should leave. This is between Lisa and Todd. No one else." Pastor Glenn looked to Todd, his expression clearly asking him to request his father leave.

Todd avoided looking at either Lisa or his father. He remembered thinking this before: Why did he have to choose between his wife and his father?

The silence hung on so long, Pastor Glenn sighed and shook his head. "Why did you care about how Lisa would react to your suspicions, but you didn't care about making such a hurtful accusation?"

"I don't know!" Todd gripped the arms of the chair to keep from leaping to his feet.

"Where did you get the idea that I'd fool around?" Lisa said, nearly whispering. She didn't look at him. Her knuckles were white on the armrests of the chair. "Maybe the problem isn't me, after all. Maybe the problem is you. I think you've been cheating on me from the beginning."

Chapter Seventeen

"I'd never cheat on you!" Todd felt as if someone had slammed him across the chest with a two-by-four.

"That's the only explanation," she continued, still staring straight ahead. "You've got a lover somewhere, so you accuse me of cheating to make yourself feel better. Remember what you said once? It's the people who can't be trusted who don't trust anyone else."

"I don't—"

Todd stopped as a clear memory slammed into him. Riding in his father's car on the way to the airport because his car had a flat tire. His father telling him to change his job and stop spending so much time on the road away from his family. Then he added, as if he didn't really care, that Lisa was probably very unhappy at being left alone so much. Silly girls with artists' temperaments got lonely easily. He wouldn't be surprised if Lisa went looking for companionship because her husband was gone from home so often. His father had hinted at such things many times before but had never said it so clearly until that morning.

"Dad," Todd half-whispered. "You got me thinking about it."

"Stand up and take the blame like a man, Todd," his father said in that cold tone he had only used on his daughters and Lisa, until now. "You don't need any help figuring out what kind of a self-centered, lying little tramp you married."

"Arthur Montgomery!" Pastor Glenn roared. His volume surprised all three. He stood and motioned toward the door. "The time has come for you to wait outside while I speak privately with Lisa and Todd."

"But this is my grandson's future I'm protecting," he protested, standing and moving to lean over the desk. Pastor Glenn leaned across it first, stopping him from towering over him.

"I am just as worried. Mending this marriage is uppermost in my mind. As a deacon and an elder in this church, I'm sure you'll be fully cooperative in this effort."

He waited, staring down Mr. Montgomery with that calm, pleasant expression on his face that had equal measures of concern, pity, humor and curiosity. A face that could make people angry, and yet laugh a moment later, and think hard once he had left their company. Todd had seen Pastor Glenn defuse many potentially explosive moments at church with that expression, his careful words, his patience, and his silence.

It occurred to him, in that moment of waiting quiet, that his father had been involved in many of those situations poised on the edge of trouble for the church family. Todd pushed that realization aside immediately. Right now, his only concern was fixing things with Lisa.

Mr. Montgomery finally took a deep breath and nodded. He stalked toward the door without looking at either Lisa or Todd, to his son's deep gratitude.

"What did he want?" Lisa asked, the moment the door closed with a slightly louder thud than necessary.

She smiled a little, but it was all ice, as Pastor Glenn outlined her father-in-law's agenda.

"Let me tell you something right now, Todd." Lisa still wouldn't look at him. "Kevin already has paperwork set up to deny your father any access to my baby. I didn't ask for it. I didn't even think of it. Kevin offered. All he has to do is file it. Your sisters will all stand as my witnesses that your father is a threat and danger. I didn't ask, they volunteered. I'll file it without hesitating if your father goes near a courthouse. And if you force me into a genetic test to prove who the father of my baby is, *you'll* never see this child, either."

"Lisa!"

"You know what you just told me? You *do* think I've been sleeping around. You've been worried about it for a while now, haven't you?" She turned and met his gaze. Todd couldn't look away.

"Yes."

"How long?"

"Lisa, I don't think that's really necessary," Pastor Glenn broke in gently.

"Yes, it is. I want to know how long Todd has thought I was a whore." She turned away when Todd winced at her choice of words.

"A couple months now, I guess." He looked down at his clenched fists.

"So for a couple months now, you've been suspicious about me, but you never said anything to me. That means you didn't care enough. You used me for sex and to cook for you and clean for you. You didn't want a wife—you wanted a housekeeper and a toy."

"Lisa, that's not—"

"The only thing you care about is whether I bring another man's child home. You don't care about *me* at all."

"Yes I do!"

"I hate you, Todd Montgomery. As far as I'm concerned, you're not my husband. My baby doesn't have a father."

Then the tears started.

When Todd reached to put his arms around her, she jerked free and stumbled across the room to a seating group next to the bookshelves. Todd looked helplessly at Pastor Glenn. The man just gazed impassively back at him.

"What am I supposed to do?" Todd pleaded.

"You say you're wrong, that you're sorry. That's always a good place to begin."

"It'll never happen," Lisa gasped between silent sobs. "Todd never apologizes to anyone."

"Lisa, you know that's not true. And I am sorry." Todd got up and took a step toward her. She backed into the corner, away from him. "More sorry than you'll ever know."

"You think that means anything to me now? Do you think an apology someone forced you to make *means* anything?"

"Lisa, I love you!"

"You don't mean it. You never meant it." Her sobs broke out, loud and harsh, shaking her whole body.

"Lisa!" Pastor Glenn pressed a button on his desk.

Jeannette hurried in. Between the two of them, they got Lisa out of the office and down the hall. Todd tried to follow, but Pastor Glenn gestured for him to stay back.

"You see?" his father muttered from his seat in the corner of the church lobby. "A silly artist's temperament. The sooner you sue for custody and divorce, the happier everyone will be."

"I am not suing for divorce," Todd said from between gritted teeth.

"She abandoned you!"

"I leased a house and called the moving men and never told her what I was doing. What was she supposed to think?"

"You had the most thoughtful surprise a woman could ever want and that ungrateful little slut—"

"Lisa never fooled around, Dad. She doesn't even like sex, but she puts up with it because she loves me. *Loved* me." His voice cracked as he remembered the pain in Lisa's voice. "You know why she got her own apartment? Because she thought I was moving us in to live with you. She knows how much you hate her and she wasn't going to put up with it. Not even for me."

"I don't hate her!"

"She has tapes from the answering machine, Dad. Tapes of you calling her a slut, yelling at her, and threatening to have us live with you. Threatening to take her baby away from her. All my sisters have heard those tapes. They're siding with Lisa against you and me. How do you like that?" Todd turned on his heel and stomped out of the church.

He was getting very good at running away, he realized as he got into the car. That thought didn't make him turn around and go back, though.

~~~~~

Charli stopped in to visit Lisa that evening after work. Each of the sisters had called or stopped by at least once since helping Lisa settle into her new apartment. Any other time, she would have resented the attention, but she didn't want to be alone. Pastor Glenn had made her lie down on the little cot in the church infirmary until her shaking and tears stopped. He had insisted she eat something. Lisa knew better than to argue with him. He might start questioning her and find out she hadn't been able to eat anything solid since Tuesday morning. Tea wasn't going to keep her going much longer. When she was steady on her feet, Pastor Glenn brought her home and made her go to bed.

Lisa hadn't been able to sleep. She spent the afternoon setting up her office in the tiny corner that was supposed to be her living room. The apartment had only two bedrooms; one for her, one for the baby. The baby's intended room was empty. Lisa didn't know how long it would be until she could plan decorations. So, she threw herself into making her office comfortable; she would spend most of her life there, after all. She set up the shelves she had found at the second-hand store and refinished, and arranged her art tables so they faced each other, pressed up against a wall. There was even room to put her couch against one wall. The apartment had cable hookup. She supposed she could buy a TV and put it on one of her bookshelves and be entertained when she didn't want to think anymore.

Charli liked the apartment, now that there was something visible besides stacks of boxes and disassembled furniture leaning against the walls. She settled down on the couch and looked around, nodding approval.

"Cozy. You'll be fine up here. And half the rent of the other place won't hurt." She opened up her suede jacket and really looked at Lisa. "How are you doing?"

"Fine." Lisa shrugged and contemplated offering her sister-in-law something to drink, just to evade those penetrating eyes.

"Haven't slept much, have you?"

"Better than I have in weeks."

"Yeah. Todd snores." Charli smiled, but the usual twinkle wasn't in her eyes. Lisa wanted to hug her, grateful for the attempt to make her feel better. "Something happen today?"

For a moment, Lisa wanted to shake her head and change the subject. She opened her mouth to ask how Charli's new job was going, then the whole story of the afternoon spilled out. By the time she was done, she was shivering again. Charli held her, rubbing her back, making soft, sympathetic noises.

"Well, at least he tried. Your pastor," Charli added, when Lisa
~~~~~

stiffened and opened her mouth to protest. "He sounds like a great guy. Except for Dad and Todd, everybody who goes to your church sounds great."

"How come you don't come?"

"If you had my father pounding you with a Bible even when you didn't do something wrong, do you think you'd keep going to church once you hit eighteen?" Charli shrugged and managed a lopsided smile.

"My folks died when I was little, but I know they both were good Christians and nice people."

"See, that's the problem. Until I met you, the only Christians I ever saw were Todd and our father. He wouldn't let us go to Sunday school after our mother died. We figured out a long time ago, he didn't want us to have any fun. We had to sit in services with him. We got swatted as soon as we got home, if we didn't sit perfectly still. Not good for making us think of spiritual things, you know? You should have heard the lectures we got when we hit eighteen and stopped going to church. We got our own apartments, just so he couldn't tell us how to live. When you asked me to visit your church, I saw a lot of people there were like you. I wondered how great they were if they could let my father be a leader."

"Maybe they can't see what kind of a man he is away from church. I was impressed with him, until I had to meet him face-to-face," Lisa offered.

She thought of the confrontation in Pastor Glenn's office. Would anything good ever come out of her pain? Would Pastor Glenn finally see the Pharisee her father-in-law really was?

"Exactly."

"Huh?"

"I can't believe in a God who lets that nasty old man get away with all he did to my mother and sisters and me, and now to you. I thought maybe there was something to what you believed. How you can sit there and take the garbage they've heaped on you—"

"What?" Lisa saw some hesitation, had an idea that Charli wanted to say more.

"I'm kind of disappointed God didn't protect you."

"Me, too. I guess." She surprised herself with a bitter little laugh. "No, actually, I can see why He hasn't intervened."

"Why?" Charli really did look interested.

Lisa wondered why this opportunity to share her beliefs with her sister-in-law would happen now, of all times.

"I didn't ask for help. God doesn't want robots, and He isn't going to interfere in our lives unless we're headed for a lot of trouble. Maybe I've been enjoying all this pain, in a weird sort of way." Lisa paused, savoring the revelation. "I've swallowed all the abuse and neglect for so long, it's time to either explode or break down. Maybe it's partly my fault, letting Todd get away with it so long. I should have complained more."

"You love him too much to nag. You're not the nagging type."

"Thanks. I try."

They managed grins. Then Charli sighed and rubbed her eyes.

"I'll tell you something, Lisa. If what you believe about God gets you through this, I might just be a believer. I'll start attending your church. No matter how much Father gloats."

Lisa had a long, sleepless night to think about Charli's words. She curled up on the mattress on the floor and stared at the sheet-draped window. The soft streetlights of downtown Tabor Heights made a warm glow through the pink sheet.

What kind of Christian had she been? From Charli's words, she had at least done a halfway decent job. Recently, though, Lisa wouldn't even try to fool herself into thinking she had been a good Christian. There *were* other ways to have handled Todd's accusations and his neglect and his refusal to admit he was wrong. Other things she could have done. Bekka had made suggestions, but she had been too angry, too hurt to listen.

Was it too late to start over? Try something else?

First of all, she should have prayed about the problem, about her hurt and anger and sense of betrayal. Lisa suspected her prayers had slacked off just about the time Todd asked if the baby was his. Her devotions had faded away to little more than a glance at her Bible whenever she went into her office. She had let her anger devour her and had thrown herself into her cartoon strips as a means of escape.

Putting her feelings on paper had only escalated them. Pastor Glenn had the right of it, when he said he knew something was wrong because she hadn't shown him her latest strips. Maybe she had avoided it because she suspected he would disapprove and guess all her anger and hurt from the cartoons. Until that afternoon, Lisa hadn't been ready to tell anyone what Todd had said and done to her. It had been too much like an admission of failure.

"That's over with, isn't it?" Lisa whispered in the quiet of her apartment.

In the darkness and solitude, she could admit that pride had kept her angry and silent. What if she had just lashed out at Todd and told him how much he hurt her? What if she had pointed out, repeatedly, how cruel and thoughtless he had been? What if she had demanded he apologize, and then made conditions in their marriage, rules to keep this from happening again?

She hadn't said anything because it had been easier to just put up with the petty remarks, the neglect, the promises forgotten and feelings stepped on, the wilted flowers and vacations that never happened, and miserable Sunday dinners with his father.

Love endured all things, yes, but enduring didn't mean becoming a doormat. Love did not allow dishonesty and abuse. Had she contributed to Todd's emotional abuse and neglect by letting him get away with it for so long?

Was it love on her part, to let him hurt her? Or was it stronger, better love to correct him and stop him from continuing down the destructive path established by his father? She had been right, at the very start of their troubles. Todd was more like his father than she had ever guessed. If she really loved him, shouldn't she help him break the cycle?

How could she expect Todd to know what he had done, and to apologize and change, if she didn't tell him?

"How can you expect him to read your mind when you've practically lost yours?" she whispered. A single gasping laugh escaped her, followed by a few hot tears. "God, please, I know I've been doing this wrong. I just didn't know what to—no, that's wrong. I *did* know what to do, I just didn't think about it, or I didn't want to remember. Please, what should I do now?"

The night stayed silent. Lisa lay curled up, staring at the light coming through the sheet, until the first shift people came in to warm up the ovens and start the day's work in Rick's Bakery downstairs. With the comforting scents of sweet rolls and bread baking coming up through the air vents, she finally fell asleep.

Thursday, March 20

She woke just after 10a.m. Lisa drank a cup of tea left over from last night, cold, because she couldn't stomach anything else. She had to walk to the Bluebird Café for her first appointment with Tyler Sloane, to show him the preliminary sketches for the first few posters for the theater season. He had insisted on buying her lunch. She would eat then.

Kevin McNeal had advised her to bring in another lawyer, just in case they had to go ahead with what he called their contingency plans. Lisa considered her father-in-law's threats about custody and DNA testing yesterday. Definitely time to consider the contingency plans. Her walk up Main to Sackley on her way to the Bluebird Café took her past Common Grounds Legal Clinic. She stopped in, on the off chance that Xander Finley was available.

Hannah Blake was busy at the front desk with Bekka, assembling what looked like hundreds of envelopes with mailing labels and several sheets of paper inserted in, and then shoving them through a postage machine. Bekka grinned at Lisa and crossed her eyes as her hands flew through the motions, keeping the machine fed.

"What can we do for you, Lisa?" Hannah asked with a smile, not pausing even for a moment in her part of the routine.

"Is Xander here? Or one of the other lawyers? I have some legal... questions." Lisa carefully looked away as she said it, but she still caught the sharp jerk as Bekka looked at her again.

"No, he's due about—ah ha, speak of the devil." Hannah handed one last envelope to Bekka and stepped back from the desk, breaking the rhythm. "Lunch break."

Bekka shoved the envelope through the postage machine and tossed it in the box of sealed and marked envelopes and dropped dramatically into the nearest chair. Lisa almost could have laughed, but at that moment, Xander stomped his way through the door, carrying a pizza box topped by plastic cartons of salad. The aroma of fresh pizza immediately permeated the office. Instead of awakening hunger, it made Lisa's stomach twist into knots.

Xander took Lisa into the conference room, waving away her offer to come back after lunch. She looked around the office. This was the first time she had stepped into the Tabor branch of the legal clinic. After all the unpleasantness her father-in-law had created trying to keep Common Grounds from moving into their town, she had felt awkward about visiting, even though she had remained on friendly terms with Xander and Hannah at church.

Chapter Eighteen

Even as she explained what had happened yesterday at church and her brother-in-law's advice to get another lawyer involved, she wondered if she might be causing Xander trouble by coming to him with her problems. It couldn't be easy attending the same church with Arthur Montgomery. After the embarrassment of his clerk pretending to be the White Rose, targeting Hannah to do harm to Common Grounds, the rift between supporters of Common Grounds and the Montgomery clique at church had grown a little wider and a little more visible.

"You're right," Xander said, when Lisa finished by asking if involving him would cause him trouble. "There are some tricky ethical questions here. That's probably why your brother-in-law suggested you get another lawyer involved. Those ethical questions concern him more, since he's a member of your extended family." He sighed and rested a hand on Lisa's on the table. "I'm so sorry, Lisa. I can't help wondering if I want to help you *because* it would irritate Arthur Montgomery. Doing the right thing for the wrong reason isn't very mature, no matter how you try to justify it." He offered a crooked smile that lit up his homely face. "But I won't abandon you. I'll call Kevin and we'll check with the ethics committee of the local bar association, see what their advice is. At the very least, we should do some preventative work. A restraining order might help prevent the need for any other legal work."

When Lisa left Common Grounds ten minutes later, Xander was sitting down to call Kevin. She wasn't sure how she felt, but she thought maybe the quivering feeling in her middle was relief, maybe a lightening of the burdens and tensions that had been twisting and crushing her for so long. If she wasn't carrying her portfolio case with all her sketches for Tyler to look at, she might have wrapped her arms around herself, just to brace against the shivering that kept pushing out from deep inside. If it was glee or terror or just a reaction to the icy wind, she couldn't be sure.

Despite her stop at Common Grounds, and slowing down on several icy patches of sidewalk, Lisa reached the Bluebird Café a few minutes ahead of schedule, and was glad of it. She felt a little wobbly in the knees, with the oddest sensation that her head was going to separate from her shoulders if she moved too quickly. She sat on the restored park benches in the cozy lobby of the cafe and closed her eyes to catch her breath and regain her balance. It didn't help much. She had to open her eyes every time the door opened and someone walked in. The cold blasts of air helped, though, so by the time Tyler hurried in, shaking snow off the black trench coat draping his lanky frame, Lisa was ready to smile and stand and walk normally as she followed the waitress to their table.

"I wish I drank champagne," Tyler said, after glancing over her folder full of sketches. He laughed at her little frown of confusion, his voice smooth and deep and his dark brown eyes sparkling. "Your talent is worth celebrating. And my good luck in finding someone like you. I'm a firm believer that every tiny detail makes a big difference in a production. With you to design my posters and programs, that's one less thing I have to worry about. More energy and time to devote to bigger concerns. Not that your artwork isn't an important detail. Are you going to say something so I can stop tripping over my tongue?"

Lisa laughed. It hurt her throat, as if she had forgotten how to laugh. She choked a little and Tyler patted her back as she snatched at her water glass and sipped it to help steady herself. The icy water hit her stomach hard, sending a reverberation up into her head.

"I'm sorry. I just—I love your voice—and I didn't see any need to say anything so..." She shrugged.

"Don't let me steamroller you. When I get excited, I have a tendency to do that. It's okay with arrogant freshmen, because they come into my classes thinking they know everything. By the time they're seniors, they have the talent and the discipline, and I've beaten some manners into them, but they don't want to stand up to me by then." He winked and fanned himself with the pale blue menu. "What's good here?"

"I have no idea. I haven't come here since I was a freshman myself. Todd used to date the owner's daughter, so he avoided this place once we started dating. Stupid, I know, but what can you do?" Lisa managed a smile and reached for her water glass again to hide the tremble in her lips.

"Todd?"

"My husband."

"Ah. The lucky Mr. Collins."

"Montgomery. Collins is my professional name and my maiden name." If God didn't intervene soon and fix things, it would be her only name again. She wouldn't put it past Mr. Montgomery to slam a divorce through so fast she wouldn't know what hit her.

Lisa thought back to the pain in Todd's eyes and voice, and his stumbled apology. What would have happened if she had let him apologize? If she hadn't held onto her hurt and anger like a shield?

But no, she knew if she forgave him that easily, if she didn't make him suffer as she had, he would never learn his lesson. Everything would be smoothed over, but it wouldn't fix anything, any more than a coating of paint on rotten wood made rickety steps safe to climb. In a few weeks, a few months, he would slide back into his old routine and mindset. Those rotten wood planks would snap, and someone would be badly hurt.

Tyler had questions, she could see it in his face, but the waitress came to take their order. Lisa thought back to an afternoon with some friends from her freshman art class, how they had come here for a late lunch and stayed, talking and nibbling, until it turned into a late dinner and an enormous bill they had barely been able to pay. She remembered what she had eaten and liked. Would it taste as good, six years later? That had been a wonderful, carefree afternoon. If only she could turn back the clock.

She decided to take it as a good sign when the menu still had the chili fries and cheese and the tuna salad deluxe pita. Tyler laughed at the combination and chose cinnamon cappuccino, spinach salad, chicken fire strips with onion rings, and a side of spicy fries.

"Believe me, I'll use it up this afternoon," he said, after the waitress had left, laughing with them over their order. "I have my second board meeting, and if it's anything like the first..." He gave a dramatic shudder and wiped his forehead clean of imaginary sweat.

"There's always some part that we can't stand," Lisa said, thinking aloud, "but what we love makes up for it. Doesn't it?"

"Just about. I loved teaching, waking the kids up to the talent and potential and energy God had put into them. I loved dreaming up sets and costumes. I hated the administrative end of it, the reports and grades. Ten years of teaching was enough for me. When this opened up and I could come home to Ohio, I jumped at it."

They spent a few more minutes talking about his family; his parents, Brock and Grace, both retired and enjoying being free-wheeling seniors, his sister, Tanya, and her children, Danny and Pam. Tyler barely mentioned his brother-in-law, and Lisa found some comfort in knowing other people had in-law problems.

When he asked about her family, she turned the conversation back to the sketches she had done. That was why they were meeting, after all.

"You outdid yourself, that's all I can say." Tyler reached under the table to take the folder of sketches off the seat opposite him. He glanced over Lisa's head and offered a smile. "Hello. Can I help you?"

Lisa felt a cold draft flow down her back even before she heard Mr. Montgomery's hard voice.

"So you finally have the gall to meet in public." He kept his voice mercifully low. None of the nearby diners even looked around.

"Excuse me?" Tyler glanced at Lisa, questions in his eyes. He stood, holding out his hand. "I've seen you at church, haven't I? I'm Tyler Sloane."

"I know who you are. Another hypocrite like those Randolphs with their filthy theater. You have the nerve to come to *my* church? To meet your lover in God's house?" Now his voice rose, growing louder, sharper, and people turned to look at them.

Lisa breathed a prayer of thanks that she and Tyler had met after the lunch rush. Would Mr. Montgomery have approached them if the cafe had been crowded?

"Lover?" Tyler managed a half-hearted chuckle. "I fear you're mistaken, sir. Lisa and I are discussing business."

"This is Mr. Montgomery, Todd's father," Lisa broke in. She knew, even without looking at her father-in-law, the more Tyler said to smooth things over, the worse the situation would get.

"You've got a really talented daughter-in-law, sir. Your son's a lucky man." Tyler retrieved the folder of sketches and opened it, balanced on one hand. "You should see the preliminary work she's done—"

Mr. Montgomery slapped the folder out of Tyler's big, capable hands, sending a snowstorm of sketches across the cafe, landing on the floor, on tables, in plates of food. Silence rippled through the room as people turned to stare.

"Is the baby yours?"

"Baby?" He frowned, but he didn't look at Lisa.

She was grateful, even as she wished she could sink down in her seat and melt into the wood. Tyler had to be alert and able to think on his feet, putting together whole pictures from inferences and hints, to be director and producer and handle dozens of other jobs in a community theater. She wondered how much of his confusion and innocence was an act, and how much was real. How much did he cover how he truly felt, and how much was politeness to protect her and avoid making a scene?

"You're her lover, the one she abandons her home to see every day, when she should be taking care of my son."

"Todd abandoned me," Lisa spat. She gripped the edge of the table to keep from leaping to her feet and facing the man. She never wanted to look at Mr. Montgomery again.

"Lying little—"

"Hold it." Tyler kept his voice low, but it vibrated in Lisa's chest. His entire frame radiated a power and authority she envied. "I only know Lisa by her reputation as an artist and what other people say about her. This is the first time we've met face-to-face. Your accusations are unjustified and slanderous."

"You're a fine one to tell me that. An actor, living in sin, come to town to corrupt brainless girls and destroy marriages."

"I was a teacher for the last ten years at a Christian college, sir. Never once did I give anyone reason to suspect my integrity. The Bible demands two witnesses before any accusation can be believed. Do you have a second witness?" He jammed his fists into his hips and looked around the room.

Everyone looked away, unwilling to be drawn into the confrontation. Lisa looked down at her hands, her fingers interlaced and white from the pressure of her clasp.

"No witnesses. Only your word against hers. And mine." Tyler stepped back and took a deep breath. "I've only been in town a little more than a month, sir. I've seen you in church. The Randolphs brought me. Fortunately, I saw a lot of other people before I saw you. If you were the first person I saw when I entered the church, I'd have turned around to leave. Which is what I suggest you do right now."

Lisa waited. She imagined she felt her father-in-law breathing down the back of her sweater, deep, rasping breaths through his nose. She knew the struggle on his face. Appearances were so very important to him, she knew. After what Karla said about how he treated her mother, and what he said about her after her death, Lisa understood a great deal more about how the man thought and acted. His reputation in town and as a leader of their church was more important to him than anything. Tyler had challenged it, without saying a single thing about the stern, judgmental, loveless face Mr. Montgomery presented to the world.

A floorboard creaked. The dim shadow cast over the table retreated. Lisa bit her lip against the pins-and-needles ache as she loosened her hands and the blood returned to her fingers. Tyler glanced around the room, giving sheepish little grins to various people. He finally sank down into his chair.

"Sorry," he murmured.

"Thanks."

"For what? I probably made things a whole lot worse for you. What's with the man?"

"He doesn't know how to love or trust, basically." Lisa flinched when Tyler rested his hand over hers.

"Sorry."

"Not your fault. This has been building up a long time." She tried to smile.

It was a relief when the waitress brought their orders. Tyler thanked her. Lisa could barely raise her head. Her fingers didn't want to close around her fork. The food caught in her throat.

Tyler again came to her rescue by doing all the talking, retrieving each sketch from where it landed, going through each one and pointing out what he liked, what matched or didn't match the thematic image he wanted for each play. Lisa tried to make notes on each one. Her hands shook whenever she saw a smear of sauce or grease or snow-melt or dirt marks on the sketches.

She nibbled at her pita and only ate ten of her chili fries. Tyler said nothing about that. The waitress offered to box up the leftovers without either of them having to ask. When they left, Tyler offered to drive her home. Lisa asked him to take her to the church instead.

"He's really gone and done it now," Jeannette said, when Lisa came through the door alone.

"Who?" She barely looked at her friend before turning to watch Tyler's black Corvette glide out of the parking lot.

"The hanging judge, who else?" She attempted a smile. "Reminds me a lot of my ex mother-in-law. If we locked them up together in one room, they'd probably kill each other in a day."

Lisa felt as if the floor lurched up underneath her and dropped her box of leftovers.

Pastor Glenn came out while they were cleaning up the spilled chili. He said nothing, merely went to retrieve more paper towels, with a few squirts of hand soap to take the grease out of the carpeting.

"I wouldn't worry about it," he said, as he helped Lisa get to her feet. "It's an orange carpet, anyway. Good, institutional color that fades like a champ. You're here to see me about that scene at the Bluebird?"

"He came here?" Lisa swallowed an urge to burst into tears. "What did he say? Poor Tyler. He doesn't deserve to be treated that way."

"Neither do you, and I let your father-in-law know what I thought of his actions and attitude in no uncertain terms."

"I'll bet he didn't like hearing that." She let him lead her into his office and gratefully sank down on the couch by the door.

"Not at all. He claims every man in the church watches you and wants you. He says you're a danger to all the single men, and quite a few married men. And quite a few other things not worth repeating."

"Danger? How? What have I done?"

"You're a lovely young woman who is so in love with your husband you don't notice the admiration of others. You're the kind of girl all of them want to take home to their mothers, or they wish they had taken home to their mothers." Pastor Glenn took hold of both her cold, shaking hands in his big, warm, calloused hands, reminding her that he spent as much time working with his hands as he did in study and counseling. "He does have a point, though. Quite a few men are jealous of Todd. Oh, not in the 'I want to take his wife away' kind of jealousy. It's more in the order of 'How did Todd get so lucky?' Understand?"

"No, not really." Lisa wondered if he could hear her heart pounding. It muffled his words, it was so loud.

"I'm afraid we're going to have to look for a new head deacon and trustee. And all the other positions Arthur Montgomery has held in this church."

"What?" Lisa looked for anger, for shame, for regret, maybe even relief in her pastor's face. All she saw was weariness, and she felt guilty for that.

"He demanded I bring Tyler Sloane before the Deacon Board to face an accusation of leading you into adultery. When I pointed out that he hadn't been here long enough to be the father of your child —" Pastor Glenn squeezed Lisa's hands tighter and held on when she tried to jerk free. "Well, he wouldn't listen. He's very sure you have a lover because you're never home." A tired chuckle escaped him. "I pointed out all the things you do for the church and the Mission, your regular schedule, and all the witnesses who could vouch for your whereabouts. He didn't like that at all. He still wants Tyler kicked out of the church."

"You can't do that. Not just on his word alone."

"Exactly. Oh, I'm sure he has some supporters among the more self-righteous element, the ones stuck in the past who never let a grudge or slight go unpunished... but they're too self-righteous to lie, even to support him. He knows it, too. It's his word and his inflexible reputation against your word and your sterling reputation. I meant what I said, Lisa. You've been a shining example to the young women in this church."

"Until now," she whispered.

"Well, we all fail. If we were perfect, we wouldn't be here. God would take us home." He finally released her hands. "In a way, it's a good thing this happened. He's a bitter, cold man, but you can't force someone to step down from his position of authority and service just because he has an unpleasant personality."

"He quit all his jobs?"

"He quit the church. Since I wouldn't throw Tyler Sloane out, he gave me an ultimatum. I wouldn't bend to him." Pastor Glenn chuckled. "I'm a little ashamed to admit that I enjoyed the verbal tussle we had. That man had the gall to demand that Tyler and others like him should give him more respect because he was a leader of the church. I told him that if he wants respect, he should first act worthy of respect."

"He blew up, didn't he?"

"Nearly took the roof off. I know the finance committee will miss his large checks when they work on the budget, but I've always believed God blesses gifts that come from the heart, more than gifts that come from pride."

"I'm sorry, Pastor. Really. If I had just faced Todd a long time ago..." Lisa swallowed hard and blinked rapidly, fighting tears.

"Sometimes God uses our worst pain to teach us very important lessons. He'll bring good out of this situation, Lisa, if you'll let Him."

She tried to keep that in mind, to accept it and apply it as she walked home. The wind had died down and the afternoon sun was warm enough to start some of the snow melting. Lisa moved at a brisk pace, trying to generate some heat. Somehow, she couldn't seem to build up the heart-pumping sweat that always made her feel glad to be alive.

Lisa tried to think of everything Pastor Glenn had said to encourage her. It was hard. Her thoughts kept going in circles, leaping off track, bringing up bits and pieces from totally unrelated conversations. As if her brain thought those soundbytes would help her make sense of her life.

She was nearly to Rick's Bakery, ready to take the back stairs to her apartment, before she remembered she had meant to get her mail before she went home. There was nothing to be done but retrace her steps now. Lisa sighed and turned around and went back up the hill to the post office.

Her stomach ached strangely. Lisa thought about her leftovers, now sitting in the wastebasket in the church office. She hadn't eaten much. She should probably get home and eat something, but the thought of food made her feel nauseous. Sweat beaded her face and for a few moments, the chill air felt good. Lisa told herself all she needed was some fresh air and exercise. Maybe the walk would help her build up an appetite.

"Hey, kiddo, how's it going?" a scratchy voice greeted her. A lumpy figure lounged on one of the benches by the sidewalk.

Maggie, one of the town characters, seemed to have no past, no home, and always seemed to be available when people needed help. The children at the Mission loved her and called her Maggie Raggedy. Lisa smiled and waved to the woman, dressed in bright green rubber boots, several layers of sweaters in a rainbow of colors and lengths, baggy camouflage pants, and two stocking caps jammed down on her shaggy, iron-gray head.

"Fine," Lisa said. "Nice day to be out, huh?" she called as she passed the woman and continued up the street.

"Yeah, if you're a penguin. You take care of yourself, you hear me? Don't go straining your heart any."

Lisa frowned, wondering what had brought that on. She liked the ragbag woman. She cared, she was trustworthy, all the children in town loved her, and she was easy to talk to. What, she wondered, would Maggie say about her problems with Todd?

The short walk up the hill to the post office seemed to take forever. Coming down the steps outside after checking her box, Lisa suddenly ran out of breath. She clutched at the railing, a dizzy giggle catching in her throat as the world twisted around her feet. When she hit the steps with her knees, she slid down three to the bottom and her body went limp.

"Kiddo?" Maggie appeared in Lisa's field of vision. "Hey, it's going to be okay. You just get some rest. Maggie'll get help."

Lisa tried to say something, but the words died in her throat and her eyes closed against her will.

Chapter Nineteen

"Todd Montgomery? This is the emergency room at Northeast General. We just brought your wife in—"

"How is she? Where is she? No, don't bother." Todd leaped from his chair, trailing the phone cord behind him. He snatched at his suit coat. "I'm on my way."

He left his briefcase and topcoat behind as he ran down two flights of steps. He wouldn't have told anyone where he was going, but the receptionist was a friend and asked what was wrong.

"Lisa's in the hospital," he called back over his shoulder, just before he hit the front doors.

It took nearly ten minutes to find the emergency room once he reached the hospital, and another ten before he could get hold of someone who would tell him what had happened and where Lisa had gone.

She had fainted at the post office. The people there had called the emergency squad. The doctor in charge was doing more tests, but preliminary results said Lisa hadn't been eating or sleeping properly. For a long time, the man at the information desk added, and gave Todd a speculative look that made him feel cold inside, even as his face burned. He mumbled his thanks and made his way through the maze of elevators and halls until he found the room where they had put Lisa.

She sat up in bed, sipping at a cup of something that steamed, while a silver-haired beanpole nurse towered over her. Lisa's hair hung loose, making her pale face seem even paler. The smears under her eyes looked like she had been punched. Several times.

"Hi." He grinned foolishly, feeling like he had the first time he asked Lisa out on a date, almost praying she'd say no because he had no idea what to say to her.

"What are you doing here?" Lisa sounded more tired than anything. At least she didn't sound angry.

"The hospital called me. Your insurance card, I guess." Todd dared to take two steps into the room. "How are you feeling?"

"Like she's been starving herself and not sleeping and worrying about her baby, that's what." The nurse picked up a bowl of gelatin on the little tableside tray and held it out to Lisa. "Eat this right now."

Lisa's lips quirked up a little. She closed her eyes and took a deep breath, then put down the steaming cup and picked up the gelatin.

"How long are they keeping you here?" Todd took another step closer to the bed.

"Until her tests are done and she's strong enough to walk down the street without passing out, that's how long," the nurse replied.

Lisa put a spoon of gelatin in her mouth and wouldn't look at him. Todd didn't know if he should take that as a bad sign or not.

"I'm really tired," Lisa whispered.

"You go on home." The nurse made a shooing motion at Todd.

"When can I come back?" he asked.

"Don't," Lisa said without looking at him. Still in that dead, not-feeling voice. "Not for a while. There are things I have to work out—"

"*We* have to work them out, Lisa." He stepped up to the bed and rested both hands on the railing. "You and me, talking for a change. All this happened because you won't talk to me."

"You better not use that tone of voice on this little girl here, or I'm going to have to ask you to leave." The nurse smiled and patted Lisa's head when she presented her with the empty gelatin cup. Her tone was steely cold and loaded with thorns, compared to her expression.

"Why should I talk when you won't listen?" Lisa picked up her steaming cup again. From the golden color, Todd guessed it was chicken broth.

"Sure, blame it all on me," he growled.

"Get out, Todd." She sipped.

"No. We're going to talk. I don't care how long it takes."

"Get out," Lisa repeated. She paled, making the smears under her eyes look black. "I don't want you here."

"Lisa, you can't—"

"Yes, she can." The nurse stepped around the bed to grab at Todd's arm.

"If you don't leave when I ask you to, Todd, then what's the use of talking? You won't listen anyway. You just care about what *you* want, not what I want." Lisa rubbed at her eyes, smearing her tears before they fell.

"You're hysterical, Lisa." He reached for her, and got yanked back nearly three feet by the nurse. She was ten times stronger than she looked.

"Maybe I am, but that's no reason to ignore what I want. Until you show that I matter for a change, don't bother coming back." She turned her back on him and curled up on her side in the bed.

"Lisa!"

"Get out! Please, get him out of here?" Her voice cracked with more tears.

"You heard the little lady," the nurse said through gritted teeth. She caught hold of Todd's other arm and half-dragged him to the door. Once outside, she hooked the door closed with her foot and gave Todd a shove down the hall.

Several patients, a dozen nurses and a handful of visitors stared at Todd as he stumbled. Worse, Terri was only a few steps down the hall. She carried a backpack Todd recognized. It had been Lisa's in college.

"You really blew it, didn't you?" His sister looked up and down the hall, then gestured toward the waiting room. It had a door that Terri closed after they stepped inside.

"What are you doing here?" he demanded.

Terri sat down and shrugged out of her heavy coat. He paced the narrow room.

"Lisa called and asked me to bring some things for her. You know what hospital gowns are like." She patted the backpack. "What are you doing here? She wasn't stupid enough to call you, was she?"

"The hospital called. Paperwork. What is wrong with her? I just wanted to stay and talk and find out how she's doing and she practically screamed for me to leave."

"Toddy..." She sighed and rubbed at her eyes with her gloved hands. "I was listening in the hall. After you gave her those stitches, I wasn't going to take a chance you'd get violent again."

"I'd never — It was an accident!"

"The first time, probably. Just don't repeat it, hear me?" Terri seemed to tower over him, even seated.

"I promise."

"Toddy, you blew it. You made a good start. At least you wanted to talk. But you forgot the most important thing here. Lisa is sick, she's in the hospital —"

"Duh."

"She's sick because you broke her heart. I still don't understand how she can love you so much, but she does. Did you ever apologize for saying the baby wasn't yours?"

"Yes, I did."

"Did she accept it?"

"No." Todd sank down into the chair opposite her. "She said an apology someone forced me to make didn't mean anything."

"Then maybe you should keep saying you're wrong and you're sorry until she believes you."

"How? She won't let me come back." He gestured in the direction of Lisa's hospital room.

"That's because you didn't leave when she asked you. Start thinking about this from her side for a change." Terri surprised him by reaching out and squeezing his shoulder. She had never been one for any personal contact between them when they were growing up. "Our father has made her miserable since before you married her. Maybe it's time you stood up for your wife instead of following in his footsteps."

"I do."

"How much? Or do you just shrug and let it slide, like you did everything else when we were growing up? If you tell Father he's wrong about Lisa, instead of just ignoring it, sooner or later he'll get the idea and he'll shut up."

"Dad doesn't hate Lisa."

"Do you really believe that?"

"You're trying to put all this on him, aren't you? It's all Dad's fault, not mine or Lisa's?"

"It's your fault for not growing up and defending your wife, and it's Lisa's fault for letting you walk all over her."

"You're a lot of help." Todd jumped to his feet and stomped to the door.

"He killed our mother."

"What?" Todd was positive he really hadn't heard the whispered words, but when he turned around, Terri watched him with fiery tears in her eyes.

"Everything he's said about Lisa, and to Lisa, he said to our mother. I heard him. He punished her for giving him four daughters when she should have given him four sons. He accused her of cheating on him every time one of us girls was born until blood tests showed he was our father. He watched her, constantly. He'd say he was going out for a few hours, and then come back and park across the street and watch the house, just waiting for someone to show up. Her lover."

"You're crazy."

"I was there, Toddy. I heard him. Every nasty word. I saw every tear our mother cried."

"He never made her cry. He loved her. She adored him."

"Just like you hope Lisa still loves you? One thing I can say for that nasty old man, at least he never beat our mother or injured her so she needed stitches, and then claimed it was just an accident."

Todd groaned and sank down on the couch again, feeling sick. He could still hear Lisa cry out in pain, see the fear in her eyes, see the blood on the carpet. It was an accident, he kept trying to tell himself.

But if you had just trusted her and listened to her, would it have happened at all? a quiet voice asked, deep inside the aching core of him.

"One thing I can say for you, Toddy, at least you don't use the Bible as an excuse for your nastiness." Terri stood up and headed for the door. "Are you man enough to admit you're stupid, and try to fix things?"

When she left, Todd knew better than to follow her. He had too many images and thoughts spinning through his mind.

Hadn't his sisters told him years ago that their father had been cruel to their mother? He listened to his father speak in reverent tones about his perfect mother, and he had chosen to believe him, even when his father sometimes grew angry and said his recalcitrant daughters were just like their mother. Was he treating Lisa like his father had treated his mother?

If his sisters had been right all along, the Montgomery family tradition was far different than the one he had grown up believing in. Todd had the awful feeling Lisa had figured out the family pattern long ago, and she had left him to protect the baby as well as herself.

What was he going to do about it? What could he do?

~~~~~

Todd pulled into the parking lot of the church, not quite sure why he had come. He sat in his car and stared at the door, wondering what he would say, or what he wanted to do. He only knew he was miserable, Lisa had left him, his sisters all hated him, and a growing certainty in his gut said they were right and this really was his fault.

The door opened and Pastor Glenn came out, his arms loaded with grocery bags. Todd panicked. Pastor couldn't leave now, when he really needed to talk with him. He couldn't!

"Pastor? Have you got a minute?" Todd trailed along after the minister for a few steps, until it occurred to him to take a few bags and lighten the man's burden.

"Whew. Thanks. Those canned goods are heavy. This week's contribution to the food cupboard at the Mission is bigger than ever," Pastor Glenn said with a proud smile. "What can I do for you, Todd?"

"Lisa's in the hospital. No, I didn't hit her again. I don't even know where she's living now. What am I going to do?"

"In two minutes or less? That's a little hard to say."

"Anything. Just get me started." Todd hated it when he sounded like he was pleading. Especially when he was pleading.

"The basics are this: let Lisa know you love her, every day. Don't take it for granted that she knows. Apologize as soon as you do something wrong, and show her you really are sorry by changing whatever habit or attitude it was that hurt her."

"I've told her I'm sorry and she won't believe me. You were there."

"True." Pastor Glenn unlocked the door of his car. "I also saw the anger on your face when you apologized. I don't blame Lisa for not believing you."

"What's wrong with us? Everything was fine up until a few weeks ago."

"Are you sure? Problems like these don't just appear out of thin air. Lisa isn't the flighty little temperamental, selfish creature your father claims. If you thought things were 'fine,' then I would hazard a guess that Lisa was doing all the work to keep your marriage running smoothly, and
~~~~~

she finally ran out of energy and motivation." He sighed. "You accused your wife of breaking her marriage vows. Did you ever apologize for that?"

"No," Todd whispered. "Not really. I've never really... I've never really apologized before. Lisa always knew I was sorry, and she always forgave me. Why won't she now?"

"My guess would be that she's second-guessing every decision she ever made. Maybe since you *keep* hurting her, she believes you were never sorry. True repentance means changing, not just saying the words." He finished loading the grocery bags into the back seat. "Consider this, Todd. The Bible says that when a man marries, he leaves his father and mother and cleaves to his wife. They become one flesh. I emphasize *leaving* your father and mother. They're still a part of your life, but they don't take precedence any longer. Your wife has first place in your love and loyalty and support. Did you leave your father behind when you married Lisa?"

"Of course!" Todd winced, recalling how his father grumbled about the money "wasted" on an apartment when he had empty rooms in his house. Or how his father expected them to spend every Sunday with him. Or how his father expected Todd to tell him about major events in his life before he told his wife.

Why had that never been so clear before?

"I don't think so, Todd," Pastor Glenn said, shaking his head. His smile looked touched with a little sadness. "From what I've seen of your father and sisters and the byplay between them, between him and you, and what he's said of Lisa, your father hasn't let go. Your sisters had to run away to establish lives of their own, and your father has never forgiven them. You think you've gone out on your own in the world, but you haven't."

"So what do I do? Stop talking to my father? Move to another city?"

"It might be good to isolate you and Lisa so you have a chance. Make a fresh start. But unless you and Lisa are willing to put in one hundred percent *each* and work together, your marriage won't survive. You could be orphans and totally alone in the middle of nowhere, and you'd still have the same problems."

"Is that supposed to help?" Todd felt like laughing and crying at the same time.

"Lisa feels abandoned. I imagine she feels you lied in your marriage vows. She devotes herself to you, but you believe your father's accusations rather than your wife's actions. You have to decide, Todd, and decide soon. Are you going to be one person with your wife, or are you going to follow in your father's example?"

Friday, March 21

Kevin and Karla came to the hospital to visit, just after the doctor decided to keep Lisa another day, to make sure she was a little stronger before sending her home. By this time, Lisa felt embarrassed by the balloons and bouquets and planters that filled all the horizontal surfaces in her room. At the same time, something quietly gloated and gloried in the proof that people cared about her. Bekka, Kat and Amy came by the night before with flowers and her favorite trail mix and offers to loan her DVDs and videos and books when she got home from the hospital. Jeannette Marshall had visited that morning before the doctor had stopped with his orders, and nearly burst into tears when Lisa asked her for advice on raising a baby on her own.

"You won't be alone," Jeannette had insisted. "You'll have the entire church behind you, just like I did. But I'm sure Todd will straighten up and do what's right."

Lisa hadn't been able to argue with her, but she had given up hope of Todd ever proving his love, so she didn't agree with Jeanette, either.

She was too tired to pay much attention when Kevin and Karla got the doctor's report. If only she could get warm. The air felt and tasted thick and smelled like a greenhouse, thanks to all the flowers and planters. Lisa tugged the blankets a little higher and wished Terri had brought her winter robe instead of her summer one. Why couldn't her room be as warm as a greenhouse, instead of just smelling like one? Would she ever feel warm again?

"Sorry. I know the doctor said to avoid stress," Kevin said, once they were finally alone.

"What?" She blinked several times before realizing Karla held out some folded sheets of paper to her.

"The restraining order against our father," her sister-in-law said quietly. "And one for Todd. I think in the interest of future reconciliation, you should just keep it on hand, don't sign it right away. I do want you to sign the first one. Kevin and I, and the other girls, have signed it already. It takes your signature, since you're the one in danger."

"Does Xander—"

"I agree with him. Filing the restraining order will have some bearing if Arthur Montgomery tries to file for custody of your baby before it's born," Kevin said. "Public figures can get away with stunts like that when the mothers of their babies are drug addicts and thieves and a danger to everyone around them. If you've registered a complaint against him first, it will go a long way toward defeating his claims against you."

Lisa wondered why she hesitated before she signed all three copies of the request for a restraining order. Kevin was doing this in her best interests. She was grateful that someone was looking out for her, ready to take whatever measures necessary to protect her.

Maybe, she decided later, once she was alone, the problem was that if her husband had been doing his duty, she wouldn't need anyone to protect her but him. And if something didn't change soon, she might end up signing those papers with Todd's name on them.

Saturday, March 22

For the next several days, Lisa did nothing but sleep, eat, and read. When she went back to her new apartment, she planned to keep away from her work table. She was weeks ahead of schedule, anyway. She didn't look forward to going back to *P.K.* and working her way out of the story hole she had created.

She had sent all of the baby-and-problems strips to Genevieve just before the move, up to the accident that killed Bob and the baby. It was a stupid, vindictive move on her part, but what could she do to change everything? When she got back from the hospital, there was a message from Genevieve telling her how thrilled the publisher was with the "gritty, realistic, face-the-consequences" story she had created. She had no idea how to change the story line without doing a lot of backtracking. She simply didn't have the energy to call her agent and explain and beg for time to change everything.

Lisa didn't have the energy to even think where to begin to make changes.

Chapter Twenty

Even at the beginning of the story line about the baby, the cartoon strip was full of bitterness and hurt. The panels sitting on her art table, waiting to be colored, showed Katie refusing to forgive Bob, and Bob's mother viciously blaming Katie for the accident. Lisa would have taken it all back if she could have, but she couldn't. Not without lots of embarrassing explanations. And she just didn't have the strength. She knew when she had her energy back, she would still be angry with Todd, and the panels might just suit her fine the way they were. Nothing had changed between them, had it?

The doctor had chewed out Lisa for neglecting her own health and the baby's. He was red in the face when she admitted that even though she was almost three months pregnant, she had yet to have her first examination. No blood work. No checking her blood pressure or any other tests to see how healthy she was.

Did she want to lose this baby? That was the doctor's biggest, most often repeated question.

Lisa thought about it during her long day and night at the hospital, enduring tests that made her think she was preparing to enter the space program. She didn't know what she really wanted until the tests came back and the doctor told her there appeared to be no harm done to the baby. Lisa's relief answered her question. She did want this baby. Maybe she couldn't recapture the joy she had first felt, but she could still love this baby and be happy it was hers.

Flowers arrived for her that evening before she turned off the lights to go to sleep. They had no name on them, just the card for the flower shop that had delivered them. Lisa suspected they came from Todd. She knew all she had to do was call the florist and they would probably tell her. She decided not to.

Another arrangement from the same florist, again with no name, came Saturday morning before she signed out of the hospital. Lisa smiled a little and ran her fingers over the pale green ceramic baby bootie that held the tiny arrangement. Andrea, who had volunteered to pick her up and take her home, said nothing. Lisa was grateful. She didn't know what she would say if anyone asked her any questions.

At home, she settled in to recuperate, mentally and physically.

When the phone rang that evening, she nearly jumped out of her slippers. Lisa stared at the phone through a second ring, wondering who would call her.

Plenty of people, of course. Bekka, Amy, Kat, the Randolphs, Genevieve, her friends at the *Picayune*.

Todd.

Her hand shook when she reached to pick up the phone. If Todd had called her, she was ready to tell him to leave her alone. Kevin had a restraining order just itching to be filed.

"Lisa?" a half-familiar female voice asked, when she answered.

"Yes."

"It's Anne Hachworth. How are you doing? I've been getting these nudges to call you. Really big nudges. Like, I'm bruised all over, know what I mean?"

"No, not really." Lisa sniffed, even as she smiled.

How could she forget Anne? Her career rested largely on Anne's generosity. She had sent some of Lisa's panels to Genevieve, using Arc Foundation connections. Anne had showed up to assess Common Grounds for more help from the Arc Foundation. In exploring the town and BWU campus, she had met Lisa and they became friends.

Lisa burst into tears and sank back down into the couch where she had been daydreaming for the last two hours. It didn't take much prodding from Anne before she spilled the entire horrid, painful, embarrassing story through the phone lines.

"You still love him, don't you?" Anne whispered, when Lisa had finished and her sobs had dried up and she only felt empty and achy and cold, huddled on the couch.

"That's the stupid part."

"Not really. Despite what the poets say, we can decide whether to love or not. Maybe something inside you refuses to fall out of love."

"What am I going to do?" Lisa nearly wailed. The sound turned into a choked, desperate burst of laughter.

"Well, you do have a few choices. You stay with Todd because you made a promise to him and to God. Because the witness you live could bring others closer to knowing Jesus."

"Maybe." She thought about her sisters-in-law. What kind of a witness had she been so far? "It's just not fair, you know? Todd's sisters didn't marry Christians, but their marriages are happy. Their husbands treat them like human beings."

"So? Who said life was fair?" Anne responded, with a slight touch of a whining Brooklyn accent. That earned a tiny gasp of laughter from Lisa. "The thing is, maybe you were wrong to listen to them? Maybe you walked out too soon? Maybe you should have been yelling at Todd, instead of playing submissive little housewife?"

"Yeah, probably."

"Lisa, you were the victim at the beginning of all this." She sighed, sounding very tired. Lisa wondered where in the country the Arc Foundation had sent her friend tonight. "But you're holding onto your bitterness. You're becoming part of the problem. You aren't innocent anymore. Yes, you do have rights, and you've been abused, but maybe it's time to forget about what you want, and start thinking about what you're willing to sacrifice."

"But how can you—"

"When I was in Cleveland, when we first met, I ran into a man I hated the way only a wounded child can hate." Anne paused, swallowing audibly. "I was molested by a neighbor when I was a kid. On a regular basis. And when my mother caught him, he killed my parents. His lawyer tried to prove that *my parents* molested me, that I didn't know what was going on, that I was crazy when I told the police what had happened. His accusations hurt me worse than what the neighbor did to my body.

"And when I came to Cleveland and I was working with Xander over at Common Grounds... I met that lawyer, up at the Justice Center. I had to forgive him. It was the hardest thing I'd ever done. But I had to, or the anger and hurt would still be inside me, waiting to burst open and poison my whole life."

"I have to forgive Todd, or I'll never get past this." Lisa closed her eyes and leaned back into the corner of the couch. She waited for more tears to come, but there was just an empty, waiting feeling inside. "I can't."

"No, you can't. Trying to do it alone is like trying to do Lamaze alone. You need a coach. Someone who was the ultimate innocent victim, and still forgave."

"Jesus," she whispered. Somehow, she smiled. It hurt, but Lisa thought maybe this was a good pain.

"You won't have any victory over this until you let go and forgive. Even when your oppressor is offended at the idea he needs forgiveness, because he believes he's right and you're wrong. Like your father-in-law."

"He's the most self-righteous... Todd's sisters never wanted anything to do with church. One said she'd consider giving Christians a chance, because she could see I was different. I guess I ruined that now, huh?"

"By proving you're human like the rest of us? No, there's still plenty of time and room for victory. You just have to take that first step. But I gotta warn you, it's a killer. It hurts worse than anything your worst enemy ever did, because you're killing part of yourself. But Jesus is there at the bottom of the fall, and He's waiting to pick you up and heal you and carry you the rest of the way."

"Promise?"

"He sure does."

Anne didn't hang up until almost an hour later. Lisa sat there in the darkness, hugging a blanket around herself, yet the darkness in her apartment didn't seem quite as thick. The cold had left her chest. She knew she should pray and ask God to help her forgive Todd right that moment and get started on the healing, as Anne told her. She couldn't.

Still, she felt lighter, stronger. She could smile at herself when she went into the bathroom and turned on a light to scrub away the stiffness on her face from what had seemed like gallons of tears. And she slept the entire night through, for the first time since Todd asked his cruel question.

Sunday, March 23

Dr. and Mrs. Holwood came to the apartment after church, bringing chicken stew and fresh bread, fruit salad, and a card signed by everyone in Lisa and Todd's Young Marrieds class. Lisa managed not to hesitate or stutter as she thanked them, but her thoughts kept circling back to the same questions while they visited for a few minutes: Was Todd in class when someone passed around the card for her? What was the story going around the church, and especially among their friends? How many knew she had left Todd? Lisa had welcomed the quiet and lack of visitors, except for the small circle of those who had supported her from the beginning, meaning Bekka and her roommates, and her sisters-in-law. The enormity of what she had done, the thought of the division she was probably causing among her and Todd's friends in church, struck her with enough force to make her feel as hollow and dizzy as she had just before she slid down the post office steps.

It didn't help as much as she had thought, when Dr. Holwood and Doria both gave her tentative support in her decision. Their reasoning came from the viewpoint of being part of the foster parenting system, and considering the needs and rights of the children.

"There is a lot of good in Todd, and we've spent quite a bit of time in prayer, trying to see beyond our problems with his father," Doria admitted with a deprecating little shrug and smile. She reached across the shallow trunk that served as a coffee table in the cramped living room-office. "But we've also seen too much hurt done to children by parents who stayed together too long. The ideal is for children to be raised by two parents who work together, who put the needs and the good of the children above their own. Unfortunately, in this sinful world, that doesn't happen, even in Christian homes."

"Sometimes it's better if the family is dissolved, or at least temporarily divided, until the parents can grow up and heal from their wounds," Dr. Holwood said, taking up the line of thought. "Sometimes it's better if a child has foster parents, or only one parent, rather than subjecting him or her to the constant tension, the battles, the toxic environment. It's not your life anymore, Lisa. The moment the Lord entrusted that child to you, your life changed. It's up to you to trust in Him, and obey, and make sure that change is for the better. For you and Todd, as well as for your baby."

Monday, March 24

Monday, Pastor Glenn came to see Lisa at lunchtime, bringing a basket from the Dorcas Circle at church. Lisa had helped the ladies a few times, contributing casseroles and bread to the meals that usually went to families hit by illness, new births and deaths. It embarrassed her a little to find herself on the receiving end.

"I didn't tell anybody who it was for," Pastor Glenn said as he brought the basket in and set it down in her tiny kitchen. "I just mentioned that a lady in our church had been in the hospital. Looks good, doesn't it?" He held up the clear plastic box full of salad, with a tiny bottle of vinegar and oil dressing taped to the top with masking tape.

"Stay for lunch?" Lisa offered, before the idea quite registered in her conscious mind.

"Tempting." He pulled a foil-wrapped oblong from the side of the basket. "Mrs. Grayson's Swiss cheese bread. Sometimes I suspect people purposely get sick, so she'll make them a loaf."

Lisa laughed. Little more than a few soft, breathless chuckles, but it was a start. Her chest hurt a little, as if it weren't used to the effort.

"Please? You're probably dying to give me a sermon on forgiving Todd, aren't you?" She laughed again when Pastor Glenn blushed, reached into his coat, and pulled out a thin booklet titled *Forgiveness: Ten Simple Steps.*

It took only a few minutes to warm up the bucket of broccoli cheese soup and the bread. They sat down in the kitchen at the tiny folding table and Lisa let Pastor Glenn hold her hands when he asked the blessing on the food.

"It's been a long time since I could really pray. About anything," she said, after they had opened their eyes again.

"That's a big step, right there." He lifted the first spoon to his lips and blew on it gently.

"Do you think I was being unfair to Todd?"

"I think you had a lot of hurt building up for a long time, and when you finally released it, you burned both of you in the explosion."

"That's a nice way of putting it." She broke off a piece of bread and took a bite. "This really is good. I ought to get the recipe."

Grinning sheepishly, Pastor Glenn produced a folded piece of paper from inside his coat.

"What's Rita doing right now? You didn't abandon her for cheese bread, did you?" Lisa was surprised at herself that she could make a joke so easily, after so long feeling like she was going to drown in her gloom. Her talk with Anne two nights ago had helped more than she could quite explain, even to herself. It wasn't just the benefit of talking to someone who understood the situation and yet was outside of it. Anne's words had hurt a little, but they had served to slap Lisa out of her self-pity.

At one time, she had indeed been the victim, but somewhere along the way, she had become as guilty as Todd. Hadn't she?

"She's spending the day at Homespun. Emily had some ideas for this year's children's theater program that she wants Rita to help with, so..." He shrugged. His wife was known for her love for children and for theatrical productions. When she could combine the two, she was never happier.

They chatted about church and friends and goings-on in the community. Lisa loved Tabor Heights. She had come here because of the reputation of the art department at Butler-Williams, and gladly stayed because of the town itself. It was a nice, small, comfortable town with all the conveniences provided by being close to Cleveland, and none of the disadvantages of traffic and congestion and industry.

"What are you doing next with your strip?" Pastor Glenn asked, when they had finished the soup and turned to the cookies Lisa had bought that morning in the bakery.

"I don't know. Maybe big confessional time?"

"You were much more honest with Katie than you realize. It was quite obvious that even though she was the injured party, she wasn't giving her husband a chance."

"You think that's what I was doing with Todd?" Lisa shrugged a little, knowing the answer already. Pastor Glenn didn't say anything. "I guess I was just tired of having to do all the work to keep our marriage going."

"Once you put your hand to the plow, you can't look back."

"Huh?"

"I tell every couple who comes to me for pre-marital counseling that marriage is a one hundred and one hundred proposition. Remember?" He winked at her, and chuckled when Lisa blushed. She did remember. "Each partner is expected to give one hundred percent. Period. No conditions on how much the other partner gives. Their complete effort isn't just between them and their spouse, it's between them and God. Do you think God accepts the excuse that just because your partner dropped to ten percent, that means you can drop to ten percent, too?" His eyes twinkled as he asked the question, but Lisa knew he was serious.

"No. God doesn't accept any excuses," she murmured.

"I don't think that baby of yours will accept them, either. If he — or she — could talk right now, what do you think he'd say about how you and Todd have been treating each other?"

"He'd cry. He'd be mad. He'd probably laugh at how stupid we've both been."

"You're on your way to healing." Pastor Glenn reached across the tiny table to pat her cheek.

"Oh!" Lisa knew she probably looked strange, sitting there with her eyes wide and staring at nothing, her mouth starting to curve into a smile.

"What is it? Is the baby kicking already?"

"Better. I just got a great idea for the strip."

"Then get to it. Right now." Pastor Glenn took hold of her hands and lifted her to her feet. He gave her a gentle shove in the small of her back, toward her neglected art tables.

~~~~~

After half an hour of quick sketching, Pastor Glenn looked at the sheets of paper Lisa handed him and nodded, his smile growing wider and brighter as he looked over the preliminary sketches for five new panels.

"You're going to get some angry mail with this, I think," he said, nodding. "Lots of women in your position who will never admit that they are just as wrong as their husbands."

"You think it's a start?" Lisa curled up in the corner of the couch and wrapped her arms around herself, tight. For the first time in weeks, she didn't feel chilled through. It had started with Anne's call. She had told Pastor Glenn about the conversation while she worked, and he agreed with what her friend had said.

"It's a grand start. You've learned a great deal."

"Did I learn enough? I don't know if I can ever face Todd with this. It's so much easier to put my feelings into the strip than to actually say them."

"You have to learn to speak for yourself, Lisa. That's the only way you'll know if your message is getting across."

"The silent treatment didn't work, that's for sure." Her wry tone prompted laughter. "It's hard enough to learn to forgive him in my heart. I don't know if I can ever get the courage and strength to say it to him, face-to-face."

"You have to. Don't let this gulf get any wider between you."

"What went wrong? We were so happy. At least, I think we were happy." A hiccupping little laugh escaped her. "I was able to put up with so much garbage from his father because I loved Todd and I thought he loved me. It wasn't all one-way, was it?"
~~~~~

"No. And it still isn't one-way, if the conversations I've been having with Todd are any indication. You know what Dr. Harris tells couples who come in for counseling?" He waited until Lisa shook her head. "Pull out your photo albums. Remember the good times. Relive the love and happiness that you think you've lost."

They talked for a little while longer. Pastor Glenn was especially intrigued by the idea of the Arc Foundation, what it did and stood for, and what Anne Hachworth did for the foundation. He knew Arc was responsible for the Common Grounds Legal Clinic, and that Nikki James had gone to work for the Arc Foundation after she got her life straightened out. Lisa knew he and Pastor Wally were concerned about the Mission, the plans they had for expanding the services to the community, and how slowly things were moving because of the lack of money. Fire Song, a musical group at Tabor Christian, was to hold a concert in April to raise funds. Lisa had volunteered to design posters to help publicize the concert.

Suddenly, she couldn't wait to get Pastor Glenn out of the apartment, so she could call Anne and ask what Arc could do for the Mission. She barely heard when he urged her again to go back through her memories and fill her mind with the good times she had known with Todd. She had a call to make.

Chapter Twenty-One

Tuesday, March 25

"Hi, Todd. Getting the shopping done early?" Joel Randolph greeted him, appearing out of nowhere in the middle of the crowded aisles of Macy's.

"Huh?" Todd jerked, startled, and then ashamed to be caught in one of his recurring dazes. He couldn't seem to concentrate on anything lately. He had gone to Padua Mall just to get out of the house, and he had no idea how he had ended up in the department store, standing in the aisle between linens and the baby department.

"Shopping. For Katie Green and Andy Paul's wedding," Emily said, appearing from behind her husband. She looked past him. "Where's Lisa?"

"Gone." Todd tried to smile, but his mouth ached so much he wished it would fall off.

"Gone?" Joel exchanged a worried frown with his wife. "Not back to those cousins of hers? Are they sick?"

"No. We are, I guess." He looked around the store, glad to see so few people around. It was a beautiful, late March afternoon, and he felt like he was caught in a blizzard. Indoors. The last thing he needed was a heavy crowd of witnesses if he started falling apart.

"What's wrong with Lisa?" Emily asked. She put a gentle hand on Todd's arm. "We've been worried about her. We don't see her in church, she hasn't called lately, and Max said she hasn't been her usual self when she goes to the Mission. Even the children have noticed."

"Lisa's... She moved out. I... I've been a real jerk." Todd took a deep breath, positive he was going to break down crying. His father had always mocked him for crying, even when he was little. Instead of keeping him from tears, it only made them worse when they finally came. "Look," he managed to say, "can we go somewhere and talk? You know Lisa, and I really need to figure out what I did—no, I know what I did wrong. I just need to talk to someone." A choked, half-laugh, half-sob escaped him. "Someone who won't knock my head off for being such a louse."

The three settled into a table tucked into a corner by a pillar and several potted trees in the food court of the mall. It wasn't quiet, but the acoustics were such that no one could overhear. Todd spilled the entire story. He knew he wasn't coherent at times, and Joel and Emily had to ask pointed questions to get him to backtrack and confess events and words he had hoped he could leave out. When he confessed what he had said to Lisa, which had brought all their troubles into the light, his lips actually burned with the shame of it.

How could he have said that to her? How could he ever have suspected her of being unfaithful?

"History repeats itself," Emily murmured. She shared a long look with Joel, and Todd was surprised to see tears glisten in her eyes. "Oh, Todd, you need to talk with Lisa right away. Both of you are long overdue for a long, deep talk. You have to get everything out in the open."

"Months ago," Joel added.

"Yeah, I kind of figured that out." Todd sighed and studied his hands, pressed flat against the slightly sticky surface of the table. "The thing is, I keep telling myself Lisa should have spoken up a long time ago and told me what I was doing. But then I wonder if I would have listened."

"It's a start." Emily dabbed at her eyes with a corner of the pale yellow scarf that had been holding her hair back. "Todd, you have to talk with Lisa. I did exactly what she did, a long time ago. I was in love with a wonderful man, and I let all my little resentments and hurts build up and didn't say anything because I knew they were petty. And I knew I was wrong, because we were living together but we weren't married. Everything built up and it became easier to stay silent and just get angrier. And it turned into a wall between us. A wall that has remained for twenty-five years. I left him when I left Hollywood. I made it impossible for him to find me. And Max's father doesn't know she exists. Because of *my* anger and *my* choices."

A tiny, bitter, thin smile was Emily's only response when Todd's mouth dropped open in shock.

"She wouldn't run away with the baby, would she?" he choked out. His stomach twisted as he remembered his father's threat of getting custody of the baby, and Lisa's promise that he would never see their baby if he tried anything.

"No." Joel shook his head. "Lisa's not the running kind. Even if she did move out. She probably feels she's protecting the baby, if anything. She won't leave town, and I don't think she'll raise the baby to hate you. But that baby will feel the division, and Lisa's pain, and who do you think he'll blame?"

"I've told Max dozens of times it was my fault," Emily said. "It was my choice to leave her father and keep the silence between us. I know she blames him, in her heart, even if her head knows the truth. You have to root out the problem now, Todd, while it's still small."

"No." Todd felt his face crack in a sickly smile. "Right now, it feels enormous. Bigger than this whole world."

Saturday, March 29

Lisa tried to do as Pastor Glenn suggested, once she calmed down from the excitement of her idea and Anne's promise to pass the information on to Arc's directors. She avoided the wedding album at first, choosing to pull out her college scrapbooks. Looking through them, she couldn't find any gaps to show where she and Todd had broken up, sometimes for months on end. He simply seemed to be everywhere.

Photos of days on the beach on Lake Erie or walking the trails in the Metroparks. Or trying to sail a boat. Or at Cedar Point amusement park. The two of them always together, no matter how many other people were around them.

Picnics. Dorm parties. Family picnics she had agreed to attend, even after she met his father and knew the man despised her because she was an artist. Lisa looked at the pictures of Todd's sisters and wondered why she hadn't seen the stiffness and coolness between Mr. Montgomery and his daughters even then.

They did have good times. Lots of good times. Tears came to her eyes, but she managed to laugh as she remembered all those simple or silly good times they had together. Back when it was enough just to walk through the Metroparks and talk.

Lisa remembered how happy she had been the day Todd put that gumball prize ring on her finger. He couldn't afford an engagement ring the first time they became engaged. She had been so happy with just a bit of cheap plastic and glass on her finger.

The day after she moved into her apartment, Lisa had looked at her wedding band and the diamond engagement ring Todd gave her right after his first big raise at DeWitt-McGregor, and contemplated taking them off. But no, she had decided to keep her rings. Was that her subconscious telling her to keep hoping?

Friday night, she finally looked through her wedding album. She didn't open the fancy, formal album full of staged and posed pictures, but the one full of photos taken by friends. The joy and innocence and dreams shining in her and Todd's faces made her cry. When had they lost that simple happiness and love?

She went walking through town on Saturday, when the sun was out and the last of the snow had melted so the side streets were brown and muddy green instead of dirty white. Lisa followed her memories, letting her feet take her down paths that had been neglected in the last few years. She walked through the campus of Butler-Williams, remembering all the hours she and Todd spent sitting under a tree or on a bench, looking up at the sky and planning their future together.

They had talked a lot, then. The more Lisa thought about those distant school days, the more she was convinced that part of the problem was that she and Todd had forgotten how to talk. Despite their busy academic schedules and work-study programs, she and Todd had packed more talking, more honest communication into a few hours each day than they had managed lately in a week of marriage. Maybe two weeks.

"That's really stupid," she told herself, as she stared at a boulder in the stone garden by the library, where she and Todd had perched for hours, planning all the places they would go, the things they would see and do, once they got married. What had happened to those plans?

Forgotten in the rush of daily living. Or maybe, put aside. When their old dreams and plans never came up in conversation anymore, had they both simply assumed the other one no longer cared?

Lisa decided to make herself face the largest hurt, the biggest piece of evidence of broken dreams and plans. She went to see the dream house.

Images from her wedding album fluttered through Lisa's mind as she trudged through downtown Tabor Heights. She shivered when a gust of damp tried to reach down her collar, and remembered a totally different shiver whenever Todd kissed her fingertips on their wedding day.

Lisa turned the corner onto the street and made herself look at the house from five driveways away, instead of waiting until she was directly in front of it, as she usually did. As if she could control what she saw.

The *for rent* sign was gone, just as Kevin had said. Tears pressed on her eyes as she recalled all the work Kevin had done to help her. She had mentioned once she wished she could be in that house for her baby's birth, and he had checked into renting it for her. Just like that. Lisa hoped Karla appreciated her wonderful husband.

There was a car in the driveway, clouds of exhaust billowing from the tailpipe in the cold afternoon air. Lisa slowed her steps and prayed the owner would get in and drive away, so he or she wouldn't see her staring at the home that would never be hers.

A man in a long black overcoat came down the driveway with a sign in his hands and a mallet tucked under one arm. He stepped out onto the melting, messy lawn and pounded the sign into the ground. It said *for rent*, the same sign she had looked at with such joy only a month ago. She stopped and waited until he tossed the mallet into his car, climbed in and drove away. Then, she continued down the sidewalk to the house, until she stood in front of the sign. Maybe the same place where she had stood, dreaming and happy and hopeful, the day before everything fell apart.

"Please, God, is this a sign?" she whispered.

The front door opened.

"Lisa?" Todd stopped on the second step down, caught in the middle of putting on his overcoat. "What are you—"

"—doing here?" she finished for him. She tried to smile, but it was hard, caught in that hopeful, aching expression that made his face gleam.

"I live here." He nodded at the sign. "For the time being, anyway. I'm pretty lucky, really. I signed a lease for a year and they're letting me out of it without a penalty, if I'll just stay until they find a renter."

"Why do you want to leave?"

"It's not the dream house without you decorating everything and making plans and..." Todd shrugged and finished putting his coat on.

"So you weren't—" She refused to let the angry word come out.

"Lying?" He shook his head and came down one more step. "I really did rent this place. I really did plan on moving us in as a surprise."

"Todd, I'm sorry."

"No, don't be. I don't blame you. I shouldn't have kept it a secret. Heck, I just wanted to surprise you with something you really wanted."

"Some surprises shouldn't be," she offered, trying to smile. It got a little easier every time she tried.

"Why didn't you tell me what my father was saying? All you had to do was play the messages back."

"He was coming in during the day and erasing them. Todd, he's been checking up on me and watching me and—" She choked, remembering that scene at the Bluebird Cafe. Could she ever face Tyler Sloane again, after what Mr. Montgomery had done and said that day? "He drove your mother into a nervous breakdown, and I couldn't let him do it to me, too."

"My mother?" He took one step out onto the snowy lawn and slid a little, wearing dress shoes instead of boots.

"Ask your sisters. I bet there are hospital records you can access, since you're a relative. She had a nervous breakdown because your father hounded her. He didn't trust her, just like he's never trusted me."

"I suppose my sisters told you all that about my parents." His voice was neutral and his face was a blankness worse than hurt or anger.

Lisa bit her lip against further words spilling out. She needed to stay reasonable and calm. She hadn't fully recovered from being sick. Her suddenly racing heart and sweaty palms were evidence of that.

"Please, just talk to your sisters. Get the truth. Then, maybe we can talk. We haven't really talked, about anything, in so long."

"I've been trying, but you won't listen." He didn't sound half as angry as he would have two weeks ago. Lisa thought that was a hopeful sign.

"Well, maybe I stopped listening because I figured you didn't want to listen to me anymore."

"Makes sense."

"Remember how we used to just sit and talk for hours? We didn't need anything to be happy, just a quiet place to sit and talk."

"And a couple bottles of ginger ale. Kind of thirsty work, talking." He shrugged, jamming his hands into the pockets of the overcoat. "Look, I have to—I have a meeting tonight. But maybe we can talk some? With a referee, I mean. If I make some appointments with Pastor and Dr. Harris, will you come?"

"Sure. Just let me know when."

His grin made her heart skip a few beats. Lisa remembered the first few times Todd had asked her out. How he had almost glowed when she said yes. Could they ever get back to those simple, happy days, when it was enough just to talk?

"Look, I have to get going. It was—it was great to see you, Lisa. I've been worried."

"Have you?" she murmured, so he couldn't hear.

"I've even been praying. Can you believe that? Me, the guy who used to fall asleep during the really long prayers at church. Guess it's never too late for a second chance, huh?"

She shook her head, not trusting her voice.

"Can I give you a ride somewhere? Dumb move, huh?" he hurried to say, when she took two steps backward, almost tripping over her own feet. "I really am trying, Lisa."

"I know."

"Well." He shrugged. They stood looking at each other for a few more moments.

One of them had to move, before they froze in that position, staring at each other from across the muddy, trampled lawn. Lisa turned to go back down the sidewalk. She waved good-bye. Todd waved back. Neither of them said anything. He stayed still, watching her, until she turned the corner onto the next street.

Monday, March 31

After a long weekend with nothing to do in the house but think, since he hadn't made any arrangements to hook up the cable, Todd was ready to listen to his sisters. He spent most of Sunday writing down all the bits and pieces he had heard and dismissed over the years and compared it to what Terri had told him at the hospital. He ignored his cell phone, which rang five times through the afternoon. He didn't want to talk to his father, who would be checking up on him since Todd had skipped the service and the Young Marrieds class at church.

Considering how hard it was to keep anything secret from his father, Todd chose not to talk to him at all. Ordinarily, his father would have come to see him after the second missed call, but he hadn't given his father the address of the dream house, so it would take some work to find him. Todd smiled sourly as he imagined his father huffing and grumbling because his secretary wasn't available today to do the research to find him. Plus there was the embarrassment of admitting his son had moved without clearing it with him. Why did Todd need his father's approval for all his decisions and actions?

"Maybe I already believe you," he told his absent sisters. When had he become so cynical about his father's actions and motives?

The trigger had been the cold look in his eyes, his words to and about Lisa during that altercation in Pastor Glenn's office. Todd had always believed his father's claims to care about Lisa, but if he cared, wouldn't he have acted differently when it was clear that Lisa was in distress? Why did he threaten to sue for custody of the baby if he cared about Lisa?

Monday morning, Todd got to work tracking down the records of his mother's hospital stays and the accident that had resulted in her death. He felt some surprise and a little guilt, and a growing sense of gratitude when he put in more than an hour using the office computer and phone and no one came in to ask what he was doing, to gently remind him not to use company resources for personal reasons, or give him something that needed to be done ASAP.

After an hour of talking to one department and authority after another, finally getting closer to his mother's records, he came up against a wall. His father had slapped a legal order on the records, sealing them.

Why was that necessary? Was there something to hide?

Using his father's name and invoking authority he didn't have got Todd nowhere. By lunchtime, he had a headache and there was nothing more he could do, short of calling his father and asking him to open the records.

"Yeah, like that'll happen?" he muttered as he got to work on untangling problems in a customer's network.

He jumped, nearly out of his chair, when the phone rang as if in response to his words. Todd laughed at himself and reached to answer the phone.

"I hear you're trying to get into your mother's medical records. Do you want to explain yourself?" his father said, his tones so icy Todd swore the temperature dropped in his office.

Lisa was right. His father did have spies all over town, reporting to him and serving his interests.

I'm sorry, honey. Now how do I find you so I can tell you?

"I've been doing a lot of thinking lately, Dad," he said slowly, and stared at the picture of Lisa that sat on the corner of his desk. It had been taken while they were dating, during a picnic with some friends from her art classes. She sat on a rock, perched high above the camera's level, looking down, laughing at him, drenched in sunshine. "With everything happening with Lisa, I've wondered about my mother's health. I don't remember much about her, and this is a way to learn some more."

"What do you need to know that I haven't told you already?"

"It's all your viewpoint, Dad. You're biased," he offered with a chuckle. *Yeah, but the bias is completely different from what you've been telling me.* "I want a complete picture of her, from other people's memories."

"What do you think you can learn from hospital records? Or her accident records?" That growl Todd only heard directed at his sisters threatened in his father's voice.

"Her problems, for one thing."

"Your mother never had any problems!"

"Then why are the records sealed? If she didn't have any problems, there wouldn't be anything to hide, would there?"

"Why are you asking questions now? Your sisters are siding with that slut, aren't they? They're telling their filthy little lies and you're stupid enough, desperate enough to get that tramp back into your bed, you're willing to believe them, aren't you?"

Todd sat back, holding the phone three inches from his ear. He could still hear his father's words loud and clear, but they didn't register as he realized something interesting. His father accused his sisters of spreading lies, but Todd had yet to mention them.

That was just more validation that Karla, Andrea, Terri and Charli had been telling the truth all along. His father couldn't accuse his sisters or even guess they were the source of Todd's questions and doubts, unless there was a lot of truth in what they had been saying all along.

Chapter Twenty-Two

"I haven't talked to any of the girls in… weeks, Dad. Not since they helped with the move." Todd rationalized that he was talking about all his sisters. He had only talked to Terri at the hospital. "I'm just worried that there might be something wrong with Mom that might get passed down to the baby. And I wonder sometimes if having me might have hurt her. There aren't any pictures of me and her, like there are with my sisters. Like maybe she didn't want her picture taken, to hide the fact she was sick."

"Your mother was too busy getting pictures of you. She was so proud of you." The growl smoothed out of his father's voice and that jolly, proud tone came back. It sickened Todd to hear it. "I know she loved you more than all your sisters put together, Toddy. You were the apple of her eye."

No, Dad, that's not true. You loved me more than my sisters all put together. I'm lucky they don't hate me for it. Or maybe the truth is that you didn't love them at all.

Todd stumbled through more reassurances, sickened by how easily he convinced his father that he would give up the search into his mother's records, and he still believed the façade of their family. He didn't feel a speck of shame when he pretended that someone had come into his office and he had to get off the phone.

"I'm just as much a liar as you are, Dad," he muttered, staring at the phone once he had hung it up. "The only difference is that I can see that, and I'm ashamed, and I'm going to do something about the mess I've made. I just don't know how, yet." Todd sighed and rubbed his eyes with his knuckles. "If one lawyer put up a wall, maybe another lawyer can help me tear it down, or get around it?"

An hour later, he had managed to convince his brother-in-law that he was in earnest about finding out the official story of his mother's illness and death. In turn, Kevin McNeal suggested that Todd talk to Xander Finley, because he was sharing the legal tasks of helping Lisa. Todd was shaken to realize that Lisa was indeed taking legal action.

"You wouldn't happen to know if…" Todd sighed and closed his eyes, resting his head in the hand not holding the phone. "She said if I did anything, she'd make sure I never saw our baby. She wouldn't file a restraining order, would she?"

"Funny you should ask. She's filed one against your father. I'm guessing you don't know anything about it," Kevin added, a questioning note in his voice.

"He deserves it. I'd deserve it, too, if she filed one against me. But I'm hoping she won't."

"There might be hope for you yet. Call Finley. He works more closely with the Tabor PD. He might know how to get around those seals on the reports."

Todd called Common Grounds, both offices, and wasn't able to talk to Xander. He left a message detailing what he wanted, and his reasons, at the Tabor office. If he was going to reform himself and break out of his father's shadow, this was the place to start.

~~~~~

Xander Finley called back just before Todd was ready to admit he was useless to DeWitt-McGregor and considered going home early from work. His news wasn't good. Short of going to court and petitioning to have the seal lifted from the orders, the only way to find out what was in those records was to have Mr. Montgomery rescind his instructions. Todd didn't want to do that. He wasn't ready to face down his father. He needed a firmer foundation, and that required solid facts.

"You know," Xander said, after Todd had stumbled through his thanks, trying not to admit his cowardice, "there's no gag order on the officers who were on-scene at your mother's accident. That part of the record isn't sealed."

"Who?" Todd felt as if the oxygen in the room had tripled.

"A certain lieutenant named Cooper."

It took a moment for Todd to realize Xander meant Chief Cooper. He didn't think the chief had been serving with the department that long.

"He hasn't," Xander said, when Todd spoke his thoughts. "He trained here, then transferred out of state when he married, then came back after his divorce."

Todd got off the phone, then everything ground to a halt in his head. How exactly did he ask the chief of the Tabor Heights Police Department about an accident twenty-four years ago? He could almost laugh at himself. The first step was to just call to ask to talk to Chief Cooper. He could think of what to say on his way to the station. This was a talk that needed to be face-to-face.

Fifteen minutes later, Todd headed out the door, still feeling a little dazed at how easily Chief Cooper had agreed to talk to him as soon as he could get to the station. Somehow, he had been sure that his name, his father's constant unpleasant clashes with the police, would have been a roadblock to any kind of cooperation.

"Okay, Lord, I know I haven't been doing enough praying, but that was You, wasn't it?" Todd muttered as he got into his car. "Please, all I want is to make things right with Lisa. I need to hear what he has to say,
~~~~~

to help me figure things out. Please, God…" He closed his eyes and rested his forehead on his steering wheel. Why was it, when he needed most to pray, he couldn't find the words?

Maybe he was in such a mess because he hardly ever felt the need to pray?

~~~~~

Chief Cooper brought Todd into his office and offered him coffee. Todd explained with as few details as he could manage about his need to find the truth. The chief didn't react when he heard that Mr. Montgomery had sealed the records. He sat quietly, nodding a few times, for several minutes after Todd finished speaking. Todd waited, afraid that the police chief would refuse to speak about the accident that had killed his mother, simply because the bad blood between Arthur Montgomery and the police department created an ethical dilemma.

"I remember. A day like that stays with you. It was a heavy, wet snow that day," Chief Cooper said, his voice soft but clear. "The temperature was dropping pretty fast, and we were trying to get the schools closed early and the kids home before conditions got deadly. We had accidents all over town, more than the ambulances could handle. And then with the ice forming everywhere, the ambulances couldn't get through. Your mother suffered a long time, stranded there in the taxi. We didn't dare move her because of her injuries, and there was no shelter other than the taxi. She was frantic. Sometimes I thought she didn't feel the pain, she was so terrified. A couple times, she laughed through her tears, and said she was trying to escape the hospital, but here she was, getting sent back."

He paused to sip at his coffee, and watched Todd over the rim.

"It took two hours between the time the accident was called in and when the ambulance took her. And another hour to crawl down streets like ice skating rinks, to get her to the hospital. Your father never got there, so I rode with her in the ambulance."

"So you were there when she died."

"No. I stayed with her in the ER for another hour. She begged me to stay. Your father still didn't arrive by the time I had to get back out on the streets."

"But Dad said she died instantly," Todd whispered. "More and more lies, the deeper in I get."

"Once she got something for her pain, it was easier for her to talk." Chief Cooper sat back in his chair, resting his elbows on the arms of the chair, cradling his mug in both hands. "She claimed that your father was chasing the taxi, and that's why it went into the ditch and flipped over." He watched Todd, unblinking as he spoke.

"What did the taxi driver say about it?" It was easier to ask questions than to deny something he was half-ready to believe. If his father had been
~~~~~

chasing the taxi, maybe contributed to the accident, then it made perfect sense that he wasn't there when the police called his office. Maybe he refused to come when he did get the message.

"Never got a chance to talk to him after the initial report. He left town two days later. One of his co-workers said he came into a large amount of money, while another one said he was getting dozens of phone calls at work, from a man who sounded very angry."

"You think my father threatened him and then paid him to leave town, so no one would know the truth." Todd felt nothing but tired as he said the words.

"We don't have anything but the word of a woman who had recently suffered mental illness, who died before she could be questioned about statements made in a time of great distress." Chief Cooper sipped at his coffee again, then put the mug down on his desk. "I never put her claims in my report. There have been times over the years, I wished I had."

When Todd reached home, he sat more than an hour in the darkness, wishing for the lamps Lisa had taken to her apartment, wishing for Lisa, even more, and thinking hard. Finally he fumbled his way across the room, bumping into boxes he suspected he would never unpack, and found the switch for the ceiling light. He dug his cell phone out of his coat pocket and punched in Karla's number.

"Hey, it's me," he said, glad to get the answering machine instead of his sister. "Todd," he added, in case she didn't recognize his voice. "Look, can you call the others and—can we meet at your place? You have things to tell me about Mom and Dad, and I'm ready to listen."

Wednesday, April 2

Jeannette and BJ Marshall stopped by Lisa's apartment on their way home that day. BJ went to the Mission's daycare center while his mother worked at their church, and he brought in several pictures he had done, to give Lisa. She treasured the hug and wet kiss from the little boy even more than the scribbly crayon drawing he solemnly handed to her. It took all her self-control not to laugh when he explained that the markings in big black swoops were messages from several other children in his class, saying they hoped Miss Lisa would get better fast and come draw more pictures for them in story time.

"You are going to be in such trouble when he's old enough to date," Lisa told Jeannette when they had a few moments alone, while BJ used the bathroom. "He's a charmer. Those thick black curls and those big, chocolate eyes don't hurt any, either."

"Just like his daddy." Jeannette sighed, and for a moment sadness wiped away the glow of laughter and chilly evening air from her face.

"Is it hard, raising a baby by yourself?"

"In some ways. But in a lot of ways, I was never alone." She settled down on the edge of the couch and looked around the cramped room. "And for what it's worth, I don't see you raising your baby alone."

"Oh, I know the church family—"

"I'm talking about Todd getting himself straightened out and being there for you." Her lips quirked up a little when Lisa stared at her, not quite sure she had heard right. "He's been in for counseling every other day, Pastor Glenn and Dr. Harris. He really wants to get things straightened out. In his head and heart, and with you."

"It's not that easy." Even as she shook her head, Lisa felt something leap inside.

"You have a second chance. Don't throw it away." Jeannette reached out and caught hold of her hands. "In some ways, I was lucky. Brody always chose me over his family. We agreed, when we were first married we would try living in his hometown to be a witness to his family. Either two years, or until we had a baby. Then, if nothing improved, we would leave." She stopped, inhaling sharply, wincing as if in pain. "I was pregnant before our first anniversary. Brody died in a car wreck before he could tell his mother about our baby." She tightened her grip on Lisa's hands. "You have a second chance, to get back the man who promised to love and protect and cherish you forever. Don't throw it away."

"It isn't up to me," Lisa murmured, and as the words left her lips, she wondered if that was exactly true.

"That doesn't matter. God doesn't ask us to be responsible for what *others* do. We're only responsible to Him for how we live, and the decisions *we* make. Live like it *is* up to you. Don't make your baby grow up without her father, if you can at all help it."

"And if nothing gets better?"

Jeannette sighed and raked her fingers through her dark auburn hair. "Then I'll help you and teach you everything I know about being a single mother. You won't go through this alone."

Friday, April 4

Lisa saw Todd's car sitting in front of the church office entrance when she went to church for her afternoon counseling session. For a moment, panic had her heart racing, but she wasn't quite sure why she should be afraid. Since meeting up with Todd at the dream house, she hadn't seen him anywhere in town. It didn't make sense to her that he would be here in the middle of the day just to try to find her, but there was his car. Dr.

Harris was waiting at the front desk when Lisa reached the office and ushered her back to her office immediately. Lisa half-expected Todd to be waiting for her, like he had been waiting when she stepped into Pastor Glenn's office that disastrous afternoon only a few weeks ago.

"Actually, I'd like to talk to you about that," Dr. Harris said, when Lisa confessed her mix of disappointment and relief at not seeing Todd. "I think he's progressed enough that the two of you can have a counseling session together."

"You think I won't have another hysterical fit, you mean," Lisa offered with a wry twist to her mouth and voice.

"You were under physical stress, and you were essentially ambushed. I think Pastor had the right idea, but... well, let's just say I've never seen eye-to-eye with your father-in-law and his interpretation of scripture, and leave it at that." She shook her head and got up from the seating group in the corner of her office to cross to the table set up with a carafe of hot water for tea. "You and Todd need to start talking. With a referee, if that will make you feel secure."

"Am I ready?"

"From what you've told me about that accidental meeting last week, yes." She offered with a gesture to make tea for Lisa, who declined. "The love is still there. On both sides. You didn't fall in love in silence and being absent from each other, did you?" She sat down again and put her mug of tea on the coffee table between them. "It was silence that made your love die. Just like we can't grow spiritually if we don't have regular devotions and prayer and meeting for worship, love can't grow if there isn't communication."

"That's how we got in this mess in the first place," Lisa murmured. "Okay. When?"

Lisa was halfway down the street to her apartment before she shook herself free of her tangled thoughts and paid attention to her surroundings. The thought of sitting down and talking with Todd, of trying to work through their marital problems, didn't frighten her as much as she had thought. Knowing he was coming for regular counseling encouraged her. Then again, the lack of response from her father-in-law when the restraining order was served against him encouraged her as well.

She stopped short, only twenty feet from the enclosed staircase at the back of Rick's Bakery, leading up to her apartment. A crawling sensation tingled up and down her back and cupped her scalp. Was someone watching her? Following her? For two seconds, as she forced her feet to get moving again, she wanted nothing more than to race up those stairs and unlock her door and get inside.

That wouldn't be smart, would it? If someone was watching her, following her, that would reveal where she lived. She didn't want Mr. Montgomery to know where she lived now.

A restraining order didn't do much good if she wasn't alive to complain that he had violated it. Lisa continued down the street, intending to go in the door of Rick's Bakery, pick out something decadently rich, and waste as much time as she could inside. She couldn't shake off the memory of what her sisters-in-law had revealed about their mother's death, fleeing for her life in a snowstorm, dying in a traffic accident.

"Don't be an idiot," she scolded herself, her voice a harsh whisper, just before she reached the door of Rick's Bakery. "He can't hurt you. There are too many people around. If you panic, he wins, and you give him proof that you're doing something wrong. Innocent people don't run."

Innocent people could drown their fears in gooey bakery, however, and she planned to do just that.

Please, Lord, protect me from my enemies? And while I'm praying – which I don't do often enough – please fix things between me and Todd? Please?

Sunday, April 6

Todd nodded, not really listening to his father complaining about the new church he had test-attended that morning. He toyed with the remains of his stroganoff noodles and let his mind roam.

Lisa had been in church this morning. He stayed away from her, and felt a pang of guilt when she didn't go to their Young Marrieds class. It was good to see her in church, and he chose to take it as a good sign, a good reaction to Dr. Harris's suggestion that they come in for counseling together from now on. He had stayed behind her, trying to stay lost in the crowd, watching her during the worship service, paying more attention to her than to the sermon. When she went home, he followed her, to make sure she got home all right, trying to build up the courage to approach her. Like he had been doing for the last two weeks.

Todd might have laughed at how he felt starved for every glimpse of her. Concern for Lisa, and fear of making things worse, hardened the wall between watching for her and actually approaching her. Meeting up with her at the dream house was a fluke. A miraculous fluke, and she hadn't been upset to see him. But he was afraid to push his luck and her patience.

Ever since Lisa got home from the hospital, he had driven by her apartment every morning and evening on his way to and from work, just to look up at her windows for any sign of activity. Three times he had seen her come down to the bakery to buy something. She had smiled at the clerk. She looked better, more color in her cheeks, and had a little spring in her step as she hurried around the corner of the building to the private entrance to her apartment upstairs.

He only knew where Lisa lived because he had followed when Karla brought her home from the hospital. Despite the improving relations with his sisters, Todd knew better than to push his luck with them and ask them where Lisa lived.

"I knew she was trouble from the moment I met her," Mr. Montgomery said. "I told you not to marry Lisa. I told you she was unstable and unreliable and self-centered, but you wouldn't listen. Thinking with your hormones instead of your brain."

"What?" Todd's thoughts jolted back to the present moment. As usual lately, somehow his father found a way to blame all his problems on Lisa. She was to blame for the need to find a new church, apparently. After having heard three different versions of the argument that had led to his father resigning his membership at Tabor Christian, Todd knew better than to believe it was Lisa's fault.

He had learned and realized quite a few unpleasant things about his father. Especially his tendency to change the truth to suit him. Todd had met twice with his sisters to talk about what they remembered of their parents' marriage. It would take a long time before he could digest the whole truth. He supposed the biggest miracle of all was that his sisters were willing to forgive him for being so stupid. They were better Christians than he had ever been, and they refused to have anything to do with church because of their father.

His father had probably said dozens of cruel, untrue things about Lisa all during dinner, only Todd hadn't been paying attention.

Maybe that was the problem. When he didn't like the things he heard or didn't like what happened, he just ignored them, hoping they'd go away. That tactic definitely didn't work.

"I said, I told you not to marry Lisa," his father repeated.

"No, you didn't."

Chapter Twenty-Three

If his father could lie about one little thing, then he could lie about hundreds of things. Thousands of things Todd's sisters had always told him, but he had chosen not to believe because they went against what his father said.

"Todd!" Mr. Montgomery stared at his son.

His father was wrong, and Lisa was more clearly a victim every time Todd thought about what had happened between them.

"A man shall leave his parents and cleave to his wife," Pastor Glenn had said, *"and be one flesh."*

Maybe, Todd decided, it was high time he left home.

"You made a thousand little complaints about Lisa's taste in clothes and her lack of responsibility and how much a liability she would be to me when we got married. You made her blush with your double-edged compliments. You tried to take over the wedding when she didn't do things your way. You weren't paying a cent, so what did it matter if you didn't like the music or the food? For heaven's sake, Dad, you tried to pick out her bridesmaids and who would give her away!"

"It was your wedding, too. You had the right to some dignity," his father muttered into his coffee.

"You wanted my wedding to be done *your* way. I happened to like the colors and the dresses and the food and the music. I helped Lisa pick everything out. I have been so stupid!" He stood up, jarring the table.

"Where are you going?"

"I'm going away. I've been married two years, and I still haven't left home!"

"What are you talking about? Is that Lisa's craziness coming out of your mouth? You went to see her, didn't you? After I told you to stay away from that girl. Todd, I know what's best for you."

"No, you don't." Todd leaned down, bracing himself on the table, towering over his seated father so he had to lean back or be nose-to-nose with him. "You don't know what's best for me. You only know what's best for *you*. Power. Control over other people's lives and minds. Lisa is what's best for me, and I nearly killed her because you wouldn't let me grow up, and because I kept seeing the world through your eyes. Well I'm sorry if your marriage wasn't happy, but that's no reason to ruin mine!"

"I had a wonderful marriage with your mother," Mr. Montgomery growled.

"If it was so happy, why did she have a nervous breakdown?"

His father sat still several seconds too long. That was all the confirmation Todd needed. Not that he really needed it. He had believed his sisters long before this.

"Why have you been spying on Lisa?"

"She's never at home where she belongs. The girl's a slut, bouncing all over town when she should stay home. Pretending to be an artist. Pretending to be a good Christian girl."

"She *is* a good Christian girl. She's a far better wife than I ever deserved. And I'll bet Mom was a lot better wife than you ever deserved," he added, almost nose-to-nose with his father. "You want to know why Lisa wasn't at home every time you called to check on her? Which wasn't your job, and certainly wasn't any of your business! Because she's working at church and reading to little kids at the Mission and cooking for the homeless and taking food to sick people and helping out wherever people need her. That's why!"

"You really believe that trash she's been feeding you?"

"I have only two things to say to you, Dad." Todd stepped over to the back door, where his coat hung on a peg. "First, it isn't trash, because I helped Lisa when I took days off work. And second, I believed all the trash you've been handing me all my life, so I ought to know trash from real. I *ought* to," he said as he shrugged into his coat. "I guess it's time to learn, huh?"

"Todd Montgomery, you listen—"

"Not anymore!" He grinned, delighted at the shock that shut up his father before he could work into a roar. "I don't want you to ever speak Lisa's name again unless it's to say something nice about my wife, do you understand? No, that's not good enough." He took one step back toward the table. "Don't ever talk about my wife again. Maybe you shouldn't ever talk to me again, period. It's about time I left home."

Todd slammed the door as he stepped down to the sidewalk into the rainstorm. He paused to listen to his heart thunder in his ears. He took a deep breath and the chill damp filled his lungs. It felt good to be alive.

He drove by Lisa's apartment as he passed through town. Todd saw only one light on. He wasn't sure if it was her bedroom or kitchen or living room window. When he envisioned getting out, walking to the side entrance and ringing the doorbell, he broke out in a cold sweat.

At least she had smiled a little when they talked at the dream house, and she believed what he said. At least she was willing to go to counseling. Could he take it as a sign that she still loved him, even if only a little?

On a whim, remembering that there was a church board meeting scheduled for that afternoon, he turned the car down the street, heading for the church.

There were only two cars in the parking lot. One was Pastor Glenn's. Todd parked and ran from his car to the office door. It was locked. Panic made him pound on the door until he split a seam in his leather glove. He had to talk with his pastor before everybody else showed up for the meeting. Then it occurred to Todd that the meeting was probably to discuss what to do about all the vacancies in various boards and committees and the deacons, now that his father had quit the church so abruptly.

Pastor Glenn appeared in the hallway, his raincoat slung over one arm. He turned on a light outside and one inside the doorway and pushed the door open.

"What can I do for you, Todd?"

"Have you seen Lisa lately?" he blurted. "Do you think she'd forgive me if I asked her again?"

Pastor Glenn grinned. Then he started to chuckle. Beckoning, he led Todd into the church and down the hall to his office.

"Lisa brought these over today before church, to get my final approval before she sends them off." He held out a sheaf of papers holding Lisa's cartoon panels.

One caught Todd's eye. Katie lay in bed, crying herself to sleep. It turned into a dream of a little baby coming down to visit her in the arms of an angel. In her dream, Katie's tears stopped. She smiled and took the baby into her arms.

Katie and the baby talked. The baby was sad because Katie didn't love Bob anymore. The baby wanted her parents to love each other, no matter how mean they had been to each other.

"Lisa's sending this out?" Todd's hand trembled a little as he shuffled the paper to the back.

"First thing tomorrow morning," Pastor Glenn said, nodding. "Did you know she has a book contract she's working on?"

"No, she never ..." Todd groaned as he recalled, through all the anger and pain and harsh words, something Lisa had mentioned about a contract. She had told him that he didn't care. Well, maybe she had been more right than either of them realized. "I'm glad for her," he said, after swallowing hard and fighting the pressure of hot tears.

He continued reading.

The next panel showed Katie crying again, assuring her baby she did love Bob and she missed him and she wished she could tell him. The baby hugged her and smiled and said she would tell her daddy when she went back to heaven.

"That's not—" Todd choked. He put down the papers to wipe at his eyes. "That's not theologically correct, is it?"

"I don't think God minds if we take some artistic liberties, do you?"

"Do you think it's the truth?" he whispered.

Tuesday, April 8

"I'm not so bad after all," Lisa murmured, surveying the changing table she had assembled all by herself.

True, it had taken the entire afternoon to unpack the parts of the changing table and figure out the instructions. They were printed in Spanish and Japanese and French, with no English anywhere. She had turned all the pieces and parts upside down and inside out and finally found the English instructions inside the bag of screws and nuts. Lisa had put it together and taken it apart three times until it finally stood up on its own, with all the pieces used and nothing left over.

She had done it. She had put something together all by herself without breaking something or shorting out a fuse or cutting herself in the process. Lisa wanted to run to the phone and call Todd and tell him what she had done. He would be so proud of her.

At least, she hoped he would be proud, and not laugh at her for interrupting his evening with something that might strike him as silly. Wasn't tonight a church baseball league night? Hadn't he said he was playing this year? Sure, she could call his cell phone. She still remembered the number, no matter how she had tried to forget it.

If only they had talked a few times before now. For the first time, she regretted cutting him off so completely.

Still, maybe she should call him anyway? Even if all she could do was leave a message? Wouldn't that be a good step toward instituting communication, like Dr. Harris advocated?

"We're going to be okay, honey," she whispered, and pressed a hand over the barely noticeable bulge in her abdomen. "I can put things together and I bet I'll even do a good job with diapers when you get here. If I can fix things with Daddy like I did with this changing table, we might just have a chance."

A tear pressed at the corner of her eye, but Lisa refused to let it fall.

"See, honey, Daddy and I are such stubborn people. We get hurt and we think the other one never gets hurt, and we don't think about being sorry and forgiving. It's a lot my fault Daddy isn't here right now. But that'll change. We have to keep trusting God and praying, and sooner or later, Mommy and Daddy will get things fixed and put together like they belong. Just like this changing table."

Lisa took a deep breath and went to her knees to open up the box with the crib parts. It was going to take all her courage to face assembling the crib. Maybe she should wait until tomorrow, when she had lots of time and she wasn't so tired.

"You'll like your Daddy when you finally meet him. He really is a sweet guy, when I'm not giving him a hard time. I hope you don't grow up like either of us. I hope you're smart enough to tell people when you're mad, and forgive them before they ask you to."

She cut the plastic straps holding the box closed and lifted the lid on the pieces of the crib. No, she didn't think she could handle this huge job tonight. Lisa sighed and got up and walked out into the living room. Her notebook full of wallpaper, carpet and drapery samples lay open, waiting for her final decision on what colors and designs to use for the baby's room. She knew it was foolish to buy furniture and assemble it before the room was decorated. It would only get in the way. Still, she needed to do something, make some progress in preparing for the baby.

At one time, the nine months of pregnancy looked like they would stretch on forever. Filled with misery. Now, though, her six remaining months looked all too short.

The doorbell rang. Lisa sighed, caught halfway down to the couch. It wasn't like she had an extra load to lift, but this late in the evening she just wanted to collapse and never get up again.

Todd stood in the doorway at the top of the stairs with his hands behind his back. He gave her that nervous grin she hadn't seen in years.

"How did you—"

"I followed you home a few times." Todd brought his hands from behind his back. Peppermint stripe carnations in one hand. A pint of peanut butter chocolate ice cream in the other. "Look," he blurted, speaking so rapidly she almost couldn't understand the words. "I was wrong. A lot of times. Probably more times than you can remember. I'm sorry. Really. Nobody is making me say this, either. I love you. Can you let me in to talk? Just talk?"

Lisa held her breath, fighting the pressure that could have been tears or laughter or both. When he held out the ice cream and flowers to her, she took them without thinking.

"I'll stand on the edge of the step if you want to push me down them," Todd offered with a crooked grin. "Just to start to even things up, y'know?"

The grin faded, bit by bit, when she could only stand there and stare at him. Her thoughts raced, twisting and spinning so she had no idea what she felt. Todd nodded, swallowed hard, and started to turn to leave.

"Wait." Lisa bit her lip and turned away, quickly putting down the ice cream and flowers. Her bare minimum tool kit sat by the front door on the shelves she had bought two days ago. She picked up the screwdriver she had been using just a few minutes before. Todd frowned when she held it out to him. "How good are you at putting cribs together?"

"Cribs, huh?" His hand closed around the screwdriver. "Whatever you want me to do, just tell me."

"Instead of expecting you to read my mind?" Lisa swallowed hard against an urge to cry. "I was wrong, too."

"I want to make this work, Lisa. More than anything in this whole world. I want you to take the dream house, okay? Just think about it? Maybe someday you'll let me come back, and we can be together like we always dreamed. You should have the house, because I left you a long time before you left me."

"Todd..."

What could she say? She wanted the house. She wanted the promise of what it meant. She wanted to say no and slam the door in his face. She wanted to drag him inside the apartment and show him all the things she had found for the baby's room. There would be plenty of room in the dream house, wouldn't there?

Okay, God, I know You answer prayers, but I'm not used to getting answers this fast. Please, please, help us so we don't mess this up. Please?

"It's going to take a lot of work. I have a lot of bad examples to avoid. I've been spending some time with my sisters, getting the lowdown on Mom and Dad." His voice broke. "You're going to have to tell me when I act like him, okay? Because there are some family traditions I just don't want to pass on. Not when I love you so much. Okay?"

"Okay," she whispered around a choking sensation that filled her throat and threatened to go down into her chest. She took a step back and pushed the door wider open to let him in.

The End

THANK YOU!

Thank you for reading this book from Mt. Zion Ridge Press.

If you enjoyed the experience, learned something, gained a new perspective, or made new friends through story, could you do us a favor and write a review on Goodreads or wherever you bought the book?

Thanks! We and our authors appreciate it.

We invite you to visit our website, MtZionRidgePress.com, and explore other titles in fiction and non-fiction. We always have something coming up that's new and off the beaten path.

And please check out our podcast, **Books on the Ridge,** where we chat with our authors and give them a chance to share what was in their hearts while they wrote their book, as well as fun anecdotes and glimpses into their lives and experiences and the writing process. And we always discuss a very important topic: *Tea!*

You can listen to the podcast on our website or find it at most of the usual places where podcasts are available online. Please subscribe so you don't miss a single episode!

Thanks for reading. We hope you come back soon!

About the Author

On the road to publication, Michelle fell into fandom in college and has 40+ stories in various SF and fantasy universes. She has a bunch of useless degrees in theater, English, film/communication, and writing. Even worse, she has over 100 books and novellas with multiple small presses, in science fiction and fantasy, YA, suspense, women's fiction, and sub-genres of romance.

Her official launch into publishing came with winning first place in the Writers of the Future contest in 1990. She was a finalist in the EPIC Awards competition multiple times, winning with *Lorien* in 2006 and *The Meruk Episodes, I-V,* in 2010, and was a finalist in the Realm Awards competition, in conjunction with the Realm Makers convention.

Her training includes the Institute for Children's Literature; proofreading at an advertising agency; and working at a community newspaper. She is a tea snob and freelance edits for a living (MichelleLevigne@gmail.com for info/rates), but only enough to give her time to write. Her newest crime against the literary world is to be co-managing editor at Mt. Zion Ridge Press and launching the publishing co-op, Ye Olde Dragon Books. Be afraid … be very afraid.

And please check out her newest venture: Ye Olde Dragon's Library, the storytelling podcast. Interspersed between the chapters will be interviews with authors of fantastical fiction. Listen to the podcast on your favorite podcast app or listen on the website: www.YeOldeDragonBooks.com, and click on the Ye Olde Dragon's Library link.

www.Mlevigne.com
www.MichelleLevigne.blogspot.com
www.YeOldeDragonBooks.com
www.MtZionRidgePress.com

NEWSLETTER:

Want to learn about upcoming books, book launch parties, inside information, and cover reveals?
Go to Michelle's website or blog to sign up.

Thanks for reading!
If you enjoyed this book, would you help Michelle by posting a review on Goodreads?

Are you a member of Book Bub? If so, please follow Michelle on Book Bub, and you'll get alerts when new books are coming out.

As a way of saying thanks, Michelle invites you to the Goodies page on her website. It will change regularly, offering you a free short story, a sample audiobook chapter, sneak peeks at new cover art, inside information on discounts and new release dates, etc.

Please go to: Mlevigne.com/good-stuff.html

Also by Michelle L. Levigne

Guardians of the Time Stream: 4-book Steampunk series
The Match Girls: Humorous inspirational romance series starting with **A Match (Not) Made in Heaven**
Sarai's Journey: A 2-book biblical fiction series
Tabor Heights: 18-book inspirational small town romance series.
Quarry Hall: 11-book women's fiction/suspense series
For Sale: Wedding Dress. Never Used: inspirational romance
Crooked Creek: Fun Fables About Critters and Kids: Children's short stories.
Do Yourself a Favor: Tips and Quips on the Writing Life. A book of writing advice.
To Eternity (and beyond): *Writing Spec Fic Good for Your Soul.* A book defending speculative fiction.
Killing His Alter-Ego: contemporary romance/suspense, taking place in fandom.
The Commonwealth Universe: SF series, 25 books and growing
The Hunt: 5-book YA fantasy series
Faxinor: Fantasy series, 4 books and growing
Wildvine: Fantasy series, 14 books when all released
Neighborlee: Humorous fantasy series
Zygradon: 5-book Arthurian fantasy series
AFV Defender: SF adventure series

Young Defenders: Middle Grade SF series, spin-off of *AFV Defender*
Magic to Spare: Fantasy series
Book & Mug Mysteries: cozy mystery series
Quest for the Crescent Moon: fantasy series
Steward's World: fantasy series reboot and expansion
The Enchanted Castle Archives: fantasy series